miracle girls

miracle girls

a novel

Anne Dayton and May Vanderbilt

NEW YORK BOSTON NASHVILLE

Copyright © 2008 by Anne Dayton and May Vanderbilt

FaithWords

237 Park Avenue

New York, NY 10017

Printed in the United States of America

First Edition: October 2008

10   9   8   7   6   5   4   3   2   1

Library of Congress Cataloging-in-Publication Data

Dayton, Anne.

Miracle Girls / by Anne Dayton and May Vanderbilt.—1st ed.

p. cm.

Summary: "Meet the Miracle Girls of Half Moon Bay! They may look ordinary, but each one is living out her second chance at life. Too bad it's their last chance at surviving high school!"—Provided by publisher.

ISBN-13: 978-0-446-40755-7 (trade pbk.)

ISBN-10: 0-446-40755-0 (trade pbk.)

1. High school students—Fiction.   2. California—Fiction.   I. Vanderbilt, May.   II. Title.

PS3604.A989M57 2008

813'.6—dc22

2008000758

Anne: To Mom and Dad, for letting me dream big.

May: To Sapna, who made high school bearable.

acknowledgments

Special thanks to Claudia Cross, Seth Fishman, Rolf Zetter-sten, Harry Helm, Anne Horch, Katie Moore, Jody Wal-drup, Jaime Slover, Dylan Hoke, Grace Hernandez, Lori Quinn, Amy Biter, Jana Burson, Laini Brown, and Preston Cannon.

Anne: Wayne, thanks for cooking, cleaning, shopping, rep-resenting us at social functions, and mostly for putting up with me. You deserve a medal. Mom, Dad, Nick, and Peter, you're my favorite people in the world, even when I don't act like it. And Jeff, Annie, May, and the Beths: I thank God for giving me friends as amazing as you. Thanks for making me laugh.

May: Thanks to Mom for teaching the writers of tomorrow, to Dad for always calming me down in a crisis, to Matt for loving me no matter what, to Diem for giving me honest shopping advice, to the boys for the hilarity, and to Sandy for being my Miracle Girl. Thanks to Bransfords for all the laughs, the hugs, and the support. I need it! And, of course, to Nathan. Here we go, and I couldn't be more excited.

miracle girls

'm not even surprised when Mr. Mackey announces a pop quiz in Algebra 2. That's just the kind of day I'm having. No, scratch that. It's the kind of life I'm having.

I was happy in San Jose. It's a *real* city. I had friends there. But this summer my dad moved us to Half Moon Bay to open his own law practice, and my early conclusion is: this place is lame, lame, lame. The people here wouldn't know a decent person if she walked right up to them and said, "Hi, decent person here." Trust me, I thought about doing it.

And even though I've been going to school here for three weeks, I can feel in my bones that today is going to be my worst day yet. I mean, look how it all started out. This morning I overheard Maria telling my mom she has lupus, and that's why she's been sick so much. I wasn't supposed to hear, but the walls in our brand-spanking-new Easy-Bake Castle are so thin you can fall through just by leaning against them. That's what Mom and Dad get for buying a McMansion in Ocean Colony. (It's really called that. I gag every time I see the sign at the gates.) I don't know what lupus is, but I'm pretty sure it's deadly.

Maria may be just the housekeeper to my parents, but to me she's like a second mother, the non-crazy one, the one who doesn't spend her life decorating and redecorating our house, the one who actually gets what I'm going through in this town.

Then, when Dad dropped me off, I noticed a run in my tights, which only got bigger when I had to take them off and put them back on again in PE. (It's not like we really needed to suit up to be herded into the gym, sit still, and learn the rules of volleyball anyway, so the enlargement was entirely pointless.) Next, I found out my Key Club meeting at lunch had been canceled because the adviser, Mrs. Galvin, was sick, which means I didn't have to spend all last night drawing up proposals for service projects after all. Instead, I could have taken a little extra time to make sure I understood polynomials. But, of course, I didn't do that, so naturally we're being tested on them today.

Mr. Mackey begins to write the first problem on the whiteboard, and I copy it onto my paper carefully. The soft click of the clock hands sweeping around the face is almost drowned out by the furious scratching of pencils.

My dad's colleagues seem to think it's impressive that I'm in Algebra 2 as a freshman. I used to think so. Back in San Jose, I was always a year ahead of everyone else in my class in math and was even given a special tutor last year to learn geometry in eighth grade, but it turns out here in Half Moon Bay there are a lot of freshmen who took geometry last year. It was a lot more fun being in advanced math when it made me special. Now it's just a lot of work.

Math has always been hard for me. I can breeze through a novel in an evening and remember history timelines until my eyes roll back in my head, but even though I like numbers, they don't like me back.

Which, I guess, I should be used to. I glance at Tyler, but he's already crouched over his paper, his curly blond hair falling over his forehead. Tyler's a sophomore, and he's the lead singer in a band called Three Car Garage. He doesn't know I'm alive.

I sigh, then lean over to start working when I hear rustling behind me. I shoot a quick glance over my shoulder in time to see Riley McGee shove something into her purse. She sees me watching her and gives me a big fake smile, then pulls out a mechanical pencil. Sketchy. I turn back to my test, shaking my head. She wouldn't really...would she?

Okay, Ana. Focus. You're just trying to solve for X. I stare at the problems, trying to figure out the first step. The tricky thing is that X is different every time. And I don't like change. I like things to happen when and how they're supposed to.

I make a tentative mark on my paper, then hear a soft thud behind me. I sneak a peek under my arm and see that Riley has knocked her pencil onto the floor. I watch as she picks it up, then peeks into her bag. She grabs something, frowns at it, then shoves it back into the bottom of her bag and quickly sits up and starts to write.

She really would. Huh. I wondered how she got such a good grade on the last test. I should have known.

Riley McGee is a cheerleader and the most popular freshman in school. In my short time here, she's been rumored to be dating two different first-string football players. That's almost one upperclassman a week. Not exactly the kind of freshman you'd expect to find in Algebra 2. Thankfully, I've totally got her beat because for one thing, I've got a brain.

Math may not come easily to me, but I work my butt off to get good grades and so far that has worked pretty well. I intend to walk out of this dump in four short years as valedictorian.

Riley peers into her bag again and smirks at what she finds. Isn't cheating hilarious?

What do I do? I didn't exactly see her cheat, but that's definitely what she's doing. I say a quick prayer for wisdom, then turn back to my paper. It wouldn't be nice to call her out in public. I'll just hang around after class for a minute and mention something quietly to Mr. Mackey. It's kind of sad, considering that I saw her at church on Sunday. I would have expected her to have a little more integrity, cheerleader or not.

"Five more minutes, my little mathletes," Mr. Mackey says, looking up from *The Big Impossible Book of Advanced Sudoku*. Old Mackey. He's almost as big around as he is tall and has the bushiest eyebrows I've ever seen. He's very weird, but I kind of like him.

I look back at my paper. Is it possible that X is zero? That always seems to be what happens when something doesn't make sense. It's like this joke the universe has—it's this little squiggle that means nothing (literally), and it makes everything around it meaningless, too. I resist the temptation to make another comparison to my life and move on to the second problem. Maybe this one's easier.

"Three minutes," Mackey says from behind his book. I quickly scratch out as much as I can on the rest of the quiz. It's not going to be pretty. I'll have to see if Mr. Mackey will let me do some extra credit to make up for this or it's going to seriously drag down my average. And I have to get an A. I just have to.

That's when I hear it again. Riley is looking at something in her bag, and she is definitely smiling about it. I turn around and stare at her. She writes something quickly, then looks up at me, rolls her eyes, and looks down at the quiz. Okay, that's it. Youth group or no, she can't get away with this. It's not right. Jesus would stand up for what's right. I raise my hand.

"Ana, do you have a question?" Mr. Mackey nods at me.

"Mr. Mackey—" I take a deep breath and slowly lower my hand—"I saw someone cheating on the pop quiz." I turn around to face Riley, righteous indignation washing over me. Someone behind me coughs, but it sounds like they're saying something under their breath.

"I did not cheat!" Riley screeches, her blue eyes wide. Riley is only a few inches taller than me, but it's enough to make her kind of intimidating.

"Oh really?" Mr. Mackey asks, cocking his eyebrow at me, then looking at Riley. "That's a serious accusation to make, Ana."

"I know, sir," I say as calmly as I can. I look around and notice that everyone is staring at me. I feel my face turning bright red. I hate this school. "But I saw her do it. She has the answers in her purse." Even as the words come out of my mouth, I'm wondering if maybe this wasn't the best way to handle the situation. Maybe this isn't what Jesus would do after all. It's hard to tell sometimes.

Someone coughs again, and this time I think I hear what they're saying: "God Girl." Who are they talking to?

Riley is looking at me like she could tear out my eyeballs. I lean back just in case she decides to go for it.

"I don't have anything in my purse!" she says, placing her hands on her hips and flipping her long blond hair over her shoulder.

Well, now I look like a fool. I have to show Mr. Mackey I'm right or I'll always be that girl who accused Riley. That'll do wonders for the friend search. I reach toward her chocolate brown bag. The nerve.

"Get away from my bag," she yells, grabbing it and hugging it to her chest as she stands up.

"Mr. Mackey, if I could just look in her bag, I could prove it," I say quickly, but Mr. Mackey is already walking toward us with anger in his eyes.

"Ladies, that's enough." He steps between us. "Riley, return to your seat." He looks at her, and she reluctantly sits down again. "For this little outburst, you'll both be in detention this afternoon."

"But—" Riley starts, but Mr. Mackey holds up his hand and continues.

"Ana, I'd like to see you after class."

"Just me?" *What about her?!* I glare at Riley, and she rolls her eyes at me. Mr. Mackey nods. Out of the corner of my eye, I see Tyler smirk.

"Now, please pass your quizzes to the front and open your books to page seventy-three," he says, turning away, indicating that the subject is closed. I take a deep breath, trying to hold back tears. She's the one who cheated!

I try to pay attention as Mr. Mackey goes on and on about factoring polynomials, but I can't focus on what he's saying. Detention. I've never had detention in my life. Does that go on your permanent record? I bet Princeton doesn't let in people with detentions on their records.

This never would have happened at my old school. Teachers there loved me and knew that I was going somewhere. Teachers here seem to think I'm headed straight to San Quentin. I've been here less than a month, and I'm already an outcast.

Finally the bell rings, and everyone around me throws their books into their bags. They're off to the grab food at the snack bar and sit on the smooth green hillsides and concrete steps that surround the school. There's no cafeteria here, but there are lots of places all over campus where groups of friends gather to eat. Someone coughs "God Girl" one more time, and though I'm not sure where it comes from, I know who it's directed at. I have to face that I have earned a nickname at my new school. Just great. I'm really going to miss being invisible.

Riley doesn't say a word to me as she walks by. I sit still, looking down at the fake wood grain on the smooth desktop in front of me. Engraved in the desk is a message for me: "Die, maggot."

I glance out the window and see people gathering together. Maybe it's good that Mackey is holding me after class. There are only so many times you can pretend not to care that you're eating alone, and it's not like I have anywhere to be, thanks to the Key Club meeting being canceled. Guidance counselors will tell you that joining clubs looks good on your college applications, but what they don't tell you is that it also gives you somewhere to go at lunch.

Slowly, the sound of voices begins to disappear, and locker doors stop slamming shut. Mr. Mackey walks over to the empty desk in front of me and sits down, turning to face me.

"Ana?" His eyes are narrowed, and he looks at me with what seems like concern. "You're doing well in this class." I nod and stare back down at my desk. Die, maggot, it tells me again. "You're doing exceptionally well for a freshman." I swallow. Where is he going with this? "But Riley—" he clears his throat and looks around, as if worried someone might overhear what he's about to say—"Riley has the highest grade in this class." My mouth hangs open in shock. *Riley* has the highest grade in the class?! "She hasn't missed a question yet."

I shut my mouth, for fear I might be attracting flies. "But see," I say, sitting up indignantly. "She must get the good grades by cheating. How else could she..."

"She's—" He coughs, and I hear phlegm rattle in his lungs. "She's quite good at math. Always has been. Teachers have been after her to join the math team for years, but she won't. I'm afraid she wasn't cheating on today's quiz."

"But she was looking at something in her bag!" I know I'm starting to sound a little hysterical, but I can't be wrong about this. I just can't. How could she be beating me?

"She was using her phone." He coughs. "To...what do they call it? Texting? She was texting."

"But..." But what? But how could he see that from all the way across the room? And cell phones aren't allowed at school. If he saw her, why didn't he stop her? How can it be true?

"That's why you both have detention," he says before I can say anything. "I just made up the quiz questions before class, so there's no way she could have had the answers hidden in her bag."

I gulp.

"I know you were only trying to do what's right today, Ana," he says, nodding at me. "So you'll serve the detention for disrupting the class, and then we'll put this behind us, okay?"

I look up at his bushy eyebrows and nod, biting my tongue to hold back the tears. The injustice of it all is overwhelming.

"Keep up the good work, Ana," he says, and I nod, looking down at my hands. He waits, but I don't move. "You're free to go now," he says, coughing again, as if I didn't get it the first time. Slowly, I stand up. I carefully place my book and notepad into my bag, looking down so he won't see the tears welling up in my eyes. He watches me as I walk toward the door and step out into the cool air.

2

As the final bell rings, I head toward the detention room. The sooner I get there, the sooner I can leave. I have a lot of work to do tonight, and I have to practice the piano before tomorrow's lesson. Papá likes me to finish that before he gets home so he can have some peace and quiet after his long day, which is so old-school, but that's how Papá is. He grew up in a conservative family in Mexico, and there the papá is the *jefe*, the bossman. Mom and I play along, but really, he can't think we're serious. Welcome to the new millennium, Papá.

I open the classroom door and step inside, and blink when I see Ms. Moore at the front of the room. I didn't know she was in charge of detention. I start to turn around, hoping she won't see me.

"Ana Dominguez," Ms. Moore smiles and gestures toward the rows of desks. "There you are. I have to say, I was surprised to hear you would be joining us today." She gives me a funny look. "Well, come in. You won't be getting an engraved invitation, if that's what you're waiting for." She laughs at her joke, and I give a little smile in spite of myself. Ms. Moore is one of my favorite teachers, and it's not just because I love English.

I take a seat near the door, put my head down on my

desk, and let my brown hair fall around my face, acting as
a barrier between me and the world. The plastic desktop is
cool and calming. I close my eyes and picture Tyler. Does he
have dimples? I think he does. The classroom door opens
and closes a lot, but I keep my head down. Maybe no one
will notice me here.

"Okay, everyone. Let's settle in," Ms. Moore says, leaning against a desk at the front of the room. She is wearing ballet flats, an A-line skirt, and a form-fitting sweater
with a dark top underneath. I could swear it's some kind of,
I don't know, rock concert T-shirt. Some people don't like
Ms. Moore, but I think she's the best teacher this school has.
True, she dresses a little strange, but she grew up out East,
so of course she's a little different. She has a very piercing
stare and people say she butts into other people's business
too much.

But I like the way she always talks about "making a dif-
ference" and gives us weird projects. Last week she assigned
us to groups and handed out bags of supplies—paper, pens,
and staples—and told us we were our own countries now
and had to write up our own constitutions. The only problem was, some groups were given lots of paper but no pencils, and some groups didn't even get any paper, and some
got colored pencils and construction paper, and some got
lots of everything. Most people thought the project was
dumb and unfair, but I got it. She was trying to show us that
it *is* unfair how some countries always get more while others constantly seem to get the short end of the stick. She's
always thinking of interesting things like that. Plus, she
really loves books, you can tell that right away. She's always

got one tucked under her arm, and our reading list for English is miles long.

"Oh, there you are, Zoe," Ms. Moore says when that quiet red-haired hippie girl from my history class comes in. Zoe. I never knew her name was Zoe. I wonder what she's in here for. Zoe takes a desk near the back, placing a small black instrument case on the floor next to her bag.

"I've thought of a very special project for us this afternoon." I look up quickly. This could be good. Ms. Moore winks at me, but I hear a snort from across the room.

"Riley," Ms. Moore says, looking in the direction of the snorter. "I absolutely admire your enthusiasm. Why don't you and Ana be our first group?"

I stare at her. She can't be serious.

"But, Ms. Moore—" Riley says.

"Thank you, Riley. You're always so cooperative. Please move over to where Ana is sitting." Riley glares at me.

She looks like she's going to protest again, but Ms. Moore has her eyes leveled on Riley. Moving so slowly it looks like it pains her, she takes a seat at the desk next to me. Ms. Moore then divides the whole class into groups of four. She pairs Riley and me with Zoe, the pudgy redhead, and a girl named Christine, who has hot-pink streaks in her black hair and is wearing a ripped T-shirt and metal-studded belt, like some kind of wannabe Asian Avril Lavigne.

"Now, we're going to all write a short essay," Ms. Moore says, smiling as if she's just bestowed an expensive gift on us. An essay? I thought she said a fun project. "Your essay will be called 'The Day My Life Changed.'" Several people groan.

I raise my hand. She nods at me. "Is this supposed to be a positive thing?" I ask, tapping my pencil on my desk. "Like the day my life got better? Or a negative thing?"

Ms. Moore bites her lip for a long moment. "I don't think I'm going to answer that question," she says finally, her short brown hair bouncing as she nods. "I gave the assignment and I want to see what you'll do with it." She crosses her thin arms over her tiny chest.

I look around, but everyone else seems to be as confused as I feel. "This isn't for a grade," Ms. Moore says quickly. "There are no right or wrong answers." She scratches her forearm. "Two pages will suffice. Let's get started right now."

We all stare at her for a moment until she gestures with her hand to indicate that we should pull our desks closer together.

"Now," Ms. Moore says, clapping. "No thinking. Just write."

We each take out notebook paper and a pen or a pencil and stare down at the blank pages. Ms. Moore is a little disorienting. Other teachers would have specified plain, college-ruled paper, front-side only, no pencils, please double-space, write your name and date at the top, remember to use topic sentences. But she apparently just wants us to go for it. I chew on the end of my pencil and think. Zoe crunches into Doritos while she writes.

What is Ms. Moore looking for here? I guess I could write about the day my dad came home and announced that he was starting his own law practice and we were moving to Half Moon Bay. My mom had always wanted to live on the beach, and he decided he could make more money in this town because there are a lot of rich people here. Mom, who is totally into appearances, thought the town was charming, so here we are. Never mind that I was happy with my old school and my old friends. That was a pretty big day.

But somehow I don't think that's interesting enough to get a good grade on this. Ms. Moore said it wouldn't be graded, but you can't trust teachers on this kind of stuff. Everything you turn in counts for something.

There was the time I fell out of a tree and broke my arm. Hm. That doesn't seem right either. Maybe I could make something up? No one here knows I was a baby when my parents left Mexico. Maybe I could pretend I was older and remember it. That's the kind of thing Ms. Moore would love.

I glance up at Ms. Moore, and we lock eyes. I smile at her, as if to say, "Don't worry. I've got this." But she gives me one of her piercing stares. For a moment, I could almost swear she's digging through the secret memories in my mind. My heart beats a little faster, and my fingers feel icy and numb. Finally she smiles at me and gives me an encouraging nod.

I look back down at my paper. Okay, fine, I'll write the truth. What's the harm in writing it down in detention? Only Ms. Moore will see it, and she's always saying you have to be true to yourself and stuff. I take a deep breath and begin.

I was born in Mexico and had a serious heart deformity. My family rushed me to a hospital in San Diego, where the American doctors performed open-heart surgery on me when I was four days old. My parents prayed and prayed that I would be okay, but the odds of my surviving were less than ten percent. But God was merciful and he saved me. Even the doctors said it must have been a miracle. Everything that has ever happened in my life is because God spared me that day. We moved to the United States for good. My parents, who weren't very religious, started going to church. And I grew up with a sense of purpose. I was given a second chance at life so that I can go to Princeton and eventually become a doctor myself. I am called to save others just as God saved me.

I go back through and check my essay, making sure I've got the commas and the spelling right and re-reading different sections. The hair on my arm raises. It's kind of humbling to know you aren't really supposed to have made it.

"Okay, everybody. Let's stop right there," Ms. Moore says, looking up from the book she's been reading. *The Grapes of Wrath*. Steinbeck's finest.

A few people groan because they haven't finished yet.

"It's doesn't matter where you are. That's not the point of this assignment. The point is that it's always important to recognize the big moments in your life and share them with others."

I take a deep breath. Did she say share them with others?

"Humans must stay connected with one another for society to work. You must care for your neighbor."

Now we all groan in unison. Ms. Moore has really lost it now. There is no way on earth I'm sharing this essay with anyone. She tricked us. She made me be honest. I cross my arms across my chest.

"Go on," she says, looking around the room at us. "No one is leaving this classroom until every single person has read their story to their group."

We continue to stare back at her, unmoving.

Ms. Moore smiles at us a little crookedly. "I wouldn't make you do it if I didn't think it was good for you." She walks around to her desk. "And I've got all day."

A few people look around to see if anyone is moving.

Ms. Moore opens *The Grapes of Wrath*. "Say, isn't *American Idol* on tonight?"

We look at each other. Can she really hold us here as long as she wants? There must be a rule about that or something. Slowly, people around us begin to move, and the room hums as people start to read.

3

"Let's just get this over with," Riley says. She carefully avoids my eye. "I'll go first. We all wrote one, so it's no big deal." She nods, as if to convince herself.

Christine, Zoe, and I nod back, and she begins to read her essay. I can hear other people around me reading cute stories about summer camp counselors and first kisses, and I want to shove my story into my mouth and swallow it so that no one can see what I wrote. How could I have been so stupid?

Luckily, Riley's story is kind of like mine. "I am one of the strongest swimmers I know, and I've been surfing since I could walk. My dad would take me out into the ocean, and I would lose myself in the wonder and the power of the waves," she begins. Her face is pink, and she keeps her eyes trained on her paper. She reads quickly. "A few months ago, just after school let out for the summer, I went out surfing by myself one morning. I promised my mom that I would never surf alone, but Ashley didn't show up, and the ocean was calling me. The waves were perfect—big and round and fast. There were a few college-age guys down the shore a little ways, but I was perfectly and peacefully alone where I was. I had caught a couple great breaks, and I was getting tired, so I was just about to come in for the day when a big wave came up behind me and pulled me off my board."

Riley coughs. She takes a deep breath, looks around, then rushes on. "It hit me on the head, and I went under. I was stunned and disoriented as the wave tossed me around, but I tried to kick my way back to the top. I made it to the surface, but the undertow was pulling at my feet, like someone was yanking me down, down, down. I fought for a long time, bobbing up and down, but after a while, I knew it was useless. I was going to die. And I was so tired that it was okay with me. When I couldn't fight anymore, I let the frothy water take me under. The last thing I remember is saying a prayer and shutting my eyes. It's not like I'm so religious, but my parents taught us to pray and I guess it was just natural. And the next thing I know, I'm waking up on the shore. My board has washed up down the beach a little ways from me, broken in half, but I'm fine. I should have died, but I didn't. God saved me."

Riley puts her paper down and looks at her hands. Riley is so bossy and confident that I guess I assumed she never really got embarrassed. And she's actually a really good writer. Not better than me, but good. We sit in silence for a moment.

"I'll go next," Zoe says quietly. Zoe's red hair cascades around her face, and she begins to read. Her voice is soft and soothing, and at first I can't understand her because she's reading so fast. I lean in closer.

A year ago, Zoe is saying, she was horseback riding with her parents. She and her father went off on one of the trails through the redwoods when her horse heard a clap of thunder and reared up on its back legs. Zoe held on, but the horse kept bucking. She knew she was in for it. She'd been around horses her whole life and knew that people can die or be paralyzed when they get thrown. Her foot caught in the stirrup, and when the horse took off running, Zoe was dragged along behind him. Her dad said the horse ran for almost a quarter of a mile before he caught up to them, but Zoe blacked out. All she remembers is lying on the ground, dazed and disoriented, then getting up quietly. Her father called 911, assuming she was in a state of shock when she couldn't tell him what hurt, and she walked to the ambulance and sat still while they examined her. They rushed her to the hospital only to find...nothing. Nothing was wrong with her. Her father called it a miracle, the doctors called it a miracle, and it must have been.

Zoe puts down her essay and shrugs. I watch her, trying to catch her eye, but she won't look up. Something strange is going on. I look at Christine the freak girl. She glares back at me.

"Okay, I'll go now," I say. "Let's hurry up because I really need to get home." The others nod.

I start to read, pretending that I'm delivering my valedictorian speech. I try to speak slowly and clearly, enunciating each syllable. I finish my story and immediately start playing with my pen to give my hands something to do. Suddenly I feel like I don't have any clothes on.

When I finally look up, I see they are all staring at me with their mouths hanging open. I take a deep breath and nudge Christine. "Your turn," I say, trying to play it cool. "It's not that bad." I figure if we move on, they'll forget about my essay.

Christine looks at me and cocks an eyebrow. "Trust me, you have no idea."

Christine's story is only half a page long, but in the margins she has drawn amazing cartoons to illustrate her story. I can see them through the paper as she holds it up to read. She recites her words as if she's reading a police transcript.

Christine and her mother were riding in the car. Her mother was wearing her seatbelt. Christine did not have her seatbelt on. It was raining. The car's brakes locked up. The car skidded off the road into a ravine. Christine flew through the windshield. She doesn't remember that part, but she saw the shattered glass later. Her mother hit her head on the steering wheel and died upon impact. Christine walked up to the road and flagged down a passing car. Now it is just Christine and her father. That was the day her life changed.

I watch Christine's face as she reads. She carefully controls herself, as if she's not even reading about her own life. I want to give her a hug, but she won't look at us. Zoe has a tear running down her cheek.

"I'm so sorry," I say weakly. Riley and Zoe nod. Zoe puts her hand on Christine's forearm, and Christine lets her keep it there. I hold out a pack of Kleenex, but no one reaches for it.

"You guys, do you realize that all of us are, like, these freaks of nature?" Zoe asks, her eyes wide.

"We should be dead," Riley says quietly.

I try to lighten the mood. "At least we wouldn't be in detention if we were dead." Christine smiles a little at my joke.

"Okay, please let me have your attention," says Ms. Moore. I look up, startled. Our little world had grown so private over here that to hear someone else's voice is strange.

"I'm very proud of everyone today. You all did great work.

When your group is done, please quietly excuse yourselves and turn in your papers on the way out. Have a great evening," she says.

I smile at Ms. Moore. I like the way she makes us feel like fellow adults. She never even mentioned the "d" word once this afternoon.

I turn back to my group. I'm glad to finally get out of here, but . . . I somehow don't want to go.

"So, I guess I'll see you guys around," I say. It sounds lame, but nothing I can think of seems appropriate right now.

Christine and Zoe are still frozen in place. Riley shrugs and starts to get up.

"What are you doing?" Zoe hisses at her. She grabs Riley's arm.

Riley shakes free. "Um, going home? You?"

Zoe stares at Riley in disbelief. "Don't you see? This is huge. We've been thrown together for a reason." She looks around to make sure we all see this.

I glance up at Ms. Moore. She has her eyebrow raised at me again. What is with this lady? Is she some kind of magician? Can she read minds?

"Look," Riley says, letting her bag fall against the desk. "We all have similar stories. That's strange. It's a coincidence or something."

"Coincidence?" Zoe says. She shakes her head. And as much as I hate to admit it, I think Zoe might be right.

"You're so smart, and you can't figure this out?" I take a deep breath. "You think this is a coincidence?"

Riley looks at us. Zoe is staring at her intently, her face pale.

"You do realize that everyone else wrote an essay about their stupid hamster dying, right?" Christine asks, her pink hair falling in her face.

"Okay, fine," Riley says. "It's pretty weird. I get it. But what do you want from me?"

I stare at Christine, then look at Zoe. Neither of them moves.

Riley's phone begins to vibrate, and she reaches to shut it off. "See you around." As she turns to go, I swear I see a trace of bewilderment on her face.

"I'd better go too," Christine says. She stands up slowly and begins to pack her things away. Zoe stares at Christine.

"We need to talk more about this, guys," Zoe says, and Christine shrugs, then tosses her book bag over her shoulder and walks toward the door. I watch her go, and for some reason I feel sad as she walks away.

Zoe shakes her head at me. "Jeez, some people." I shrug. What can you do? Did she honestly think a cheerleader and a freak were going to hang out with us? "Do you want to get together sometime?" she asks. I look at her long tie-dye skirt and her hemp backpack. She smells a little weird, like patchouli. She's an outsider too.

"Sure."

"Good." Zoe stands up and abruptly grabs her backpack and walks to the front of the room.

I am left sitting alone at my desk for the second time today. "Thank you, God," I whisper, although even as I say it, I'm not really sure what I'm thanking him for.

4

When Papá asks how school went today, I don't know what to say. I look at him chewing his chicken and notice that he's staring over my shoulder, out the back door. Okay, good. Sometimes he gets on these "I'm an involved parent" kicks where he tries to really care, but most of the time he just asks because he doesn't know what else to say. Thankfully, this is one of those times. I can probably get out of here and onto my homework in under ten minutes.

"Fine," I say, then quickly stuff ginger chicken into my mouth. When he's home in the evening, Papá insists that we all eat dinner together. Thankfully, his new law practice keeps him busy most of the time. "I practiced my piano piece for a while, and I think I'm really getting it now."

"That's good," he says. "Hard work is the only way to get ahead, Ana." He takes another bite. Hard work is Papá's favorite topic, at least when it comes to me.

It's not that he doesn't care about what's really going in my life, but he just doesn't seem to know how to ask. Even if he did, I'm not sure I'd know how to answer. We have some kind of communication gap. It started around the time I got boobs.

I look straight ahead, staring at the pink wall behind him. Who paints their dining room pink? Mom is doing the new house in what she calls a "beach palette," and apparently this room is Sandy Sunset, which is supposed to be stimulating or something, but is not helping our conversation here.

Mom picks at the broccoli rabe on her plate, steering clear of the fattening wasabi mashed potatoes. The potatoes are for Papá and me, and, well, to decorate her plate a little. "Did your Key Club meeting go well?" She looks at me sweetly, as if she actually cares, but I know what she's really asking. Did I make any friends at Key Club today? I weigh my options on how to answer. I could tell her that the meeting was canceled, but then I'd have to explain what I did instead. I could answer what she's really asking and tell her I met someone named Zoe who seems kind of cool, but then I'd have to explain about detention, and Papá would flip out. So far my detention is a secret between me and Maria, who picks me up from school. I could distract Mom by mentioning that I aced my history test, but she might pick up on the fact that I am trying to change the subject. I look at her smiling at me hopefully, and my heart sinks. I wish I could give her the answer she's looking for, but instead I just nod.

"It was fine," I say. I hope God will forgive me. I know you're not supposed to lie, but surely Jesus remembers how hard it was to be a teenager. I guess they didn't have college admissions quotas to worry about back then, but I doubt much has changed with the whole parents thing in the past two thousand years.

Thankfully, Maria breaks the awkward silence by coming into the dining room to check on our "water situation," as Mom likes to call refilling our glasses, and Papá is distracted by a new e-mail on his BlackBerry, so I use the opportunity to change the subject.

"How was *your* meeting, Mom?" Mom has already made herself indispensable to the women's group at our new church, and she is in the throes of organizing some tea or something. I can never keep it all straight.

"We're working on the most interesting project." She purses her artificially plumped lips. "We're organizing volunteers to visit the elderly and shut-ins in town." She puts her fork down. "You wouldn't believe how many people there are in Half Moon Bay who have no one to talk to. They're so lonely. It's tragic."

"Wow," I say, unsure how to respond. I mean, I'm not elderly or a shut-in, but I wonder if I can sign up.

"And the community service will look good on your applications, honey, so I volunteered you to do visits at the nursing home. Oh, and Michelle McGee's daughter is going to do it too. Isn't that great? She goes to your school, so this will help you get to know someone." She smiles as if she's just handed me an adorable puppy. God, you were pretty clear about honoring and obeying, but what if my parents are crazy?

"Super." I shove a bite of potato into my mouth so I won't have to say any more. I have too much homework to do to waste my weekends visiting old people. Besides, if I got one guess as to who Michelle McGee's daughter is, I wouldn't even need to use one of my lifelines.

Papá grunts, and I turn to him quickly. "Anything good, Papá?" He puts his BlackBerry down on the table but doesn't seem to hear me. "On your e-mail?"

He shakes his head. "Just a client issue. No need to worry." He pokes at his chicken with a fork.

"George, did you look at that color I selected for the bedroom?" Mom asks. His real name is Jorge, but Mom only calls him George. I personally like the way Jorge sounds better—not so reminiscent of that curious little monkey—but again, it's not like anyone in this house is like, "Ana, what do you think we should call Papá?"

"It's more on the pastel blue side, and I know we'd talked about a lighter aqua, but I think the greeny hues are too sea and not so beachy. What do you think?" Mom waits expectantly. He stares at her, and I use the distraction to make my escape.

"May I please be excused to do my homework?"

Papá nods, and I breathe a sigh of relief. Polynomials are calling my name, and this time, I really have to answer.

5

The house is finally quiet, just the way I like it. The only light comes from the chandelier above the kitchen table, and the silent shadows make the rest of the house feel calm. I spread my textbooks out on the thick oak table, delivered fresh from Pottery Barn two weeks ago, and pull a blue pen out of my bag. I lay my papers out carefully, arranging them by subject, then turn toward the kitchen. I pull open the refrigerator door and grab a can of Diet Coke, fill a glass with ice, and pour the cool dark liquid over it. It fizzes and pops, and I take a sip.

I blame my mom for my Diet Coke habit. She would never let real sugar pass her lips, but she drinks this stuff by the gallon. It has no calories, but I'm pretty sure it's completely toxic, because you just can't cheat nature like that. I try not to think about it as I sit down on one of the straight-backed kitchen chairs.

First period. Biology. I look my homework over quickly, then clip it into the bio section of my binder. Done.

Second period. French. I skim the textbook and scan my homework, correcting a missing accent in question three. Check.

Third period. P.E. What a waste of time. And by the way, who decided a sport where you knock the ball back and forth with your wrists was a good idea? There's a reason most sports involve rackets or bats of some sort. It's called bruises.

Fourth period. Math. Argh. Just thinking about it makes me want to impale myself with a spoon. I can't go back there. Maybe I can go to the office first thing tomorrow and get them to transfer me to a different class. Mackey didn't seem like he was going to hold it against me grade-wise, but everyone else will hold it against me for the rest of high school. Tyler definitely thinks I am the biggest loser since...since...no, I'm the biggest loser anyone has ever seen. Historic lows.

Okay, focus, Ana. Factoring polynomials. You can do this. I take a sip of Diet Coke, get out my mechanical pencil, and turn my attention to the word problems I didn't have the guts to face earlier.

I've only been working for a few minutes when I hear something in the other room. It sounds like my parents are trying to keep their voices low, which means that I have a job to do. I'm an expert level spy. I'm just waiting for my top-secret recruitment letter from the CIA. They probably want me to complete high school first. Of course, it wouldn't have to be this way if anyone ever told me anything, but they don't, and desperate times call for desperate measures. I stand up and tiptoe over to the hallway, where I can hear the murmurs of Papá's voice, but I can't make out what they're saying. I take a few more steps, then freeze when I hear my name. They're talking about me. I move in closer.

"It'll devastate her," Papá says, "and the freshman year is so important in setting the foundation for academic success." My mother mumbles something, and then Papá continues. "School is more important, Andrea. She must get into a good college, or where will she be?"

The sound of the faucet in their bathroom drowns out my mother's response, but I wait. I hear something about Maria. Oh no. My mother sighs, and I make out something about insurance. Papá grunts in response; then it all goes quiet. The strip of light under their door goes out, and I know the conversation is over for the night. I sigh and tiptoe back to the kitchen, trying to piece together what I just heard. They still aren't going to tell me about Maria's lupus. How can they not tell me? I'm not a child. Don't they think I'll notice?

I shake my head, then sit back down at the table. I say a quick prayer for Maria's health and resolve to find out exactly what lupus is. I'll look it up on the Internet.

I turn back to my math. I'm halfway through the last problem when I hear footsteps behind me.

"Anita." Maria walks into the kitchen, her faded pink robe wrapped tightly around her. Her face is traced with lines, and her black hair is laced with strands of gray. She shuffles across the Italian-tile floor in her worn slippers. In our old house, Maria had a small bedroom, but here she has a large room, complete with sitting area, and her own bathroom with a whirlpool tub and everything. But for some reason, I don't think she likes it too much. In the old house, her bedroom was right next to mine. Now she's downstairs and I'm upstairs. She flips on the kitchen light.

"How was *Survivor*?" I ask.

She walks toward the refrigerator. "Predictable." She digs

around in the back, then pulls out a package wrapped in tinfoil. "The redhead should have been voted off, but she's cute, so..." She shrugs, then carefully lifts two tamales onto plates. She wraps the foil around the rest of the tamales, then puts them back into the fridge and puts the plates into the microwave.

Though Maria is welcome to eat the same food as the rest of us—i.e. whatever she cooks for us—she usually skips whatever weird food trend Mom has seized upon at the moment and eats her favorite dishes after my parents have gone to bed. Her tamales are out of this world. Let's just say it's a good thing I inherited Papá's metabolism. I've been eating two dinners for most of my life.

Maria pulls a glass out of the cupboard and pushes it against the water dispenser on our giant refrigerator, takes the steaming hot tamales out of the microwave, gets two forks out, and sits down at the table next to me.

"How is the homework going?" She unwraps the corn-husk from her tamale. I consider the question as I watch her gnarled fingers work. If it had come from Papá, I would have simply said it was going great, but I can't lie to Maria. She can always tell.

"It's okay." I slam by math book closed and slide my plate toward me.

"What's wrong?" She blows on her tamale.

What's wrong? Where do I even begin? Everything is wrong. I hate this place. I hate my school. I hate not knowing anyone. I hate that Riley is beating me in math. I hate that Maria is sick. I hate that God is letting me down.

"Nothing." The woman is probably dying, for goodness'

sake. I can't complain to her about some stupid cheerleader making my life miserable.

She studies my face for a moment, and I force myself to smile. She shakes her head. Obviously, she doesn't believe me.

"They love you, Anita," she says, then takes a sip of water. "They love you more than anything." I unwrap the cornhusk from my tamale and steam warms my face. Coming from anyone else, that statement would have sounded like it came out of left field, but Maria has this eerie way of making conversations flow according to her own rhythm. Somehow I follow.

"I know."

She has a bite, then lays down her fork. I take a quick sip of my Diet Coke.

"I do too," she says quietly.

I take her hand. Is now the time to ask her about the lupus? She smiles, then stands up and pushes her chair against the table quietly.

"I think I'll finish this in my room and let you get back to work." She picks up her plate. "Good night. There are more tamales in the fridge if you want them. Don't stay up too late."

"Good night," I say. She shuffles across the tile, flips off the light, and disappears into the shadows.

6

The game tonight is Marshmallow Wiffle Ball. I usually prefer the kind of game where I can just hide and watch other people be embarrassed (because that's all youth group games are anyway, just various ways to embarrass you), but despite the humiliation inherent in team sports, at least when everyone has to play the game, you don't end up just sitting alone. I seem to be doing a lot of that these days. It's impossible to hit a marshmallow past first base, for the record.

My parents did not ask me where I would like to go to church. They did not ask me if I wanted to be involved in the youth group with a bunch of kids who have known each other since nursery school. They believe dropping me off here on Sunday nights is their parental responsibility, so here I am. Riley isn't here tonight, and I can't decide if I'm relieved or disappointed. Maybe a little of both.

As Judy, the youth pastor's wife, gathers up stray marshmallows and herds us into the folding chairs set up for worship time, I quietly take a seat in the back row and look around. The youth room, with its high, sloped ceiling and wide floor, used to be the main sanctuary at Seaview Community Church, but they recently built a brand-new main building, complete with padded oak pews and a soundproof cry room. And even though the youth room has been transformed into a space that screams, "Please please come to church, kids," with its plywood stage, ratty couches, and foosball tables, there's still a sense of peace that pervades it when Fritz, the youth pastor, finally gets everyone to quiet down.

Worship is my favorite part of youth group. When I'm singing praise songs, that's when I feel the surest that God really is out there. I mean, not that I doubt it. Okay, well, dirty little secret here, but maybe I do lately.

Of course, it doesn't hurt either that Tyler leads worship with his band, Three Car Garage. He's wearing baggy jeans and a tight black T-shirt that shows off his broad shoulders, along with a green A's hat and Reef flip flops. He's tan and built, and his shaggy blond hair falls over his eyes a little. Tommy Chu, the drummer whose hair always looks greasy, bangs his drumsticks together, Dave Brecht the oddball bassist plucks one string, and Tyler begins strumming a chord and singing. Thankfully, Tyler didn't laugh and point at me when I came into the room tonight so I'm guessing he doesn't even know I'm in his math class. I've never been so thankful to be invisible to a boy.

I pull my eyes away from him and try to focus on the words, which are projected onto a screen at the front of the room, behind the band. I'm doing a pretty good job losing myself in the music, but just as we get to the chorus, I hear a loud bang and turn around in time to see Riley McGee, along with another freshman girl named Tanya, giggle and stumble into the room. They laugh as they make their way toward the rows of chairs. I smile at Riley. She meets my eye, then turns away as if she hasn't seen me. She and Tanya fall into chairs on the other side of the aisle.

They've accomplished their goal. Everyone is looking at them. Leave it to Riley to show up fashionably late to church.

I try to ignore them and focus my thoughts on singing, but it's difficult when I can see Riley flipping her blond hair around out of the corner of my eye. She's wearing a short denim skirt, a tight white cotton top, and a chunky yellow beaded necklace. Maybe I should get one of those necklaces.

The band fades out the final lines of the first song, and I refocus my eyes on the front of the room. I have to remember why I'm here. It's not to pick up fashion tips.

As Tyler begins to play again, I see him smile a bit, and I suck in my breath. Shaking my head and closing my eyes, I begin to tune the world out again and find a sense of peace.

I hear a snicker. My eyes fly open, and I turn toward the sound. Tanya is looking at me and laughing. I look back at the screen and try to focus my eyes on the sharp edges of the letters, but then I hear it again. Tanya, laughing. I don't even have to turn to know who she's laughing at, but some masochistic force compels me, and I look at her. Her straight, dark hair lies in a shiny sheet down her back, her face twisted in a sneer. She pokes her elbow into Riley, but Riley doesn't turn. Tears well up in my eyes, but I look away before Tanya can see me cry. I'm not that low. Not yet.

We sing a few more songs, but my heart isn't into it anymore. Adults always say you're welcome at church no matter who you are or what you've done, but they never tell you how to convince everyone else that you're welcome. Apparently being the new girl, on top of accusing the wonderful and amazing Riley of cheating, is something even Jesus can't help me overcome.

If I were back in San Jose, I'd be having Jamba Juice from the shopping center across from church with Holly and Claudia right now, after an awesome evening of real fellowship.

After the last chords fade away, the worship team quietly puts their instruments down and moves to the back of the room. Fritz jumps onto the stage, clapping to get us riled up to learn about God, but for some reason I glance back at Tanya and Riley again. Tanya is not looking at me for a change, but Riley and I catch each other's eyes for a quick moment. The look in her eyes is loud and clear: It didn't mean anything; we are not friends.

As soon as the final amen is said, I slip out the door, slide under the eave, and stand out of the rain to wait for Mom to come pick me up. It's good that it's raining. It's stupid, I know, but I always feel like Jesus feels my pain when it rains. Though I guess Jesus has more important problems to worry about right now than me, like you know, world hunger and stuff.

I keep hearing noises from inside, running and high-pitched squeals and the clang of cymbals being hit by someone who doesn't know how to drum, but I prefer the soft patter of rain on the roof above me. I stand right next to the door, but no one who comes out seems to see me as they breeze by.

I look at my watch. Youth group ends at seven thirty, but Mom always comes a little late, which is annoying because I have a few hours of studying left to do tonight. The raindrops hit the pavement and pool in shallow puddles in the parking lot. I practice looking deep and brooding, just in case anyone notices me.

Fifteen minutes later, Mom still isn't here, and since my parents won't let me have a cell phone, I can't call her to see what's wrong. The noise inside has quieted, and more kids are dashing from the youth room across the parking lot to waiting cars. Tanya and Riley squeal as they walk outside and scream and laugh as they run across the lot to Matt Hershey's beat-up station wagon. Matt is a senior who drives his parents' discarded car, but even I know it's an honor to get a ride as a freshman. They blast the radio, but the rain deadens the noise as they peal out of the parking lot. It's not like I'm allowed to ride in cars with boys anyway.

Something has got to change. I'm tired of being an outcast. Maybe I need to be more proactive. I'm not about to go up to just anyone and ask if they want to be my friend, but it's definitely time to do something about this situation. Maybe I should see if that girl Zoe wants to have lunch sometime. She might not be my first choice of friend, but beggars can't be choosers, right?

The gray sky darkens, and I wonder what to do about a ride home. Do I go back inside and find an adult and tell them I've been abandoned? Do I ask if I can borrow someone's cell phone? I could call Papá. He won't be happy about having to come out and get me in the rain, but I suppose he'd have to make the trip. I decide I should probably just head back inside and find one of the leaders, but as I start moving, Tyler walks out of the building. Let me rephrase that—walks out of the building with Stacy Meeker, the long-legged senior.

I know it's stupid, and I know I never had a chance with him anyway, and I know he doesn't even know who I am, but for some reason it still feels like I've been punched in the gut. I twist my hair up into a ponytail to give my hands something to do, then take it back out again. It's heavy and thick, and never seems to do what I want. Why does my mom do this to me?

Out of the corner of my eye, I see Tyler lean in and give Stacy a hug. She smiles and walks calmly to her car, then climbs in and drives away. He watches her go, and I die a little inside. As her car leaves the parking lot, Tyler seems to realize for the first time he's standing in the rain. He quickly jogs back under the eave. I look down, unsure what I'm supposed to do. He's standing about four feet from me. Can he hear my heart slamming around in my chest? Does he see me? Should I say something?

I bite my lip and examine my shoes. Safer not to say anything. It's hard to hate yourself for saying something stupid if you don't say anything at all.

Tyler sneezes. There, it would be rude not to say bless you. But when I open my mouth, only a tiny squeak comes out. Did he hear that? I clear my throat, then try again.

"Bless you," I say quietly. Tyler turns to me, as if surprised to see me standing there. His eyes are darker blue than I thought.

"Thanks."

For a moment, I'm not sure who he's talking to. I'm used to being invisible. But then I realize that I'm the only one there, so I nod. The soft drum of the rain is comforting somehow.

"Do you go to my school?" He runs his hands through his hair to shake off the rain. His forearms are really muscular. I've never been attracted to a guy's arms before.

He's really talking to me. I gulp and work up my courage to answer.

"Uh huh." I try to smile, but my lips stick to my teeth. "I—" He looks at me, waiting. "We have math together."

He nods. "Tyler." He sticks his hand out, and I stare at it for a second before I realize I'm supposed to shake it. I reach my hand out. His hand is soft and warm and a little wet. I let go quickly.

I stare at him. He clears his throat. All of a sudden it feels very private under this eave.

"Ana!" I say quickly as realization dawns. He was waiting for me to say my name. Oh jeez I am totally messing this up.

He smiles slightly. "Nice to meet you."

"Yeah." I smile and wait for him to respond, but he doesn't say anything. I listen to the rain.

"So," he says, clearing his throat. "Are you new?"

"We just moved here."

"Cool." He nods, staring at the parking lot again.

I wait for him to go on, but then a bright pair of headlights turns into the parking lot. I make out the silver outline of Mom's Lexus as it comes toward us. Of course. Now that I don't want her to come, she does. She has a real gift for ruining my life.

"My mom's here, so . . ."

Tyler nods.

"Bye, Ana."

I smile, unsure of what else to do, and then walk to the car. Pulling the door open, I slide into the passenger seat and force myself not to look back at him. I also force myself not to grin from ear to ear.

"You would not believe the traffic tonight. There was an accident on Highway 1, and it's got everything backed up for miles," Mom says, panting, as if she, not the car, has been running. She backs out of the parking space, revs the engine, and drives toward the parking lot exit. "Were you waiting long?"

"It's okay," I say, resting my head against the fogged window. As we drive away, I cave in and look at Tyler, standing alone watching us drive away, and allow myself a little smile.

7

'm checking my teeth in my locker mirror (I don't want to go from God Girl to Green Teeth) when I see a flash of red hair behind me. I shut my locker quickly and turn around. It's her. I make myself move before I lose my nerve.

Zoe is putting a book into her locker when I walk up behind her. I cough, and she turns around, and smiles when she sees me.

"Hi," Zoe says quietly. She has several books and an instrument case in her arms.

"Um, hey." I say the first thing that pops into my head. "What's your next class?" The smell of french fries wafts into the hallway as the noon rush begins.

"Spanish. It's my fav—"

"Do it, Zach!" a voice says across the hall. We both turn and see Riley and her airhead cheerleader friend Ashley laughing with Zach Abramo, that huge junior she's always hanging out with. He's on the football team and kind of looks like Governor Schwarzenegger. Zach's football goon Andy comes up behind him, making whooping noises and doing air circles with his hand. A few kids whistle, and people are crowding around Riley. It's apparent that some kind of plan is afoot. I shrug and turn back to Zoe.

"I've got English. Ms. Moore is great."

I hear a whistle, and Zoe and I both turn our heads to look at Riley's group again. Zach is bent down in front of her, and she's climbing onto his shoulders. Ashley and Andy are egging her on, and others are starting to turn and make noise too.

I look up and down the hall, incredulous. Is no one seeing this? Where are all the teachers?

"Seriously, aren't there hall monitors at this crazy school?"

Zoe smiles and shrugs. "It's a small school."

Riley is now trying to stand up on Zach's shoulders, and lots of people are laughing and cheering her on. He's staggering around, but she's laughing and doesn't seem to be concerned that she might fall. I turn back toward Zoe. I can't stand to see Riley crash to the tile floor and crack her head open. This isn't to say that I care about her. I'm just worried out of common human courtesy.

"So...we should...hang out sometime...if you want or you're not busy. We could have lunch? But you probably are too busy or whatever." I sound like an idiot. There's no way she'll want to hang with me now. "I was going to go to French Club right now, but we could maybe have lunch—" I stop when I see Zach walking down the hall with Riley on his shoulders. People are giving her high fives as she passes them.

The speaker in the hallway crackles and the principal Ms. Lovchuck—sadly, that isn't her nickname—begins to speak. For someone with "love" in her name, Ms. Lovchuck has very little of it for high schoolers.

"Attention, students." The way she says "students" makes it sound like she said "cretins." A few people quiet down to hear the announcement but most go on as if nothing is happening. "Mr. Dumas, our art teacher, will be starting an Art Club."

While Ms. Lovchuck is explaining what the Art Club is, Riley and Zach stumble down the hallway. Zach puts Riley within arm's reach of the speaker. She looks around uncertainly, but when people around them start chanting, "Do it! Do it!" Riley's face breaks into a smile. She reaches out her arms, and when Zach steps closer to the wall, Riley grabs hold of the speaker and begins to pry it out of the wall. The face falls off easily, so then she begins to pull at the wires connecting the speaker.

"The first meeting will be this Thurs—" Ms. Lovchuck's voice goes dead as a cheer goes up from the crowd at Riley's feet. She has pulled the wire loose and disconnected the speaker. She raises her arms triumphantly, then totters a bit on Zach's shoulders while the group around her applauds.

"I can't believe she just did that," Zoe says.

"I don't get her." I shake my head. "A stuck-up cheerleader with a death wish? It doesn't make sense."

Zoe shrugs. I wait for her to say something, but when she doesn't, I realize that I'll have to stand alone on this one. Somehow I doubt Zoe has ever said an unkind word about anyone. I feel my cheeks flush. Who's the Christian now?

"We could hang out after school if you're busy for lunch." Zoe smiles shyly.

"Sure." I nod. "I mean, wait. I could do lunch too. I'm—" I think of the tiny and disorganized French Club meeting. "I'm free now." I cough. "I mean, if you are."

"Good," Zoe says. She smiles, and her pale face reddens a bit.

"Okay." I grab my peanut-butter-on-a-bagel sandwich out of the locker. "Where do you usually sit?"

8

"Why do you think Achebe chose to write his book in English?" Ms. Moore levels her eyes on the class.

Her outfit today just might outdo all of her past outfits, which is really saying something. Most teachers here wear really frumpy, hideous clothes that my mom wouldn't be caught dead in. Like, literally. If she were dead and I tried to bury her in them, she'd come back to life and ground me forever. They wear horrible stuff like pleated pants, polyester pantsuits, or on Fridays, acid-washed jeans up to their necks with rolled up cuffs. Rolled up! I'm not even into fashion, and I know that you should never roll up your jeans.

Ms. Moore, on the other hand, looks kind of like she was shopping in L.A., took the wrong door in an alley, and ended up in AP English. She's wearing a jumper dress with a black turtleneck underneath it and black ballet flats.

"Anyone want to venture a guess? It's English class. It's not like there's only one answer." Ms. Moore smiles at her joke.

No one raises their hand so I sort of half raise mine. I try to be subtle about it. No need to advertise that I'm killing everyone in this class. Cheerleader Girl might have me beat in polynomials, but she'd better not even try when it comes to dangling modifiers and Hemingway.

"Christine? Why don't you take a stab at this for me," Ms. Moore says, completely ignoring my hand.

Christine looks up from her copy of *Things Fall Apart* and shrugs. I hadn't realized she was even in my English class until after that day in detention. But once you meet Christine, you can't stop noticing her everywhere she goes. Her hair is pink, after all. And today she has hot pink eyeshadow to match. Christine crosses her arms. "I didn't read the book."

A few people snicker. Christine is usually really quiet in class, and this wasn't exactly the answer I was expecting. I sit up straighter.

Ms. Moore smiles as if what Christine has said is a very clever joke. No screaming, no threats, no pressing Christine to say something about the book. That's just how Ms. Moore is. She's a little kooky, but it kind of works for her.

"Well, then. You must have a punishment," she says, then turns and begins to write on the board. I crane my neck to see what it says, but even when she steps back so we can all read it, it doesn't really make any sense: "Christine Lee does NOT have detention today."

"Ana?" Ms. Moore turns around and nods at me. "Do you want to tell me why you think Achebe wrote in English?"

I clear my throat. "He wrote the book in the late fifties, during a time when the Western world saw Africa as very backwards and 'primitive.'" I make little quotation marks around "primitive." Ms. Moore constantly stresses that no culture is primitive. "He wanted to show everyone how complex and rich the Nigerian culture really was, and the only way to do that was to write a book that could have a huge reach around the world. Thus, he needed to use English."

"Good, Ana," Ms. Moore says and then asks someone else for an alternate reason. I glance over at Christine. Does she think I'm a show-off for answering her question? What does that message Ms. Moore wrote on the chalkboard mean? Who's ever heard of a student *not* getting detention as a punishment? This school is cracked.

Christine is doodling on her notebook like she doesn't have a care in the world. I guess if she wants to fail English then that's her funeral, right? I lean in closer to see if I can see what she's drawing, but all I can see are dark squiggles.

"So for your assignment this weekend—" Ms. Moore walks to the board. She does not erase Christine's "punishment," but writes underneath it—I suck in my breath—ESSAY.

A groan goes up.

Ms. Moore turns around with a crooked grin on her face. "Were you hoping for two essays? I hate to disappoint you guys." People groan again, and Ms. Moore smiles and turns back to the board. She outlines the assignment and turns back to us.

"And one final note of business." Ms. Moore glances at her watch. "I have been asked to start a club. Ms. Lovchuck's initiative for the year, as I'm sure you all know from the rally last week, is to make this your school by getting more students involved."

Ms. Moore turns around to the chalkboard again and writes EARTH FIRST CLUB just above Christine's punishment. "I am starting an environmental club. If anyone is interested, the first meeting is at lunch next Monday." She looks around the room, and maybe I imagine it, but I could swear she winks at me.

The bell rings, and people spring from their desks and start packing up their books.

Hm. Maybe joining an environmental club would be cool. I'm not really into granola and all that, but I always recycle, and an environmental club might look good on my transcript. I'm already in enough clubs, but I could drop Key Club. It's just a bunch of popular people sitting around in the cafeteria planning events that never really come together anyway.

I stand up and pile my books into my bag, then glance over at Christine. Now that I'm standing, I can see her notebook clearly. I study the picture she was working on and realize that it's a very cool cartoon of Ms. Moore. In the picture, Ms. Moore doesn't have a huge nose or a mean look on her face or big ears. If I didn't know any better, if I hadn't been sitting in this class the whole time, I could swear that the girl actually really likes Ms. Moore.

Christine catches me staring at her notebook and slams it shut. She stuffs it into her book bag.

"Hey, Christine—"

She stops for a moment and stares at me. I guess it does seem weird, talking to her like this, since I've never said anything to her since that day in detention, but for some reason I think she might want to join me and Zoe for lunch sometime.

"I..." She's looking at me like I'm absolutely crazy. I lose my nerve. "Um...never mind," I say quickly.

Christine turns and stalks out of the room. She doesn't even look up as she passes me or Ms. Moore. I find myself really hoping she joins the art club.

9

Youth group is technically over, but I promised myself that this time I would try to hang out inside until my mom came to pick me up. The last thing I need is to develop a reputation as the girl who stands outside alone all the time. I head toward the snack table. That seems like a safe bet. At least there I'll have something to do with my hands. Riley is talking to her friend Tanya in the middle of the room, and some junior girl who I think is named Tricia is standing on stage and singing into the mic like she's on *American Idol*. Thankfully, it isn't plugged in.

I'm trying to hold my head up and look like I know what I'm doing when Tyler passes by me, carrying a pick in his teeth. I put my hand into a tub of Trader Joe's cookies and watch as he puts his pick into his guitar case.

"How's school, Ana?" Judy, the youth leader, comes up behind me in a sneak attack. Judy is in her twenties and is quite stunning, with short brown hair and fine features. I think a few of the high school guys have crushes on her, but too bad for them she's married to Fritz. But I'm not really thrilled that she's talking to me. Everyone knows it's the leaders' job to talk to the kids no one else is talking to.

"Fine," I say, tucking a cookie into my mouth. Judy creases her brow and purses her lips to make a face that shows she's really listening. I think they teach that face in Youth Leader Training because all of them have it down pat.

"What's your favorite subject?" She tilts her head a bit to the right. I try to keep a straight face as I tell her about English and Ms. Moore, but she's looking at me like I'm a hurt kitten or something, and I can't help but wonder what she would do if I said something really outrageous and four-lettered.

I keep one eye on Judy but manage to watch as Tyler snaps his guitar case closed and walks over to the wonky pool table. Someone donated it to the youth group, and it leans a little to the left. I watch as Tyler gives a high five to Dave, and they start talking. My heart skips a beat as Tyler picks up a pool cue.

Judy must notice me staring over her shoulder, because the next thing I know she's pulling me over to the pool table and picking up a cue. Tyler and Dave are talking about chord progressions or some guitar nonsense and don't seem to notice us invading their territory.

"Come on, guys, let's play." Judy holds out cues.

"Uh...," I say stupidly. On the one hand, I want to say yes, because, hello, Tyler, but on the other hand, I don't exactly want to embarrass myself today. "Sure. Okay."

Dave cocks an eyebrow at us. I've never spoken to him, and he always struck me as a bit weird, but he gamely grabs another cue and moves aside to make room for Judy and me around the pool table. He's tall and gangly, and I don't think he goes to my school. If he did, I would probably notice, because in addition to his typical outfit of board shorts, flip flops, and a T-shirt, he's wearing a necktie—a bona fide paisley, silk tie like my dad would wear. Isn't he afraid everyone will talk about him? Even if he is a total weirdo, though, you have to admire his courage . . . or maybe he's just color blind?

"Shall we play boys against girls?" Judy rolls a few solid balls toward Tyler.

Tyler laughs. "Maybe we'd better switch it up." Okay, so maybe we don't look like the most formidable opponents, but that doesn't mean he has to look so certain of victory. "Judy, you and Dave take that side," he says, nodding across the table. Butterflies take flight in my stomach. Tyler is trying to get on my team. His longish blond hair falls over his bright blue eyes.

"Sounds good to me." Dave runs his fingers through his messy brown hair—it looks like he's been experimenting with his sister's styling gel. Something on his arm catches my eye. Is that a tattoo? I peer a little closer and realize that it's actually marker. He has written in all capital letters, from his inner elbow to his inner wrist: FEED DOG.

"It's so on." Dave racks the balls while I chalk my cue. I'm not sure what that's all about, but everyone seems to do it, so I play along. Tyler finds a stool and brings it near the table. He plops down right next to me, then looks up at me and grins. Okay, that has to mean something.

Dave points his stick at me. "You can break, um . . ."

"Ana." Does he really not even know my name? I try to stare him down. I can at least *look* intimidating, even if they'll quickly learn the truth.

"Ana, you can break because I want to make sure you get at least one turn," Dave says, laughing. Judy scowls at him, but I ignore the comment. I can't believe I'm actually playing pool with Tyler.

"Come on, Ana," Tyler says, clapping as he balances his cue between his knees. My heart races, but I try to stay calm. I decide to impress him with my wit.

"How can a guy who can't even remember to feed his dog be any kind of threat?" I laugh as I get the white ball in my crosshairs and pull the cue back in my hand. With a loud thwack, I scatter the balls in all directions. By some miracle, I even manage to sink two stripes.

I see the admiration in Tyler's eye. I wonder if he'll ask me to go get ice cream or something after this. He's definitely giving all the signs he will. How could I get Mom to let me go? My mind is reeling, which might explain why on my next turn I scratch and Dave nearly dies of laughter.

Just as Dave is lining up his shot, I hear a familiar voice behind me and my stomach is seized by cramps. *Please not now.*

"What are you guys doing, Tyler?" Riley asks. I love how she specified exactly who she was talking to. Tanya is watching from a few feet away.

"Hey, Riley," Judy says, her voice cheerful. "Wanna take over for me?" I know it's her job to be nice, but I could hurt her right now. Dave sinks a stripe and mumbles under his breath. Judy hands the cue to Riley, who holds it like she doesn't know what it is.

Tyler's whole face lights up, and it feels like my heart is being stabbed by little pins. He takes a shot at the orange-striped ball, but he doesn't even connect with the cue ball.

"I'm not really playing," Tyler says nonchalantly, leaning his pool cue against the wall. "These two are like pool experts. I'm just watching." Dave immediately picks up his cue and sinks a solid.

"Yeah, I figured," Riley says, looking at me. She rolls her eyes.

My stomach falls. What does he mean he's not really playing? Dave misses his next shot and sighs in frustration.

"Come outside and show me how to shoot a basketball." Riley puts her hand on Tyler's shoulder. "I'm still doing granny shots." I can feel the flush of anger creeping into my cheeks.

"Your turn," Dave says, eyeing me.

I ignore him. "Wait a minute. It's your turn," I say to Tyler, trying to keep the desperation out of my voice. "I need you here." I try to bat my eyes at him, and then I give Riley a cold hard stare. She smirks at me.

Tyler stands up and laughs. "Ana's lying. She's amazing at pool." Obviously, he hasn't even been paying attention, which only makes me angrier.

"It's *your* turn, Ana," Dave says. Keep your pants on, dude.

"I'm going to go help Riley. You'd understand if you've ever seen her play basketball," Tyler says.

Riley beams back at me, and they leave. I stand there with my mouth hanging open.

"Koot-ssh." Dave's hand is cupped over his mouth like he's holding a walkie talkie. "Earth to Ana. Ana, it's your turn. Do you copy?" He does a surprisingly good walkie-talkie voice.

I look at Dave, pretending to be ground control. There's just no comparison. How can I end this game gracefully? Maybe I can pretend my mom's here?

"Houston?"

This guy will not take a hint. Maybe I can casually suggest we go check out the basketball game?

"You gonna play or not?" Dave asks, dropping the walkie-talkie voice.

I sigh. This is a lost cause. I'll have to finish this. After it's over I can casually stroll outside and see what's going on. At least I can get to know one of Tyler's friends. That's a way to get closer to him, I guess. I force myself to smile.

I approach the table and proceed to sink another stripe.

"How'd you learn to play like this?"

He's obviously exaggerating to be nice here, but I'll play along. "My last youth group had a table too. Guess I just spend a lot of time at church." *To get away from my parents.* I don't tell him that the only social activities I'm technically allowed to participate in are school and church. I think if my parents ever actually attended youth group and saw me talking to a guy they might forbid it too, but what they don't know won't hurt them.

It's my turn again. I lean in and line up my shot and try to act normal. "So what's up with the tie?"

He looks down at his pink paisley tie and gives me a huge grin. "Dunno. What's up with your hair? Or those jeans? Or those shoes?"

For a moment, I think he might be making fun of me. But then I realize that anyone weird enough to wear a necktie with board shorts isn't critiquing my fashion choices.

"I just thought I'd wear a tie every day for a while. Just see what happens." He lines up his shot.

"Your parents will let you do that?"

"Yeah, of course. Why not?" He laughs as he accidentally knocks one of my balls into a pocket. I can't help but laugh too.

10

You never really know a person until you see where they live. That's a life lesson I learn the moment I enter Zoe's house. It's unlike anything I've ever seen. For one thing, it's got a dome. As in, the building is completely round, and the top is a clear bubble that lets in the light from the sky. When I ask about it, Zoe just shrugs and tells me her parents built it themselves when they first got married. The way she says it, I can tell she means that they literally built it themselves with, like, hammers and stuff, and not what my mom means when she tells people we built our house in Half Moon Bay. Zoe acts like it's no big deal.

But it is a very big deal. The house is so light and bright, and well, natural. And the shape is just the beginning. There's also the fact that inside the dome, the furniture is worn and the shag carpet is way outdated and the whole place smells sweet, and a little spicy somehow, and yet Zoe's family doesn't seem at all embarrassed about any of it.

We've been having lunch fairly regularly these days, so when she asked me if I wanted to come over after school, I jumped at the chance. I'll take any excuse to get away from my mom, who has not stopped asking questions about Zoe since the moment she realized I made a friend. Somehow, I don't think this is exactly what my mother had in mind for my first new friend, but I don't care.

As Zoe shows me more of the house, I start to see the appeal of living in a giant bubble. First of all, the living room is very airy, with rooms opening off it in all directions, and there's a cool metal spiral staircase to get to the second floor, where Zoe's room is.

And there's the shrine to Nick. Nick is Zoe's older brother who lives on a ranch in Colorado. He's tall and has long brown hair, a deep tan, and wears lots of leather. He likes horses and motorcycles, apparently. He has a small scruffy-looking dog and a weathered cabin. And that's just the first group of photos.

The most notable feature about Zoe's house, though, is that there's stuff everywhere: books piled on every surface, papers shoved into every available corner, and clothes strewn across all the furniture. It's a mess, but it doesn't feel overwhelming. It feels lived in.

"Do you girls want some cookies?" Mrs. Fairchild calls from the kitchen as we walk down the spiral staircase to the living room again. She bustles around the cramped kitchen with avocado-green appliances. She pulls the lid off a ceramic cookie jar and sniffs inside, then holds the jar out to us.

"Fresh batch."

Zoe shakes her head. "Carob," she whispers to me, and I nod as if I know what that means.

"C'mon, Zoe, you used to love these." Zoe's mom has long, dark hair, streaked with white, and it's pulled back into a loose ponytail. And though she is wearing a baggy red sweater rolled up to her elbows, you can tell that she doesn't have a single pound to spare. Meanwhile Zoe has long, gorgeous red hair and is pretty short and, well, a little plump. I flush when my brain throws out the word "plump." I don't care if Zoe's overweight. I guess I just expected her whole family to have the same build.

"Well, Ana might want some of my cookies, even if you don't." Her mom hands the jar to me and Zoe subtly shakes her head so that only I can see it.

"Thanks Mrs. Fairchild, but I'm still pretty full from lunch."

"Dreamy," she says.

"Um…yeah. Groovy," I say, catching on to the house lingo.

"No, *my name* is Dreamy. Mrs. Fairchild is Ed's mom." She sticks her tongue out and makes a face. I'm thoroughly confused.

"I'm going to show Ana the pond," Zoe says abruptly and starts to drag me to the door. I follow her through the living room, padding across the orange shag carpet, toward the sliding glass back door.

"Okay," Dreamy calls, fluttering her fingers. Zoe slides the big glass door open and steps outside into the overcast autumn afternoon. I step lightly on the spongy wooden deck, then walk carefully behind her down the stairs to the sloping grassy area that leads to the trees.

"Sorry about that." Zoe shakes her head. "My parents always go by their first names. It's totally ridiculous."

"Dreamy. That's a cool name," I say, though I'm pretty sure that if my parents had inflicted such a ridiculous name on me I would have changed it the moment I learned to write. "What was wrong with those cookies? I almost never say no to sweets."

Zoe stops dead still. "Trust me, they don't qualify as 'sweets.' If that's what you want, I've got a stash in my room that we'll hit up later. My parents are total health nuts. Vegans, you know? They don't eat any animal products whatsoever."

"Oh." A long list of questions runs through my mind: How do you cook without eggs? How is Zoe even still alive without ever eating bacon? Does this mean no pizza too?

"Those cookies might have looked like chocolate chip, but they were actually carob, which is this horrible, natural substitute for chocolate. Trust me, I spared you."

We walk in silence for a moment.

She stops and turns to me. "I'm not vegan, just so you know. I'm vegetarian. Dreamy calls it my 'little rebellion.'"

"So you only eat vegetables?" I shudder at the thought.

"I just don't eat meat. But I still eat eggs, milk, cheese—stuff like that."

"So you can have pizza?"

"Meatless pizza anyway. I just do it for the animals, you know? I can't eat anything that has a really cute face. It grosses me out. That's how I got landed in detention that day. I had refused to dissect a frog in Biology. I don't eat animals, and I don't hurt animals."

"Whoa." I would never, ever defy a teacher.

"My parents were all over it, of course. It's a violation of my rights. I don't have to dissect. It's California law. They got it resolved with my Bio teacher."

I keep walking behind her in silence, processing this.

Wait. I'm supposed to have dinner here later. What are they going to feed me? I try to keep from panicking. I guess I can always fill up on Maria's stash afterward.

"My parents are totally crazy, you know. But they're also real pushovers and they're pretty...cool. Sometimes I like to call Dreamy 'Mom' just to freak her out." Zoe laughs and leads me across the yard in silence. "There's the garage," she finally says, motioning at the small wooden building behind the house, then she points to a hole in the sloped roof. "My dad fell through the ceiling, so we don't use it anymore." I feel like I should ask about that statement, but I don't know what to say, and I am too distracted by the trees to put a coherent thought together anyway.

What I'm realizing is Zoe lives in the woods. Half Moon Bay is pressed right up against the ocean on one side, which is why it's foggy so much of the time, but it's also surrounded by cypress and redwood groves on the other side. Just a few minutes away from the modern downtown, you can be in the middle of an old-growth redwood forest where the trees have been alive since before Jesus was born. The natural beauty is part of what sold Mom on this town, even though I've never once seen her near a tree.

Zoe takes me down a dirt path that leads out of her back-yard, through the forest. She practically skips as she tells me about her brother, Nick, and how she went to visit him in Colorado this past summer. It's kind of cool how close her family is.

"He lives on this ranch up in the mountains," she says, gesturing to show me the size of the mountains. "And he has this little cabin, and I got to stay in one of those beds that folds up into the wall when you're not using it, and..."

"Zoe!" I suck in my breath. She freezes and stops mid-sentence.

"What's wrong?"

"Is that a horse?" Even as I say it, I know it's a stupid question, because, well, obviously it's a horse. There, right before me, standing in front of a wooden building with a pitched roof, is the most gorgeous horse I've ever seen. It's brown with white spots. Okay, it's not like I've seen *a lot* of horses in real life, but still.

"Oh." Zoe kicks at the ground. "Yeah, the stable is over there." She nods toward the building. "But the pond is farther on, and there are these cool flowers that grow there that I want to show you."

I look from the horse to Zoe, then back to the horse, hesitating. I know I should keep walking with her, but I've never seen a real horse up close.

"Hey there!" A deep voice, cheerful as all get-out, interrupts my deliberation. A slim man, clad in head-to-toe denim, waves at us from the stable. "Who's your friend, Zoe?" His bright red hair blows a little in the breeze, and I realize this must be her dad. At least he has Zoe's hair, but he's very skinny and very tall too, which throws me a bit.

She shakes her head and takes a long breath. "We're not going to escape without saying hi. Come on." I follow her down the rocky path to the stable, glad for any excuse to get near the gorgeous horse.

"Ed, this is Ana," Zoe says, gesturing to me. "Ana, my dad, Ed."

"Well hello," Mr. Fairchild—Ed—says, sticking out his hand. I shake it nervously, but his handshake is firm. "You like horses?" He raises his eyebrows hopefully.

I look from him to Zoe, unsure how to respond. Do I like horses? Zoe shrugs.

"Yes," I say uncertainly. He smiles at me, and I notice his denim jacket has running stallions embroidered on the left lapel.

"Wanna go for a ride?" He smoothes his hair down. "I can get Alfalfa here saddled up in no time, and—"

"No thanks," Zoe says quickly. "I was showing her the pond."

I don't want to be rude here, but if I had to pick between riding this horse and looking at flowers, it wouldn't exactly be a tough choice. But how do I say that nicely?

"Oh come on," Ed winks at me. One of his front teeth is a little crooked. "Zoe never wants to ride any more."

"Um..." I'm not sure how to answer that. I mean, Zoe is standing right here.

"Ever since—" His brow creases.

"Ed," Zoe whines. Her cheeks turn a little pink, and she bites her lower lip.

"Butter Bean, you just need to get back on the horse, as they say." He chuckles a little.

"I just want to show Ana the pond, okay?" She turns to go, but I stand still, unsure what to do.

"You're never going to stop being afraid," Ed says, lowering his chin to look his daughter in the eye, "if you don't give it another try."

Zoe just shakes her head. "Come on, Ana," she mumbles as she begins to walk away, and, because I don't know what else to do, I follow her.

"It could have been much worse," Zoe says as she settles into the beanbag chair on her bedroom floor. The chair, like most things in Zoe's oddly shaped bedroom, is lavender, and there's a musical theme going on. There are musical notes on everything—the bedspread, the framed posters, the mirror. I sit down on the edge of the bed, which is covered by a light purple spread. "She wanted to make seitan, but I made her promise not to serve anything too weird." She pulls a package of Sour Patch Kids out of a drawer on her nightstand and pours a few into her hand. I notice what looks like a Bible peeking out of the drawer before Zoe shuts it again.

"Satan?" I've never heard of this food of the devil.

"It's this vegetable protein thing." She bites the head off a red kid. "Veggie burgers are the most normal thing she makes."

"They were good," I lie. She hands me the package of candy, and I pop a few pieces in my mouth. I chew for a minute. "Your parents are really cool." This part, luckily, is true. They asked me about a dozen times tonight if I had enough to eat, wanted to know everything about my family, and even seemed genuinely interested in hearing what I thought of Half Moon Bay's recycling policies. They talked to me like an adult. "I really liked when they did that harmony of 'Bridge over Troubled Water.'"

Zoe shakes her head and lifts up the edge of the bedspread, then reaches under the bed and pulls out a package of Oreos. "They don't always sing at the table," she says, cringing. I laugh, remembering how her dad broke into song when Zoe asked for the salt, and how her mom joined in with the harmony as if singing like this were the most normal thing in the world. "They're on a big Simon & Garfunkel kick recently."

"I like that song." I take a cookie from the package she holds out to me.

"They're so weird." She takes a bite of an Oreo and sighs. They are weird, but in a good way, like Chunky Monkey. Bananas and chocolate sure don't sound like they'd make good ice cream, but you'd be surprised.

"I'd be okay with weird." I unscrew the top of my cookie carefully. "At least they're not tying to take over your life and ruin your birthday." Zoe looks at me like I'm crazy.

"When's your birthday?"

"Not till June." I shake my head. "But they're already planning it now." Zoe looks confused. "It's my fifteenth birthday, so Mom wants to throw a *quinceañera*. That's this big party they have in Mexico when you officially become a woman or something. It's a huge deal. Only, hello, we're not in Mexico. And do I look like the kind of person who wants a huge birthday party? All those people staring at me . . . I'd rather die. They just want to show off to their friends. It'll be mortifying, you know?"

Zoe watches me for a second. "Yeah," she says quietly. "The worst."

Fine. I guess it doesn't sound *so* terrible, having a huge party thrown in your honor. "Trust me. It's going to be bad. I've already begged them to just let me have a small, normal birthday party, but my mom is pitching a fit."

Zoe doesn't say anything. I decide to change the subject. "Do you play an instrument?"

Zoe nods. "The piccolo. I'm in the marching band." I don't really know what the piccolo is, but it sounds impressive, so I smile.

"Who's that?" I point to a photo of her and another girl on her dresser, in a handmade plastic frame painted with swirls and flowers. Zoe reaches up and grabs the photo, then tosses it to me. I see now that the two girls are on a beach, arms around each other, their long towels draped loosely over their shoulders, blowing in the breeze. They're laughing and leaning toward one another comfortably.

"My best friend, Monica," she says, taking another Oreo from the package. "She moved to Michigan this summer." She takes a bite. "We've known each other since we were born."

I squint at the picture and notice that Monica is thin and has short dark hair and glasses. Zoe's cheeks in the picture are a little thinner than they are now, and her hair is a bit lighter, but something else is different.

"We need to get Christine," she says suddenly.

"What?" I look up and see more clearly that the Zoe in front of me isn't the Zoe in the photo. I run my eyes over the picture, trying to figure out what it is. Did she grow her hair out?

"She's one of us. We need her." She takes another bite. "And she needs us."

"I don't know. She seems kind of..." What? Uninterested? Self-sufficient? Weird? "Happy to be by herself."

Zoe nods. "But she's not alone." She licks crumbs off her thumb. "She needs to know that." Zoe watches me, her gaze even and steady.

"I tried to invite her to lunch one day." Zoe perks up at the news, but I shake my head. "She wasn't interested."

"We'll have to figure out a way to make it happen," she says. "I really feel like we're all meant to be together somehow."

"All?" I raise my eyebrow.

"All four of us," Zoe says, nodding. "From detention. That was no accident, the way we lived through miracles. We're supposed to do something with that. I know it."

"I don't know." Christine I can maybe deal with. But Cheerleader Girl? No way. Even if we are called for something special, I think it's just the three of us.

"But we'll start with Christine." Zoe pops another Oreo into her mouth. There's a determined look in her eye.

"Sure," I say, unsure how else to respond. "What are we going to do, kidnap her and force her to be our friend?" My eyes travel down to the picture in my hands until I study Zoe's frozen face again.

That's when it hits me. I know what's different about the photo.

I look up and see Zoe biting her lip. "We'll figure something out," she says quietly.

I've never seen Zoe this happy in real life.

"Okay." I smile, and her cheeks redden a little. "Let's recruit Christine."

12

t's cruel to make a teenager wake up a seven o'clock on a Saturday morning. But apparently the Alzheimer's patients do better with visitors early in the day, so we're meeting in front of the nursing home at eight o'clock. There are a few adults from church here, but mostly it's the teens. Don't get me wrong. I like old people. I just don't like any people at eight o'clock on a Saturday. I pray for patience. I know these people will appreciate us being here.

"Have fun, honey," Mom says as she pulls onto the circular driveway in front of Stonehill Manor Assisted Living. I make some incoherent noise, then turn to open the door. "Oh, there's Michelle McGee," she says, her voice brightening as a blue minivan pulls up behind us. "Don't forget she's giving you a ride home later." I turn in time to see Riley climb out of the car and slam the door.

"Great." I swing my legs out and step onto the pavement, then shut the door and slowly walk toward the entrance. Mom was thrilled to have worked out this little plan, which allows her to spend all day "antiquing" and forces me to ride home with Riley, who my mother is determined to make my friend. But of course I wasn't informed of the dastardly plot until it was too late to protest, argue, or beg. Besides, if I showed any sign of resistance, she'd seize on it and use it as an opportunity to teach me a lesson about loving others like Jesus did. It's only a short ride from the assisted living facility to my house, I reason, but somehow it still feels like a plot hatched to drive me crazy. Mom doesn't even like antiques.

I trudge toward the entrance, and Judy is already there, cheerful and perky at this ungodly hour. That weird guy Dave is there too, wearing a tie with piano keys up and down it, along with a couple junior girls I recognize from youth group, and some women from church. And, of course, Riley.

Riley doesn't look at me as we stand in the early morning sunshine, waiting for someone to tell us what to do. I study my feet. There's just not much to say, and everyone is fairly quiet. Finally one of the church ladies decides it's time to go inside, and we all trudge through the door and listen to directions.

All of us, I notice, except Riley. As soon as everyone is inside, a black sports car pulls up, and she hops right into the front seat. I catch a glimpse of a guy's face as the car pull away.

What is she thinking? Is she seriously ditching this? I can't believe her. Does she even know that guy?

No one else seems to have noticed her little stunt. The woman in charge reminds us that the Alzheimer's patients are often confused, forgetting people they've known their entire lives and sometimes thinking they're back in their childhood, but though they may not show it, they appreciate us being here. She also instructs us to split up, don't be shy, ask questions, don't contradict the patients if they say something that's obviously untrue, and remember that whatever you do for the least of these, you do for God.

Most of us look at each other, a little uncertain how to begin, but Dave takes right off down the hallway, his green board shorts swishing, walks into the first room, and begins talking to the wrinkled man hunched over in a recliner. From my dumbstruck spot in the hallway, I can see that the man inside, Mr. Stanley Fisher according to the nameplate on his door, smiles and raises his head.

"Okay, um, here we go, then," Judy says nervously, and it gives me some satisfaction to see that even she is struggling with this. She turns down a different hallway and disappears. The rest of the group scatters, and I'm left standing alone. I say a quick prayer. I know I can do this, but I don't know how to start. Why is it so hard for me to talk to new people? I bite my lip and try to decide which way to go.

"There you are!" a squeaky voice calls out, and I turn to see a stooped old woman coming toward me. The weird thing is, she looks genuinely delighted to see me. She takes a timid step forward, then places her hand on the wall to steady herself. "I've been looking all over for you, Molly," she says, shaking her head as if I've been naughty. She takes another small step.

"Oh, I'm not..." I start to correct her, but then remember that we're not supposed to correct them. Oh well. I guess if she wants to call me Molly, I can deal with that. "I'm not sure where we were headed," I say uncertainly, but she smiles and points to an open door down the hall.

"You were going to show me what you bought at Woolworth's," she says.

Woolworth's? Didn't that store go out of business in like 1912?

"Did you find something for Father?" She walks slowly toward me, and I nod lamely. Does she think I'm her sister? "The stores get so crowded this time of year." She catches up to me, and we walk a few more steps to the open doorway, where she gestures me inside. I take a quick look at the nameplate on the door and commit the name Sarah Slater to memory, then nervously step in and gasp.

Sarah's room is decked to the gills for Christmas. She has a plastic Christmas tree, hung with glass balls and tinsel and little framed pictures of people she must have once known. There are wrapped packages under the tree, lights strung around the window, an advent calendar on the wall, and a Nativity scene on the table on the corner. It's festive, and kind of nice, except...it's October.

"Please have a seat," Sarah says, gesturing to the wooden rocking chair in the corner. She shuffles toward the bed and lowers herself down slowly.

"Now, who are you?" She tilts her head, and her wrinkled face puckers a bit.

"I'm..." I look around, trying to figure out what I'm supposed to say. Do I tell her I'm Molly? She seemed to like Molly. Please, God, give me the right words to say. "I'm Ana." I let my breath out slowly. She seems content with that answer.

"Have you seen my tree?" She asks, pointing toward the faux fir. I nod, then move off my chair so I can take a closer look at the ornaments. "I decorated it myself." Sarah seems kind of confused, but she smiles a lot, and something about her voice is soothing.

I stare at a black and white photo of a handsome man in a small frame on the tree. The man is clad in a crisp white navy uniform with the name Slater on the left. It looks like it's from World War II or something.

"Who is this?" Sarah leans forward, squints at the picture, and purses her lips.

"I don't know," she says quietly. Her face looks pained, and her cheeks are a little pink.

"That's okay." I pick up another picture, this one of two little girls in matching pink dresses. The car in the background makes it look like it was taken in the fifties or sixties. "How about these girls?"

She leans in, then shakes her head. "That...maybe Molly, but..." Her voice trails off. I try to smile for her, but we both know she doesn't remember who these people are. "Let me show you my Nativity," she says. I slip an ornament off the tree and look at the back while she shuffles over to the manger. A shaky hand has written "Patty and Becky Slater in front of Sarah and David's new house, 1954." I turn it over and look at the little faces again and realize these girls must be Sarah's daughters. I take a deep breath.

"Did you see this Joseph?" she says, fingering the small wooden figure. I slip the ornament back onto the tree, then walk over to see her figurines. She begins to tell me the story of Christmas, pointing out all the relevant players in their miniature form, though she calls the shepherds plumbers for some reason. I half-listen. The other half of me is praying for Sarah, and for Molly and Becky and Patty, wherever they are.

It feels like it's only been a few minutes when Judy pokes her head into Sarah's room. "Ana?" she says, her face registering surprise to see me sitting on Sarah's bed holding the stuffed bear Sarah insisted needed a hug. "It's time to go."

I turn to Sarah. "Thank you for talking to me today."

"You come back soon. We have so much baking to do before Christmas Eve," she says, her eyes lighting up. I stand up and stretch.

"Okay. I will. Thanks, Mrs. Slater."

She nods. "You're welcome, Ana."

I shake my head as I walk down the hallway and push open the clear glass front doors of Stonehill Manor. The group has scattered by the time I make it out, but Riley's freakishly blond hair announces that she's returned. At least she had the smarts to come back before her mom arrived. She and Dave are the only ones standing around waiting for rides home. The plight of the young and the carless.

"You're back?" I raise my eyebrows. "Lucky us." Riley pretends not to hear. She is focused entirely on Dave, batting her eyelashes and jutting out her hip.

"Did Tyler go surfing today?" she asks, laughing as if this is a totally innocent question, though of course it's not. I perk up and listen in.

Dave shrugs. "That's where he usually is Saturday morning." I file this information away in my mental crush file. "I guess you'd know that better than me."

"You couldn't talk him into coming to the nursing home with you?" Riley asks, as if she does visit the nursing home.

She runs her fingers through her blond hair, which I'm sure she knows shines brilliantly in the sun.

Dave chuckles. "Not his style." He finally notices me standing behind them. He smiles, then quickly turns back to Riley.

"I've only bumped into him once or twice. Where does he usually surf?" Riley asks. There are several really famous places to surf around here, so it could one of many, but her line of questioning here is totally obvious. Riley surfs, and she wants to know where to "run into him." Even though it's stupid and obvious and I'm sure Dave sees right through her, I can't help but lean in a bit to hear the answer too.

Dave shrugs. "I have no idea. I never go." Riley's face falls. "How about you, Ana?" Dave says, turning toward me. "You a surfer chick?" He makes a hang loose symbol with his hand.

"Not in this lifetime." I laugh, trying to picture where exactly surfing would fit into my packed schedule.

"Sweet." He nods. "Your brain gets pickled by the salt water, you know." He nods, pointing to his own head. "Best to stay away." Riley opens her mouth to protest, but before she can get a word out, he gestures toward the door to Stone-hill Manor. "You guys should come back next week."

I don't know. It was really nice to talk to Mrs. Slater, but it was weird. And since she probably won't remember me next week anyway...

"Maybe," Riley says. I can't even look at her or I might gag.

"It means a lot to them." Dave smiles at me, which totally catches me off guard.

"Do you do this regularly?" Riley nods toward the building.

"Mos' def. Every week." He starts to move his arms and legs strangely, and Riley and I stare. She looks as confused as I feel. What is he doing? Slowly, it dawns on me.

"Is that the Charleston?" I ask, laughing. I've seen people do this weird old dance on the History Channel. Dave snaps his fingers and points at me.

"We have a winner. Mrs. Elton in room 203 taught me last month. She's pretty nimble for a ninety-year-old."

"Wow. Your parents make you come every week?" Riley sneers.

"Parents? My parents don't make me come." He brushes a lock of hair back behind his ear. "I just like old people."

"Oh." Riley winces a little, no doubt realizing her mistake.

Dave nods. He's figured her out. "How about you, Dominguez?" He narrows his eyes and for some reason I suddenly want to hide. "You here because of your parents too?"

"Uh . . ." I swallow. "I mean, I came here because they—"

"My mom's here," Riley says as the blue minivan pulls into the driveway again.

"I'm going with Riley," I say. Dave doesn't say anything, just watches us as we both walk quickly to the car.

Riley opens the back door and slides in, leaving me to walk around to the other side.

"What a weirdo." Riley rolls her eyes. I don't know if I agree, but disagreeing seems too hard.

"Hi, guys," Mrs. McGee says from the front seat. I notice for the first time that there's a kid sitting in the passenger seat. "You must be Ana. I'm Michelle McGee," she says, her voice low and sweet. Her blonde hair is neatly tucked behind her ears and her light blue sweater looks like cashmere. "And this is Michael, Riley's brother."

"Hey," I say, nodding, but Michael doesn't acknowledge me at all. I guess it runs in the family.

Mrs. McGee pulls the car out of the parking lot while Riley stares out the window. Michael starts tapping on the dashboard, marking out a very regular beat. No one else seems to notice, so I try to ignore it.

"Mom, can we go to Nordstrom to get that dress I want?" Riley asks.

"We'll have to see, honey," Mrs. McGee says, sighing. "It depends on how your brother's therapy goes." Riley bites her lip. Man, sometimes I am so glad I don't have siblings. The tapping changes pace, and Riley sighs.

"Drummer?" I ask Riley, arching an eyebrow.

She shakes her head. "Autistic."

I have no idea what I'm supposed to say, but I'm pretty sure it isn't "Oh," which is all I can manage to squeak out. Riley stares out the window again. I swallow and try to think of something better. "I didn't know."

We're silent the rest of the way home.

13

n Algebra on Monday, Riley avoids me. The way she ignores me is not as if I don't exist; it's more like she knows I exist and is completely determined to not acknowledge me. And Tyler, who actually said hi to me at youth group last night, is experiencing AAA—acute Ana amnesia—and has no idea who I am. Needless to say, I am even more thankful than usual when the bell rings to release us.

I slip into the hallway and walk to the picnic table where I meet Zoe for lunch. Sometimes we eat here, and sometimes I drag her along to French Club, but today is the first meeting of Ms. Moore's new club, Earth First, so we're going to walk to that together. To be honest, I'm not totally sure why I'm going, but I know Ms. Moore wants me there, and Zoe is all excited about it. Dreamy and Ed are very into conservation, and Zoe is quite knowledgeable about environmental stuff.

I sit down on the picnic table bench and flip through *A Tale of Two Cities*, which I checked out from the library hoping it would make me smarter, but it's been so long since I've cracked this book that I don't even remember what happened last. I give up and decide to just enjoy the sunshine instead. The air is cool, but the sun shines brilliantly, a rare treat, and it casts a warm glow around the courtyard. I lift my face up to the sun and soak in the warmth of its rays, then say a quick prayer of thanks. Soon Zoe approaches, her long flowered skirt blowing lightly in the breeze. Her red hair is piled on top of her head in a loose knot and a few tendrils fall down around her face. It's the kind of style that looks effortlessly beautiful on her but would make me look like a Chia pet. Together, we walk toward Ms. Moore's classroom. Together. It feels so good to be able to say that. It feels good to have a friend.

Zoe pulls the door open and steps inside, and I follow. It's a small group, I can already tell. There are a couple of junior girls talking quietly together, and...it can't be. Christine Lee? I don't know why I'm surprised to see her sitting there really, except my sense is that she's not much of a joiner. I can't imagine what would bring her here. But Ms. Moore doesn't give us time for speculation as she quickly explains an overview of what she's envisioning for the club and assigns us our first task: selling organic pumpkins bars at the upcoming Half Moon Bay Art & Pumpkin Festival. It's not exactly saving the world, but Ms. Moore says that the first thing we need if we're going to be able to make an impact is buying power, and this will help us raise money. The whole thing strikes me as a little capitalist for Ms. Moore, but I can't deny the wisdom of her plan. Plus, the Art & Pumpkin Festival is no joke. Practically the entire Bay Area comes out for the festival. I know because we drove up from San Jose last year to see it, and that's when the wheels in Mom's head got to turning.

Christine stares straight down at her desk like she's not listening as Ms. Moore explains all of this. But when Ms. Moore sends around a piece of paper and asks us to write our e-mail addresses and phone numbers, Christine duti-fully adds her information to the list.

"Good, then," Ms. Moore says, scanning the sheet to make sure everything looks right. "See you all back here next week. And in the meantime, start thinking of projects you would like to see the club tackle with our new wealth." She laughs, then waves her hand to dismiss us. She takes a seat behind her desk and starts flipping through papers. I turn to Christine. She raises her eyebrow and smiles, then picks up her bag and stalks out of the room.

14

slip out of Key Club and into the empty breezeway. It's blissfully quiet after school. It feels kind of like when you've had a headache and it goes away—all of a sudden, it's just pure, unfettered relief.

Today is my last day in Key Club. I only came this one last time to tell Mrs. Galvin the bad news in person. I think she was hoping I'd run for an office next year since I'm one of the few organized people in the whole outfit. But last night, Mom sat me down to discuss focusing my transcript around a few "key differentiators" and weeding out some of the other activities. She had just read an article in the *Times* about over-scheduled kids and how what the Ivy League schools are really looking for now is kids with "passion."

Apparently if you have passion, you only have it for a few things. So we made a list of all my clubs and decided that I would eliminate Key Club (though theoretically a volunteering club, they never really do anything), French Club (not a "hot" language—Mandarin would have been one thing, but not French), and Future Business Leaders of America, which I only went to once anyway (I'm going to be a doctor, not a future business leader—duh). Mom thought I should really throw myself into Earth First (environmental issues are very "now") and my church service activities (service is a perennial favorite). And she's still trying to think of something that would be truly unique that I could start from the ground up.

I take a deep breath to prepare myself for the sweetly pungent bathroom smell that seems to permeate every school restroom in the world, then push open the door. And gasp.

There's a head in the sink with red streaming off it.

She's been shot.

Or maimed? Wait, maybe she hit her head? The figure turns her head to the side and peeks up at me.

"Christine?!"

"Hey." She turns her face back down and uses her hands to push her hair under the water. Okay, I can see now that she's not dying, but what is she doing?

"Are you bleaching your hair?"

"No, just washing that man right out of my hair."

"Huh?"

She peeks up at me again. "It's a joke. It's an old song my mom used to listen to."

The bleach is filling the white sink with pink liquid and slowly her hair is turning white. Well, not white exactly. It's more like a light orange, brown, yellow decaying color. Eventually, she shuts off the water, grabs a dark blue towel from her backpack, wraps her hair in a turban, and stands up.

She takes a deep breath. "Mmmm...I love the smell of bleach in the afternoon. You hang out in bathrooms a lot too?"

For a moment, I am so stunned, trying to figure out what is going on, that I forget why I came to the bathroom in the first place. "Oh, no. I mean, not more than anyone else

I guess. Well, except you, apparently. But, yeah, I was just going to use the bathroom."

"Why are you still here?" she asks. The implication: *School let out an hour ago. Anyone who has somewhere else to be is long gone.*

"Key Club."

"Woo." She rolls her eyes.

"Yeah, I actually quit today." I suspect Christine will like this, and for some reason I want to tell her things she'll think are cool. It's weird, because I never do this with Zoe. "Why are you dyeing your hair in the school bathroom?"

Christine turns the faucet on again and holds her hands under to rinse them.

"If you're hiding it from your parents—" Wait. Christine's mom is . . . I can't believe I just said that. My cheeks feel hot. "If you're hiding it from your dad, he's going to see it when you get home later."

"My dad's not going to care if I dye my hair." She opens her bag, and I see a bunch of tubes of paint tucked inside. She pulls out a little jar with blue goop in it. "I'm trying to avoid my dad's bimbo girlfriend."

"Really?" I briefly try to picture exactly what would happen to me if I dyed my hair, but then stop myself. Too scary.

"He won't even notice, actually. I could bring an elephant home and then announce that I've joined the space program to be the first teen on the moon, and he wouldn't even look up from his dinner. It's pretty awesome. I can get away with anything. Unless The Bimbo is around. She's always trying to butt in."

"Oh." I try to pretend like I get it, but I don't really. Why would her dad's girlfriend be at her house at this hour? And didn't her mom die this past summer? How could he have another girlfriend already? It's only been a few months at best.

"Here," she says and puts the little jar of Manic Panic in my hand. "If you're going to watch, make yourself useful." She shoots me a smile to show me she's kidding. "Once I get my hands covered in that stuff, I never know how to get the lid back on without making a huge mess." She unwraps her towel turban and drapes it around her neck, revealing her very hideous hair. It's the same color as chocolate and vanilla ice cream all melted together in a soupy pool.

"Are you sure you know what you're doing?" I glance nervously at the door. Am I going to get in trouble for being an accomplice?

"It looks like puke right now but when you've got dark hair, you've got to bleach it first if you want the new color to stick. And I'm sick of the pink. Too Barbie."

I try to picture her with blue hair. She bustles around, getting a few more things ready. The truth is she'll probably look great with blue hair. I hadn't noticed it until now, but Christine is really beautiful. She's so slender that she might be wearing kids jeans. Even though her hair is a bit fried from all of the dyeing, it's still very long and straight.

"Okay, take the lid off," Christine says. I take it off, and she dips her plastic-gloved hands into the deep blue gel and begins to smear it into her scalp.

"Whoa."

She studies herself in the mirror and works the goo in, section by section. "So you're into that guy Tyler, right?"

I nearly drop the jar of dye. "What?! Who told you that?"

Christine shoots me a look. "No one told me. I didn't need to be told. You stare at him in the halls. I thought you might actually start drooling on Wednesday."

I stare at a drop of blue on the tile floor. Okay, this is very dangerous. I barely know this girl. If I say yes, she might spread it all over school. Better deny everything. "I think I need glasses is all."

Christine digs another glob out of the jar in my hand. "I'm not going to tell anyone. I'm not like that. You already know my worst secret, thanks to that day in detention, so don't sweat it." She works the glob into a spot by her ear. "I was just going to offer to talk to him. He's in the Art Club with me."

"He is?"

"Nice guy, but he's no Van Gogh."

My stomach turns over when she says he's a nice guy. Her approval means a lot for some reason. "No, thanks."

Christine turns around and tries to inspect the back of her hair in the mirror. "Sure? I don't mind. He doesn't seem to be dating anyone."

Riley's face flashes before my eyes. "He seems to have a thing for cheerleaders."

Christine shrugs. "The offer stands. Just say the word." She turns to me. "How do I look? Is it even?"

I inspect her work and suggest a few touch-ups. Then she throws her gloves in the trash while I put the lid back on the half-used jar of dye. Suddenly I remember that I came in here to pee.

"I've got to hurry up and get back." I think about what

Zoe said about bringing Christine into our group. This is probably the best shot I'll ever get. After all, I held a jar of dye for her. You don't do that for just anybody. "But listen, you should join Zoe and me for lunch sometime. We always sit on that picnic table at the end of the courtyard."

Christine smiles. "Cool."

I'm not sure if that's a yes or no or even a maybe. "Yeah, cool."

15

Riley leans over and kisses a football player on the cheek and his friends cheer. Andy and Zach line up to pay for a kiss. I try to comfort myself with two thoughts: at least she's not kissing Tyler, and she'll probably get mono. Though at this point, I'd almost welcome her kissing Tyler because at least that would mean that he was actually here. All of my snooping around at school and listening to Dave made it sound like Tyler was going to be at the Art & Pumpkin Festival, but I haven't seen him all day. Riley kisses another guy on the cheek. Ashley is set up in an identical booth right next to Riley, but her line is much shorter.

"Just when I think she can't get any more obnoxious, she goes and does something like organize a kissing booth, and I realize how wrong I was," Christine says.

I laugh. "If there's one thing I've learned about Cheerleader Girl, it's that you can never underestimate her evil qualities."

"You guys!" Zoe says. Christine and I shut up about Riley for Zoe's sake, but not before we exchange a look. Christine has been joining us for lunch at school this week, and the more I see of her dark humor, the more I like her. Zoe reaches into a small Doritos bag and bites into a chip. "I want to get her to hang with us too."

"Good luck." Christine twirls a lock of hair around her finger and rolls her eyes.

Ms. Moore walks toward us through the thick crowd. She weaves between men and women wearing giant berets that look like pumpkins and small children dressed as Harry Potter and princesses. The fall air is brisk and smells sweet from the cider and donut booths nearby. We are sitting at a folding card table behind a big sign that says, "Organic Pumpkin Bars. Save the earth and put a smile on your face!" So far business has been slow. There are a lot of pumpkin foods for sale and it's hard to stand out among the pumpkin bread, pumpkin pie, pumpkin ice cream, and even pumpkin macaroni and cheese, which sounds disgusting. Still, that stand has seen more action than we have.

"How are my little pumpkin-bar purveyors?" Ms. Moore plants her hands on her hips and grins. We mumble something. We've been sitting out here all morning and have only sold a few bars. Ms. Moore turns to see what we're all staring at: the Key Club's Kissing Booth. I swear, the moment I quit that club, they suddenly get organized enough to show up at an event and raise money.

"Hmmm," Ms. Moore says. "Watching a show, are we?"

Christine nudges me. "We think she's going get mono."

Ms. Moore shakes her head. "Look at the three of you, staring that poor girl down."

"Poor girl? Ms. Moore, you've got to be kidding me." As if on cue, Riley leans in to kiss a senior guy but squirts him with a water gun instead. The senior grabs the gun from her hands and sprays her until she squeals in delight.

"How well do you know Riley?" Ms. Moore asks me.

"Well enough," I say, and Christine chuckles. "Besides, she has the most popular booth here, so I'm not going to start pitying her."

Ms. Moore turns to the Key Club booth, where an all-out water war has started.

"No wonder. I'd go over there too. You know why?" Ms. Moore shakes her head, and her dangly silver earrings gleam in the sunlight. She's wearing jeans today, but not teacher jeans, cool ones, extra-dark denim, boot cut. "They're actually having fun and they're a spectacle. You know, something to see."

"She's a spectacle, all right," Christine says.

Ms. Moore sighs. "That's it. I've had it with you guys. You're going to stop moping around and do something useful to drum up business for our pumpkin bars."

"How are we going to that?" I suppose we could make a sign that says, "Come stare at the girl with the blue hair." Christine is probably the biggest attraction we've got.

"I don't want to kiss anyone," Zoe says quietly. Zoe is funny. In front of adults, guys, or new people, she's so shy. But I've discovered that when you get her in her element, she'll chat your head off.

"That's not what I had in mind," Ms. Moore says. "Do any of you know the meaning of the word busker?"

I start to answer. "A busker is—"

"Other than Ana?" Ms. Moore says. Man. She never lets me answer anything.

Christine and Zoe shake their heads.

"They're people who entertain in the streets for money. They attract attention to themselves."

"You want us to beg for money?" Christine wrinkles her brow.

"No, just perk up over here. Do something entertaining. Have some fun with this. You guys look like you're being forced to sit here. If you were having half as much fun as Riley, you'd be surprised at how business would boom." Ms. Moore glances at her watch. "You've got thirty minutes to come up with something." She walks over to help some of the other Earth First members, who are unloading more bars from the back of a van, as if we need more.

"That woman is off her gourd," Christine says.

Zoe picks up a small pumpkin sitting on our table for decoration. "Maybe we could sell her a new one?"

We all bust out laughing, but eventually give way to staring at Riley and the other cool kids in the Key Club again. Ms. Moore may be right. Their charisma is the secret. They look like they're having fun, and everyone wants to be with the people who are having fun. I start wracking my brain. What could we do to call attention to ourselves?

The sun is just starting to slide behind the brown hills, bathing the gorgeous fall landscape in a luminous golden glow, when I get the bright idea to call my parents and see if I can stay at the festival a little later.

This morning we arranged that Mom would pick me up in the parking lot at six so she could take me home before she and Papá go out tonight, but as the day wears on, I hear all about how awesome the festival gets after dark. For one thing, there's a haunted house that's supposed to be really spooky. Some girl fainted in it last year. And the corn maze is apparently much more fun after dark. And there's a hayride.

After Ms. Moore told us to come up with something to make our booth great this afternoon, Christine had a brainstorm. She thought we should give away a free face painting with every pumpkin bar purchase. Christine volunteered to the actual painting and Zoe called up Dreamy and Ed and asked them to buy every color of face paint they could find. I just, um, cheered them on. And it turns out that Christine is an incredible artist. Forget simple cat whiskers—she painted elaborate designs on people's arms, ankles, and hands. She did this butterfly taking flight on a little girl's cheek that should have been framed and put in a museum. Soon, we started charging top dollar for our face painting and just giving the bars away to the family members as they waited for their kids to be transformed by the stroke of Christine's brush. An hour later our booth had a longer line than the kissing booth and I got so excited that I started acting like a real busker. I stood out in front and made rhymes to get people's attention: "Make your face a piece of art. Save the earth and do your part." Even shy Zoe stood next to me with a sign.

Now that it's almost nightfall, we're technically done, but we've decided that we want to stay later. Besides, there's all kinds of stuff that needs to be done. Like cleaning up, and counting the money, and...well, all kinds of stuff. Zoe called her parents to ask permission to stay later. They had gone back home after dropping off the paint because they've attended more than pumpkin festivals over the years. They said yes immediately and even invited us over to spend the night. Christine left a message on her dad's cell phone, since he's in Sacramento again. He's a politician, so he's sometimes there for weeks at a time.

Which leaves me. I guess I'm stupid, or maybe I'm just having so much fun that I forget for a moment who my parents are, but I really think they might say yes.

I borrow Zoe's cell phone, but when I get ahold of my mom, she's already on her way to pick me up. I calmly tell her that I still have stuff to do, cringing a little at what could possibly be construed as a bit of an untruth, and that Zoe has invited us to spend the night.

"You're going home to Zoe's house to spend the night?" Like a bomb-sniffing dog, Mom immediately knows that something is afoot. It's like she can read my thoughts and knows that I want to stay because I'm hoping to bump into Tyler later.

"We're going home soon. Is it okay? Mrs. Fairchild said she'd drive me home in time for church tomorrow." No need to alarm my mother with the fact that Zoe's mom goes by her first name and that name just so happens to be Dreamy.

"What do you mean, soon? What are you doing?"

I bite my lip, watching Christine and Zoe laughing together over at the cotton candy shack. "We thought we might check out the festival some first."

"No," my mother says immediately.

"Why not?"

"Are her parents there?"

"They're going to pick us up at nine o' clock," I say quietly. As I hear myself say it, I know that any hopes I had about tonight are gone.

"I'm sorry, Ana, but you know the rules." I hear the sounds of talk radio playing in the car in the background. "You're too young to be off gallivanting around at night." She huffs and puffs about how "children" shouldn't be out at a town festival by themselves after dark.

"But, Mom, there are tons of people here." Okay, I know I sound a little whiny, but I can't help it. I'm not five.

"Ana, the answer is no," she says.

"But—"

"No buts. I'll see you in the parking lot in ten minutes." Silence is ringing in my ear before I realize that she's hung up the phone.

I look toward Zoe and Christine and shake my head. In the dying light, I see a flash of blond hair in line for the hayride, and I turn away before anyone can see me cry.

I'm sitting on the couch, staring out the sliding glass door as they're getting ready to leave. Mom has been fluttering around, looking for the iron and a clean pair of pantyhose, but I've been watching the light disappear from the tops of the trees.

"Be good, Ana." She throws her silk wrap around her shoulders and kisses my head stiffly. She smells like *L'Air du Temps*. She's said the same thing since I was three years old. I ignore her.

I watch the sun's last rays vanish over the horizon. I thought I felt bad when I had no friends here, but tonight I decide that there's nothing lonelier than knowing you're missing out on your life. People—my friends—are out there having fun and falling in love and living while I'm stuck here and can only dream of someday taking part. Even my parents have plans. I must be the only person in Half Moon Bay who doesn't get to enjoy the gorgeous fall night.

I hear Mom sigh and then hustle my father, who doesn't even remember to say good-bye to me, out the door. They're gone. Finally. Off to schmooze with some people for Papá's new practice. I hope it works. Papá is so stressed that I feel like he might snap at any moment. But I also kind of hope they have a terrible time.

The house is completely quiet, and it feels hollow. Maria is out with friends from her church tonight. They went line dancing. I didn't even know people still *went* line dancing, but at least she's somewhere.

I go upstairs to my room and find Zoe's phone. In a flash of selfless pity, she gave me her phone for the night so I can keep in touch with them and hear about the festival. Zoe and Christine promised to report back if they saw Tyler. Christine even offered to talk to him for me again, but I declined. What's the use? I'm never going to be allowed to date anyway. I text Christine's number.

C him yet?

I flip the phone shut, and when the light from the screen disappears, I am left in darkness. Mom and I fought the whole way home from the festival and then stopped speaking to each other. I don't like fighting with my parents, but it's time that they learn that I'm not a helpless baby anymore. They think I can't take care of myself, but I can.

The phone beeps, and I look down to see that I have a text from Christine.

T is here. Just saw him @ the haunted house.

I text her back to keep him in her sights. I want to know everything, even if I will only torture myself with every single detail for the rest of my life. Just think, I could have been there. I could have bumped into him in the dark haunted house. If I had screamed when something jumped out at me, he might have taken my hand to comfort me. I fall back on the bed in a dizzy state. I should have been there.

It's hours and many text messages later when I hear a knock at my door. "Anita?"

"Maria?" I sit up as she flips on the light and sits down on the edge of my bed. She's still wearing her jeans and short-sleeved shirt. "Did you have a good time?"

"We had a great time," she says, stroking my hair lightly. "There was so much to remember, but we had a ball. I think I finally mastered the Tush Push."

"Um, good." I think.

"Have you been in here all night?" She glances around my spotless bedroom, frowning. When we moved in, Mom decided it was time to get rid of all my stuffed animals and childhood trophies and thought we should make it look "sophisticated." In other words, she wanted it to look like some model teenager's room she saw in a magazine. The all-white furniture, hot pink bedspread, brightly colored lamps, and pink faux-fur rug were not my choice. Which is basically the story of my life.

"Yep."

"They just want to keep you safe."

I don't answer. She changes tactic.

"Have you and your mother settled on a theme for your *quince* yet?"

"Considering I don't even want a stupid *quince*, no." I cross my arms over my chest. Mom thinks the party should have a fun theme, like Masquerade or Arabian Nights. "And even if I did want one, I don't see what's wrong with, oh, you know, a Mexican theme." I roll my eyes.

Maria is silent for a moment, massaging her knuckles.

"Don't forget to enjoy it," she finally says.

"What?"

"Anita, your *quince* is a big deal." She pauses. "Mine was magical. I wore the most beautiful dress because I was becoming a real woman, a *mujer*, and my friends all dressed up too. They were my *damas*, my ladies to attend me. And there was such a party—my family cooked for days and days, and I danced with all of the young men in town, and I got a tiara to wear just like a princess." Her eyes become glassy and her face lights up as she relives the party that happened so long ago.

Well, times have changed. The whole beautiful dress and tiara thing sounds okay, but the rest of it . . .

"We'll see," I mumble.

"Okay." Maria nods, then kisses my forehead and walks out quietly. She can tell I'm not going to change my mind tonight. I lie back down on my bed again. I wonder what kind of dress Mom will let me get.

It's late when I finally get up to get ready for bed. After I brush my teeth and wash my face, I take one last peek at Zoe's phone. I have two new text messages. The first one, sent a while ago, says they're on their way to Zoe's and they lost Tyler and didn't see him the rest of the night.

Then, twenty minutes ago, they sent me this:

Good night, O:-)

17

"Gossip alert." Christine slides into our picnic table. Zoe and I chose this one because it's a little broken on one end so no one ever uses it. It's amazing how little time it took for Christine to start eating with us every day. All we had to do, it turned out, was ask.

"Dish it," I say, nibbling on my bagel.

"Guess who tried to break her neck at a party on Saturday night?"

"What?" Zoe says. Her lunch is dumped over our little wooden table, and she's inspecting it. She usually eats the little baggy of almonds and tosses the "fruit leather" snack and whatever else her mother has sent her that day. Then she hits up the vending machine for two packs of Nutter Butters and a Dr. Pepper.

"You know that big ogre, Zach?" Christine makes sure he's not behind her.

We nod. Everyone knows who he is, even Zoe.

"Apparently he had a party after the festival on Saturday, and our future homecoming queen jumped off the roof at his house and into the pool."

"That's very dangerous," Zoe says, genuinely concerned. "You mean Riley, right?"

"The one and only." Christine takes a bite of Yoplait.

As if on cue, Riley and Ashley brush past our group. I hear "God Girl" as they pass by, and I put my head in my hands. So I like to wear Christian T-shirts. So what? They stop at a picnic table a few feet away and sit down. Ashley hangs on Riley's every word. It's sickening. Andy, the football goon, comes over to join them.

"Nutter Butter run. I'll be right back." Zoe stands up and walks toward the snack bar.

"What else did you hear?" I try to act like I don't care, although we both know I do.

Christine polishes off her yogurt. "I guess at first everyone thought it was really funny, and people were really drunk of course, but after she jumped off then there was, like, this silence that fell over everybody."

"Really?"

"She could have broken her neck. And I guess she stayed under the water for a while. But then she came to the top and everyone cheered."

"That's so messed up. What is she, an adrenaline junkie?" I can't believe Zoe actually wants that girl to hang out with us. I glance back toward the snack bar and freeze. Tyler.

Christine turns too and sees him. And Zoe is walking right behind him, trying to point at him without being too obvious. I sit up straight, quickly flash my teeth at Christine, who gives me a thumbs up, and throw Tyler a big smile. He continues to stare off in the distance and breezes right past us to Riley's group. My shoulders fall.

"I don't know why I even bother."

Zoe sits down next to me so that she can have full view of Riley and Tyler.

Christine studies Riley's group for a moment. "Yeah, I'd say you have some competition there."

I crumple up my paper lunch bag. "It's not really competition when the other person has already won. Tyler only talks to me at church. At school, I'm not even alive."

I shove a huge bite of bagel into my mouth and fight back the tears. God Girl, huh? If I were really God Girl, wouldn't that mean I was favored by God?

Zoe gives me a hug. "At least you've got us."

"And what a prize we are." Christine laughs.

I clink my milk carton on Christine's bottle of green tea and then on Zoe's Dr. Pepper can. I hear Riley's loud, almost boyish laugher and cringe as I look at the table.

"I kind of want both, though."

Zoe's face falls.

"You guys are amazing. I don't even want to talk about what it was like those first few weeks I went here and didn't know anyone."

"You don't have to tell us, God Girl." Christine says. She takes an apple out of her backpack and pulls the stem off.

Zoe brightens up. "We're like a real group now. We should think of a name. My parents are always joining groups, you know, and you've got to have a name."

"How about Freaks of Nature?" Christine says, taking a bite.

I laugh. "That about sums it up."

Tyler finally walks away from Riley and disappears down a hallway.

"You guys," Zoe says and picks at the flaking wood on our

broken picnic table. "I'm serious. We've all got this, I don't know, this second chance at life."

"Yeah." I look at Christine to make sure she doesn't think this is lame. "I kind of agree. It's like we're all here for a reason."

Christine snorts a little. "You mean we should have been dead a long time ago."

"It's like we're all miracles." Zoe unwraps a Nutter Butter and smoothes the wrapper out on the table in front of her.

"I guess," Christine says.

"That's it," I say as the light bulb goes on. "We're the Miracle Girls." They both stare at me for a moment. "Okay, maybe not."

"It's perfect." Zoe claps. "That's it." We both stare at Christine.

"I suppose if you guys don't like Freaks of Nature, I go could with that." She shrugs at us.

"Now there's just one more thing to decide," Zoe says. She continues to play with the shiny red wrapper. "What about Riley?"

"What *about* Riley?" Christine meets my eye, and we look at each other in horror. Zoe is sweet and everything, but she's obviously lost her mind. Even if we did invite Riley into our little group, there's no way she'd join. She hates me, for one. And she probably thinks Christine and Zoe are total nobodies.

"No," I say, shoving the last of the bagel in my mouth.

"Not happening," Christine says.

"But she's—"

"Zoe." I put my arm around her shoulders. "Three is the perfect number. It's like the three parts of the Trinity. Or three strikes. Or..."

"Three stooges." Christine nods, taking a bite out of her apple.

"And three amigos," I say, though Zoe doesn't look at all convinced by our list.

"She's a miracle too. God must have saved us all for a reason," Zoe says. She crumples up the Nutter Butter wrapper and tosses it toward the trash can, but the wrapper doesn't even come close and floats slowly to the ground. She runs to pick it up and throw it in the trash, then comes back. "I'm going to make it happen."

Christine laughs and throws the rest of her apple in the trash. It lands in the garbage can with a satisfying thud. "Not in this lifetime."

18

"It's way too cold to be wearing skirts that short." Christine blows into her hands. The cheerleaders are jumping up and down like kangaroos on crack.

"They've got their brain power to keep them warm," I say, and Christine laughs.

I pull the sleeves of my sweatshirt over my hands and take a deep breath of the cool night air, sweet with the scent of cinnamon sugar from the churros at the concession stand. The stadium lights shine brightly onto the supernaturally green field. The stadium is filled with noise, and the bleachers are packed with Marina Vista students cheering and clapping and wearing garnet and gold outfits in a bold statement of school spirit.

This just in: it's not cool to bring your English homework to Homecoming. Who knew? To be fair, I only brought *The Good Earth* in case Mom was late picking me up, but apparently that's not the kind of thing most people bring to football games. I think even Christine was a little appalled when she showed up and saw me reading. But at least I'm not prancing around, sticking my butt in the air and waving pom poms around like someone else I know, someone whose name quite fittingly rhymes with "smiley."

Okay, I do have to give the cheerleaders some credit here. It's hard to cheer like you mean it when your team is dramatically losing its own homecoming game. It also doesn't help that the school mascot is a Starfish. "Go, mighty Starfish" just doesn't sound very intimidating. Even Zach, the star quarterback, is having a tough time keeping it together while the team loses.

"We've got our hands up high, our feet down low..." The whole peppy cheer squad is lined up and clapping along to some kind of chant. They wiggle their butts and scream while I try to figure out what they just said.

"This cheer doesn't even make any sense." Christine takes a sip of her hot chocolate. "Doesn't everyone have their feet down low? Ana, can you tell me something? Are your feet up high? No? Hmm, fascinating."

I snicker and turn back to the crowd. "What do you think the singular of pom poms is?" I stuff a handful of popcorn in my mouth.

"What? Now you're asking the great secrets of life?" Christine continues to study the cheerleaders. "Zoe owes us."

"For the rest of her life."

Christine and I crane our necks over to where the band sits. I can't pick Zoe out in the sea of instruments and hideous uniforms. At least we'll get to see her march at half time.

I'm not much into football. Did a football player ever go on to pioneer a vaccine or broker a ceasefire between warring nations? No. It's not a good use of time. But Zoe begged us to come and see her perform, and friends are friends. Christine and I decided that we liked Zoe more than we hated football. Besides, Christine pointed out it could be an interesting anthropology project, you know, to observe the natives at their big powwow or something.

Besides, Homecoming seems like the kind of thing you should do once, and since Zoe's family was going to come along to cheer on the band, my parents deemed the outing acceptable. Mom kept going on and on about how she wished she could come along but just couldn't find the time. As if. But at least she isn't here. I would have died if I had been the girl who had to sit with her mommy at the football game.

Thankfully, Zoe's parents are sitting up in the back row with some other band parents, huddled under wool blankets wearing shirts that say "What's the football team doing on the marching field?" and cheering at every opportunity. I suspect there might be something stronger than hot chocolate in the thermos they keep passing around.

The crowd around us begins to scream, and I look down at the field in time to see the Seaside Spartans get the ball and run with it to the, um, end of the field thingy.

Christine makes a face. "Why do they blink so much?" She blinks her eyes in rapid succession in the direction of the cheerleaders, then screws up her face.

"They look like those dolls whose eyes open and close whenever their heads bobble," I say.

"You want some more?" She holds out her hot chocolate. I shake my head and slip more buttered popcorn into my mouth. I prefer my calories in solid form. I continue scanning the crowd.

"You're being totally obvious," she says.

"What?" I spin my head around and try to look innocent, but she rolls her eyes. "I was looking for Zoe." I quickly cast my eyes over to where the marching band is sitting in the stands. As if on cue, they launch into a rousing rendition of "Louie, Louie."

"He's over there in the front." Christine points to the section of the bleachers down in front, near the middle of the field, right by where the cheerleaders are standing. It's where the cool kids stand. I already figured that much out. I squint, and finally spot his curly blond hair. He's wearing a light-up plastic neon cord, like you get at the circus, around his head, and a dark tuxedo.

The homecoming dance immediately follows the game, and though it's a casual thing, the members of each grade's court are dressed up since the Homecoming Queen will be crowned at half time. Not surprisingly, Riley was elected our Freshman Princess, though since she's cheering, she gets to change into her dress before the halftime show. Anyway, Tyler is the Sophomore Prince, hence the monkey suit.

The three of us are not going to the dance. I'm smart enough to know that dances are nothing more than highly organized torture exercises. If I want to stand around and feel awkward, I'll go to a nude beach. Also, Papá would never let me go even if I wanted to, which I don't.

"I wasn't looking for Tyler." I think we both know I'm not being totally honest.

"You should just go talk to him."

"No way."

"You have to. It's pathetic otherwise. Before the end of the night, I will insist that you go up and talk to him."

"In your dreams."

"If you don't go talk to him, someone else will." Christine throws her hands up in the air.

"Hey there." I turn around quickly, then break into a grin when I see it's Ms. Moore sliding into an empty seat in the row behind us. "Look at you two wild and crazy girls out on the town."

"What are you doing here?" Christine asks.

Ms. Moore shrugs. "Not much else to do in this town. Might as well take in the culture."

I guess it never occurred to me to wonder what Ms. Moore does in her own time. Most teachers have families and kids to deal with, but she doesn't have any of that. Suddenly I wonder if she ever gets lonely.

"You need to get a boyfriend, Ms. Moore." Christine seems to dare Ms. Moore to argue. I suck my breath in, trying to wrap my mind around that fact that Christine actually just said that to a teacher. "Been there, done that." Ms. Moore rolls her lips in for a moment and seems lost in thought. "I came here to get away from a bad engagement, and I'm not in any rush to head back. Boyfriends aren't everything, you know."

Hmph. Spoken like a girl who's actually had a boyfriend.

"You were engaged?" I notice Ms. Moore's naked ring finger for the first time.

"Yeah." She picks a hangnail for a moment. "He proposed the day we graduated from Brown. It was so romantic. I just got caught up in it all. It quickly became clear it wasn't going to work, so I broke off the engagement. I knew I needed to move so I threw a dart at a map of the United States." She runs her fingers through her short hair. "Too bad I was never very good at darts."

We both stare at Ms. Moore for a moment. Do I say I'm sorry?

"Cool," Christine nods.

Cool?

My eyes must be wide because Ms. Moore looks at me and laughs. "It's not *that* big of a deal, Ana." She smiles at me and I try to force a smile back, but it's all so sad. "And I think that's my cue to find someone my own age to talk to." She walks toward the stairs, then down toward the section where the teachers sit. I watch her go, then turn back to Christine. How does she do it? I mean, it's one thing to tease me, but to tell Ms. Moore that she needs a boyfriend . . . and somehow she gets away with it, which is even more baffling. Christine just has this untouchable nature.

"Pee break," Christine says at the end of the third quarter. The crowning of the Homecoming Queen meant very little to me. I don't know the senior class well enough to care that Sandra Entrekin beat out Natasha Sage. But when they crowned Riley, her mother was down on the field snapping a million pictures while Riley's dad and brother cheered loudly from the stands. And, you know, I have to admit that she looked sort of pretty. She didn't wear one of those ridiculously sparkly numbers like the rest of the court. It was just a simple, elegant black dress that set off her tan skin and blond hair really nicely. But after they announced her name, the cheerleaders did a cheer spelling her name and I nearly threw up.

Christine thunks down the concrete stairs, her blue hair flying back behind her, and I follow. She throws a quick wave at Zoe, who is in her seat in the woodwinds section. When we get to ground level, Christine threads her way through the crowd expertly. It's a bit crowded down near the bathrooms since they're right by the snack bar and everyone is refilling their snacks before the final quarter. She holds the bathroom door open, but I don't need to go. I lean against the wall to wait.

I am starting to recognize more people at Marina Vista, but the sheer number of students here is overwhelming. I wonder if I'll ever really feel like I belong.

That's when I see Dave. He's waiting in line at the snack bar, his dark hair sprayed blue for the occasion. He's wearing a red Seaside Bowling shirt under a red paisley tie, and he's talking to two guys I don't know. I think I knew he went to Seaside, but it still strikes me as odd to see him here. I quickly duck around the corner, not really sure why I feel the need to hide from him. I peek back at him, but he's still there, laughing with his friends.

Bowling. I wonder if that's an ironic statement or if Dave really is on the bowling team. With him, you never know.

As I'm trying to figure Dave out, someone comes out of the men's bathroom, and the dark suit catches my eye. Tyler. Oh my gosh. I think about what Christine said, how it's pathetic if I just obsess and don't ever talk to him. Should I do it? He's away from his friends. That makes it easier. I'll just say hi. There's nothing hard about that.

Christine would be so impressed if I actually did it.

"Tyler!" Before I know what I'm doing, the word is out of my mouth. He turns his head, squints at me, then nods. He takes a step toward me, and I freeze. What am I supposed to do now? "Hi," I stammer. "I didn't know you like football. I don't like football, but the marching band was playing." What am I saying? "Do you like the marching band?" SHUT UP. Why can't I make my mouth stop saying stupid things?

"It's cool," he says. He bobs his head. He watches me, waiting, no doubt, for me to explain why I called him over.

"Well, it was good to see you," I say quickly. I stick out my hand, and he stares at it, then takes it uncertainly.

"Good to see you," he says, dropping my hand. He winks, then turns and walks toward the stands.

"What are you doing?" Christine says, popping up in front of me. "You having fun over here?" How long has she been there?

"I talked to him! I talked to Tyler!" I sort of squeal this, but Christine doesn't have the reaction I was imagining. She looks kind of annoyed.

"Woo." She nods. "You ready to head back?"

"Um..." I try to read her reaction, but she stares past me toward the stands. "Sure."

We turn back toward our seats and walk in silence. Why is Christine being so weird? I decide to concentrate on the stairs. The steps in the stands seem a lot steeper when you're actually walking up them.

"Saw a cheerleader puking in the bathroom," she finally says, her voice a bit lighter.

"Gross," I laugh, though I don't really know if I should be laughing.

"Yeah."

Christine doesn't say anything when we get back to our seats, and though she's kind of freaking me out, I can't stifle the little feeling of excitement in my stomach.

He winked at me. Maybe football isn't so bad after all.

19

've replayed the scene in my mind so many times I think the tape is broken, but that doesn't stop me from imagining the wink over and over again all weekend. I didn't go to the nursing home this morning because Mom wants me to focus on my studies and my piano this weekend, and to be honest I'm glad, because I feel kind of weird about hiding from Dave last night. I wouldn't really know what to say to him if I bumped into him at the old people's home.

I'm trying to focus on my math homework, but my mind keeps going back to Tyler. He looked really nice in his tuxedo.

My bedroom walls feel like they're closing in on me. Normally, I like to do my homework in the kitchen. I try to spend as little time as possible in my room. But when Mom is home, bustling around with the interior decorator, it's useless to try to work in the kitchen. Today they're looking at bathroom fixtures, poring over catalogs, and exclaiming over showerheads and faucet fixtures. Plus, she's been on a huge planning kick for my quince recently, and I can't deal with discussing invitations any more. No invitations would be perfect in my opinion. Papá is home too, working on his computer and brooding about taxes or something, which means it's best to stay out of his way. And Maria is lying down.

To block it all out, I hole up in my room, sit at my desk, and put on some Bach. This is the new piece my piano teacher assigned me, so by listening to it now I'm really multi-tasking. Besides, they say listening to classical music makes you smarter. I'll take all the help I can get.

The phone in the kitchen trills, and I hope that it might be Zoe or Christine with gossip about what happened at the home-coming dance. Neither of them went, but Christine somehow always knows things like that. I prick my ears to try to hear what Papá is saying. Five minutes later, he still hasn't called me down-stairs, so I let my breath out slowly. I guess it's back to math.

I really do try to study for at least twenty minutes, but then I give up and turn on my computer. This is one of the ways my parents tried to bribe me into not fighting them too much on the move. They promised me my own computer in my room, though of course they didn't tell me that they were going to use parental controls to monitor everything I look at online. Mom was disappointed to find out they don't make the brightly colored Macs anymore, because she had pictured building my whole room's theme around the tangerine one, but I was quite pleased to get the flat white screen instead.

Neither Zoe nor Christine is online. Typical. Just when I need a distraction, no one's around. I check my Gmail, but the only new messages are spam. I pull up Google and click around on a few department-store Web sites. Nordstrom has a few cute dresses, grown-up but not too fancy, that might work for my *quince*. Maybe I could live with one of those. I quickly lose patience with dress shopping, though. It's not really much fun when you can't try them on. I think. Should I? I type in Tyler Drake and hit return.

There are a few links to teen art fairs, and a bunch of his times from swim meets show up. I didn't know he swam. But I click on the Web site for his band Three Car Garage.

Jackpot. There are pictures of the band leading worship at church, playing concerts at local high schools and churches, and just hanging out. It's kind of ridiculous the number of photos they have posted of themselves, actually. I click on one of Tyler leaning against a railing on a set of high concrete steps. He's smiling at the camera, showing his adorable dimples. I briefly consider saving it onto my computer but decide against it. If Mom or Papá decides to check my hard drive, they'll just ask too many questions, and it's not worth the fight.

I click on another photo, this one of Tyler with Dave, and smile. Dave is mugging for the camera, wearing a nice button down and a striped tie, as if he's going to the office or something, but then he's paired it with black board shorts and flip-flops. Tyler is wearing perfectly tight jeans and a slim white T-shirt with his A's hat, and he looks as if he couldn't care less. My stomach warms.

I click on a few other pictures and even check out a few of the drummer, Tommy Chu, who's not bad looking now that I think about it, then click over to the band's schedule. Hm. They have a show coming up in a few weeks at Half Moon Bay Coffee Company, the café downtown. I make a mental note to find out more. Then I go back to the photos and click around some more, savoring the experience of being face to face with Tyler, who acknowledged me in public.

I hear something. Mom and Papá. Their voices are raised and strained, and I close the browser window and tiptoe over to my door to try to hear what they're saying. I hope it's not about Maria again. *Please, God, don't let it be about Maria.* I stand with my ear to the door, listening, but I can't hear any more. I wait, but the house is silent. Eventually, I tiptoe back to my desk and sit down again.

I bring up Google again, then wait, my hands poised over the keyboard. I've already read everything the Internet says about lupus. I could Google it again, but I'm probably not going to learn anything new. I type something different into the search bar instead: *autism.*

I click on the first link that pops up and read about how the developmental disorder usually leads to repetitive activities—like drumming or tapping—as well as social problems. Sometimes people become obsessed with counting, or with dates or calculations. According to the site, it's often really difficult for the family to deal with. I'm about to click on a link that talks about treatment options when I hear a knock at my door. Startled, I jump up and fling open the door. Papá is standing there, his dark hair going every which direction and his face red. Thank God I wasn't looking at pictures of Tyler anymore. And I mean that literally, as I am thanking God for that small miracle. Close call.

"Is everything okay, Papá?" I smooth my hair down and straighten my shirt. There's something about Papá that makes me always feel like I need to measure up.

"We have something very serious to discuss." He steps inside and closes the door behind him. Oh no. It's Maria. They're taking her to the hospital now.

"What is it?" I try to keep my voice steady. I don't want them to know that I've been listening in. He gestures toward my bed, and I obediently sit down on the narrow twin mat-

tress and lean back against the pillows encrusted with rhine-
stones that spell out the words "Beautiful" and "Shopping."
Papá takes a deep breath, grabs his head for a moment, and
then looks at me straight in the face.

"A boy called for you." He delivers the news in a flat, even
tone, as if it pains him to say it.

"A boy?" Confusion washes over me, then relief. It's not
Maria. Thank God. And then, slowly, I start to feel a twinge
of excitement.

"You know boys aren't allowed to call here." Papá looks at
me sternly. Actually, I didn't know that. That must be a new
rule. I know I'm not allowed to date until I'm dead, but, considering my complete lack of options, it's not really something I've ever worried too much about.

"Who was it?"

"You don't know?" Papá watches me, and I can tell he's
trying to figure out if I'm telling the truth.

"No." I shake my head. I wish.

"Then how did he get this number?"

"Probably the phone book." The number is listed, so it
couldn't have been that hard.

Papá seems to consider this. "You really don't know who
it was?"

I say a quick prayer for patience. I shake my head instead of
speaking. Who knows what I might say if I opened my mouth.

"I didn't get the name," he says. "But I told him what the
rules of this house are and then hung up."

Oh no. I can feel my cheeks starting to burn just imagining it. If I had a cell phone, I could avoid this kind of drama,
but of course my parents know that, which is why I don't

have one. "But, Papá, how am I supposed to find out what he wanted? What if it was someone calling about an assignment at school?" What if it was Tyler and my dad just scared him off?!

"Then you'll find out on Monday."

"But—"

"Ana, we only want the best for you." He plays with the strap on his watch, and the silver metal jingles as it moves around his wrist. "We know there are many distractions in high school, and we don't want you to lose your focus. Thinking about boys will distract you from what matters." As if he knows anything about high school.

"But, Papá, I'm not—"

"Ana, you will not argue about this." He crosses his arms over his chest. "You are too young for boys. End of discussion." He turns and walks out of my room, closing the door behind him softly. I sit still on my bed, staring after him. I can't believe what I just heard. I'm a prisoner in my own house. They can't cut me off like this! What if someone called about school?

I grab the "shopping" pillow and turn it over in my hands. What if someone was calling about the nursing home project? Or to arrange something for Earth First? Or about a project for church? What then?

But that's not really why I'm upset. What if that was someone calling for a completely different reason, and now he'll never call me again? I wrap my arms around the pink pillow and lean back on the bed.

I close my eyes and remember how we winked at me last night.

20

My foot slips into the small pool of freezing water, and I know I'm a goner. I land on my butt on the slimy, algae-covered rocks.

"Ah!" I scream, but no one can hear me but the seagulls, who seem to be laughing at me. I pull my foot out of the tide pool and stand up as quickly as possible, but it's too late. My right sneaker is soggy, and my butt is smeared with wet brown sludge. Just call me God Girl Poopy Pants. I pat my butt with my notebook but only succeed in smearing the stain around more, so I give up. Better just focus on the project and get this over with. Why did I think this would be fun?

I'm an extra-credit junkie. I don't know what it is, but when I hear those two little words, something inside me goes wild. So when Mrs. Morales announced that we could do a long-term extra-credit project toward our final grade, I jumped at the chance. It's not like I'm failing Biology either. In fact, if I get the full five points with this project then I'll probably get a 101 for my final grade, but I just couldn't resist. It never hurts to build up a cushion in case something goes wrong. That's when I had the brilliant idea of tide pooling.

Half Moon Bayers can barely talk for five minutes without mentioning tide pooling. The beaches here are a little unusual. They're not the sunny Southern California beaches you see in the old surfer movies. These are rocky and moody and usually shrouded in fog. At the top, they're surrounded by high cliffs, affording crazy views of the Pacific Ocean. If you take a path down to the beach below, there is a small stretch of brown sand. But what's most interesting is that beyond the sand, there is this huge bank of craggy rocks, which you can only see when the tide is low. Go down there at high tide, and it looks like a pretty typical beach: water, shore, whatever. But go down there at low tide, and you'll see a small beach leading to a huge bridge of rocks. The rocks are very, very slippery and full of holes—some as small as a pin prick and others the size of small ponds. Millions of sea creatures can be found in the spaces in those rocks, called tide pools. Apparently sea creatures don't have even half a brain, so as the tide is going out, they get trapped in these little pools. You can see starfish of every color, beautiful spiny purple and black sea urchins, small fish, and maybe even some sea lions sunning themselves out on the rocks.

Plus, the best beach to tide pool at—Moss Beach—also happens to be right near the best surfing beach. I thought...it's a slight chance, but you never know who you might run into down at the surfing beach. And as luck would have it, low tide is at seven o'clock in the morning today, which I understand is the perfect time to catch a wave. And he did call me, so apparently he does want to talk to me...

At first Mom made some noise about accompanying me tide pooling, but once she realized that it would cut into her precious beauty rest, she decided that Maria could just drop me off, as long as I brought a life jacket with me. Of course

I left that on the shore. I'm not wearing some bright orange dork-alert life jacket all day. And Mrs. Morales said she can't wait to see my pictures and profiles of all the different sea life I find. I'm not trying to prove a hypothesis or anything. It's just extra credit.

I lean over and snap a picture of a sunflower starfish. It must have twenty legs and is a little bit creepy looking—like a spider or something. I make some notes in my journal and then pick my way over the rocks carefully.

I glance to my left and through the misty morning air I see a few people surfing, way out. I put my camera to my eye and try to use the zoom function to see who they are. But even with the zoom, I can only identify them as human and nothing more. I can't even tell if they're male or female. And yet, hope is born in my heart. After I get all the pictures and notes I need, I'll have to walk down there and see if I bump into *someone*. Maybe that's why he called anyway, to tell me where he'd be.

As the sky changes from a pinkish blue to a brighter, deeper blue, I take a deep breath and let salty air fill my lungs. It's hard not to think about God when you're nose to nose with some of the most amazing and bizarre creatures he ever made. I peer into a promising pool and see a beautiful lavender starfish with the standard five legs. I start snapping pictures of him...wait, her?...aren't they asexual? It? I keep taking pictures and they all turn out beautiful.

"You're really photogenic, you know that?" I say quietly, as if I will disturb him.

I know I should move on, but I find myself oddly mesmerized by the starfish. I wonder if he was surprised when he found himself hanging out in a small puddle instead of swimming along in the vast ocean. Did he like it? Did he try to get back out to sea? I know it's stupid, but I can't help but wonder how long it took for him to adapt and begin to thrive in his new home.

Before long, water is creeping up around the base of my sneakers and I realize the tide is coming back in. Soon the rocks I'm standing on will disappear under the ocean again. I snap a few more pictures of my friend the starfish and call it a day, picking my way over the slippery rocks back to the shore.

After grabbing my life jacket, I casually swing by the surfing beach, but I don't recognize anyone down there. They all seem like older people, college kids or something. I start walking back to the top of Moss Beach, where I said I would meet Maria. It was a silly plan anyway. I mean, what are the odds that I would run into Tyler on this particular stretch of beach on this very morning?

I kick at the sand and squint down the road for signs of our car. I'm in the right spot to wait for Maria, but I'm a little early. I hear a coughing noise behind me and gasp when I turn and see Riley, wearing a dark wetsuit and carrying a board under her right arm, a little ways down the road. I turn back around quickly and begin to send Maria ESP messages to hurry up and come get me.

I hear Riley give a little sarcastic laugh that confirms she can't believe her luck either. She ignores me and walks up to the road, her flip-flops squishing with every step. She puts out her thumb and waits.

"What are you doing?!" Is she? Could she possibly be...hitchhiking?

"What are you doing?" I try again, but she doesn't look at me.

"What does it look like?" Her wet hair hangs limply on her shoulders.

"You can't do that," I say. "That's so dangerous." I may not like her very much, but that doesn't mean I want Riley to die or anything. What is she thinking?

"What are *you* going to do?" She scratches at some wax on her board. "Fly home on your broom?"

I jut out my chin. "You can't hitchhike." I don't want to do it, but I don't know what else to do, so I add, "You can come with me."

She rolls her eyes. "Mommy, may I please have permission to catch a ride home?"

"Fine!" I throw my hands up in the air. "If you want to jump off buildings to your death and hitchhike with ax murderers, what do I care?" I turn and peer down the road.

She keeps her back to me for a moment and then turns around.

"You know, Ana, I don't know what I ever did to you. Why won't you just leave me alone?"

"Leave you alone?" I gasp. "This is probably the second time I've ever even talked to you." I walk back over to her. "In case you haven't noticed, you're too cool to talk to me."

"Whatever," she says and puts her thumb out again.

"You know, the other day I almost felt sorry for you."

She narrows her eyes. "Why?"

I bite my lip. I probably shouldn't have said that. It's just that it must be hard to have a brother who has autism.

She puts her face in mine and speaks in a slow, low

whisper. "Don't you feel sorry for me. You don't know anything about me or my family." I see tears welling up in her eyes.

"Riley, I'm sorry. That's not what I meant."

She turns around and begins to flag down a pick-up truck that's approaching us.

"Please don't do this." I try to put my hand on her shoulder but she shrugs it off. "My ride will be here in just a moment. We'll drop you home."

The truck pulls up with its radio blaring.

"Hop in," one of the two college-aged guys in the passenger cab says.

Riley smiles and then puts her board in the back, hops in, and beats on the side twice. One of the guys looks at me to see if I'm getting in too, but I shake my head. They drive off in a cloud of dust, and I watch them go, knowing I should have done more, or said less, or something.

21

It's a couple miles to Christine's house, which is farther than any of us really want to walk, but Christine assures us that it's better than riding with The Bimbo. Apparently The Bimbo isn't going to be around today, which is why we're going over there at all. Well, that and the fact that we have to make posters for the upcoming Earth First "Go Green This Thanksgiving" initiative we're gearing up for, and Christine has more art supplies than God. Though I guess God doesn't need poster paints since he's got rainbows and stuff. At any rate, Christine's mom was an artist so she has a lot of supplies, and it's the first time I've even heard Christine talk about her home, let alone concede to let anyone come over.

The Bimbo is Christine's dad's new girlfriend. She's an aerobics instructor, and her schedule is as flexible as she is, which is how she is able to come over to Christine's house every day after school to "be with" Christine until her dad comes home from work, and to help out when Christine's Dad goes to Sacramento. As you can imagine, Christine isn't so into this situation.

As we trudge down Highway 1, the main road that goes through town, Zoe snacks on Starburst and talks about the new piece the piccolo section is learning, and Christine looks down at the ground. Cars zoom past us on the highway, but Christine doesn't say anything the whole way home.

Despite the cool November air, I'm thirsty and kind of tired by the time we turn onto Christine's street. But as soon as we hit her block, she freezes.

"She was supposed to take The Bimbot to the doctor," she says. The Bimbot is Christine's nickname for The Bimbo's daughter, Emma. A giant white SUV is parked in the second driveway on the left.

"What?" Zoe asks.

"She wasn't supposed to be here today." Christine purses her lips.

She points toward an adorable white bungalow with a big porch. But as I look more closely, I realize that the house would benefit from a good scrubdown and some TLC. The grass is brown and the paint is beginning to peel a little from around the bottom of the garage door. There's a graying, flat soccer ball in the front yard. Christine stands still, shaking her head. Zoe and I wait, trying to figure out what to do.

"Come on." She trudges up the flagstone walkway, and we walk behind her. I try not to notice the weeds sprouting up through the cracks. She pushes the faded front door open and steps inside, putting her finger to her lips and walking quietly down the hallway.

"Is that you, sweetie?" a voice calls from the kitchen. Christine freezes.

"Christine, we made you some cookies!" A high-pitched voice trills out, and then we hear light footsteps running toward us. A bubbly preteen wearing a Miley Cyrus T-shirt jumps into the hallway and holds out a plate of chocolate chip cookies. Her broad smile turns into a blank look when she sees me and Zoe. "Who are you?"

"These are my friends." Christine ushers us past the girl down the hallway.

"Hey, there," says a perky brunette standing in front of us. "I'm Candace." She smiles and waves at us. Her long brown hair is shiny and perfectly styled, and she's so thin, she looks like she could be a model. "And this is Emma." She strokes the peppy girl's hair.

"I thought Emma had a doctor's appointment today." Christine plants her hands on her hips.

Candace lights up. "The doctor had an emergency with another patient, wouldn't you know it. So I was able to come over, after all. That worked out well, didn't it?" Candace smiles at Zoe and me.

"Yeah, except for that other kid," Christine says, rolling her eyes.

"I'm so glad to meet your friends." Candace holds out her hand to Zoe. The Bimbo seems determined to be friendly. Zoe takes Candace's hand slowly.

"I'm Zoe," she says.

"Ana." I smile and shake her hand as quickly as possible, then drop it.

"We're just going to go to my room and make posters for school," Christine grumbles, letting her blue hair fall in front of her face. She starts walking down the hall.

"We made cookies," Emma says again and bounces up and down. I nod as if I didn't hear her the first time.

"Woo." Christine doesn't look back.

"Just make yourselves at home," Candace says as Christine slumps away.

"Yeah, I live here," Christine says over her shoulder and walks down the hallway. As I follow her, I look at the photos that line the wall. Behind the pictures, the faded yellow and brown wallpaper is starting to peel along the seams. Something strikes me as odd. There are lots of pictures of Christine growing up, and there are a few photos of Christine and her dad, but there are several empty spaces where it looks like photos have been taken down. The nails still stick out of the wall, and the evenly spaced frames on either side highlight their absence.

"Those were the ones of Mom," Christine says, following my line of vision.

"Oh." I really need to think of a better way to respond.

"Dad took them all down."

"Oh." Shoot. I did it again!

"She's here every day." She nods toward the kitchen.

Candace and Emma are laughing and talking in the kitchen, and suddenly it's clear as Technicolor why Christine tries to get herself into detention all the time. If my dad had replaced my mom with a bimbo, I would stay away, too.

22

The youth group ski trip is still two months away, but we're raising money for it now. As Fritz has reminded us for the past few weeks, the more we raise now, the less we'll each have to fork over in January, but since very few of us in the youth group will actually be paying our way out of our own pockets, the turnout is predictably low. Next time, I think he should mention that he's providing pizza for lunch, since that always seems to work.

Today we're working on Mrs. Murphy's house. She's a wealthy, elderly widow in the church. We're pruning her garden and repainting her living room, and in return she's donating money to the youth group. If it were me, I'd just hire a real gardener and painter. I've seen these people in action, and it's not pretty. But it's her funeral. Oh, bad choice of words. Well, whatever.

This isn't exactly how I would have dreamed of spending my Saturday, but I'm trying to put on a happy face. Zoe came with me today, and even though she showed up wearing patchwork overalls, I'm glad to have her along. I let it slip a while ago that Riley goes to my church, and Zoe decided that was how she was going to get to Riley to join the Miracle Girls, which is ridiculous, but here she is. She's planning to come on the ski trip with our youth group, and now we're trying to convince Christine to come, too.

Zoe, I was shocked to discover, is a Christian. Dreamy and Ed were a part of what she calls "The Jesus Movement," which from what I can tell was a bunch of hippies who started going to church in the seventies. The Fairchilds go to something called Church of the Redwoods, which sounds a little *kumbayah* to me, so I wasn't shocked that Zoe wanted to try out a real youth group. Apparently at Church of the Redwoods, she *is* the youth group. And she was predictably delighted to discover that Riley is here today as well. A little too delighted, if you ask me. It's kind of nutty.

Because I brought a friend, Fritz gave me first pick of chores, so naturally I chose painting, because it seemed more fun than gardening, but an hour into it, I'm not so sure. The fumes are starting to get to me, and poor Mrs. Murphy picked a pukey shade of green for her walls, which is making me a little ill. Still, the painting itself is much less annoying than the company. Riley won't even look at me after our little conversation on the beach. It's not like she ever made much of an effort to be polite anyway, but this is different. She refuses to look in my direction at all. She hates me even more than she used to, which is really saying something.

And now she won't shut up about herself. All morning she's been bragging about how she recently went snowboarding for the first time and tackled a black diamond without ever having taken lessons.

"I got to the top and looked down, and I freaked out," Riley says, bugging out her eyes to show how scared she was, "but then you know, what was I going to do? I was already up

there." She tosses her hair and laughs, and her vapid friend
Tanya, who hasn't touched her paintbrush to the wall all day,
laughs too. "It's really just like surfing. I think that's why it
came so naturally to me."

I can tell Zoe is listening to Riley's every word. I refill my
roller and continue painting over the lovely light blue walls,
trying not to roll my eyes. You know what else is just like
surfing? Painting this freaking wall. Really! It's so great! And
I've never even had a lesson. It's all in the wrist!

"You're probably really good at surfing," Zoe says, smiling
at Riley. Oh, Zoe. I recognize her attempt to start a conversation, and I ache for what I know is coming. How can she
be so kind to someone so horrible?

Riley spins around, smiling benevolently at Zoe. She's
such a fake.

"Yeah," Riley says, then turns back to Tanya. "I thought
I was going to die. But you know what? It was so fun." She
dips her brush back into the open paint can. "What a rush."

"Outta my way, ho!" We all turn to see what kind of a
creep is coming toward us, only to see Dave making a weird
face and wrestling with a garden hoe, which is blocking the
partially open sliding-glass door. Riley laughs as Dave sets
the offending instrument down outside and comes into the
living room. He wipes his face with a tie he has fashioned
out of an old rag.

"How's it coming, Dominguez?" Dave grabs a brush from
the ground and examines it. "You need any help?" Sweat
drips down his face and plasters his dark hair to his scalp.

"I guess." Maybe he can tell me where Tyler is today. I
introduce him to Zoe, then turn back to my painting. They

chat for a moment, then fall quiet, and we all work in companionable silence, at least on this side of the room. On the other side, the Riley Show is in full swing.

I'm working up the courage to casually mention Tyler when Dave clears his throat. "So," he says, smiling at me. "Did you enjoy the Web site?"

"The...what?" I squeak. Does he know I was looking at their Web site? How could that be? I can feel my cheeks burning.

"Three Car Garage." He smiles and brushes his hair back from his face. "The Web site? You were looking at it, right?"

"Um..." Okay, I have two options here. I could deny it all and play dumb, but I suspect that will only work for a little while. Or I could come clean and play it off like it's no big deal, though it's a very big deal. I mentally roll the dice and opt for number two. "Yeah. Great site." I clear my throat. "Um, I see you have a concert coming up."

"Yeah. And thanks," he says, smiling. "I built that site myself." He dips his brush back into the paint and begins to apply a coat of green. "Since I host the site, I can see the ISPs of every visitor, and from there I can figure out what name the browsers are registered to. I saw the name Dominguez, so I figured..." he trails off and shrugs, and I feel my face turning bright red. Oh, no. I pray that he can't see which parts of the site I looked at, too. If he can see how many pictures of Tyler I looked at, I'll actually physically die.

Zoe, who has been listening to all of this and knows about my crush on Tyler, mercifully tries to change the subject. "What's that?" she asks.

"It's a tie," Dave says, clearly hoping she'll ask more about it. She does, and he explains his tie-a-day mission and how he fashioned this one out of an old towel his mom gave him. He blots his face with it again, and Zoe admires his handiwork.

"By the way," Dave says, giving me with a serious look. "I really hope I didn't get you in trouble with your pops. I didn't know about the, um, rule."

I stop painting. "What?" He's never met Papá.

"It's just that when I called your house—"

"*You* called?" The breath disappears from my lungs. I know I'm sweating, but I can feel the hair on my arms stand up like I'm cold. It was Dave who called, not Tyler? Why would Dave call me? I cast a nervous glance at him, then look away quickly when I see him watching me. All of a sudden I feel like I'm going to throw up.

"Yeah." He watches me. "He didn't tell you?"

I shake my head. How could it not have been Tyler?

"Sorry to disappoint you," Dave mumbles almost silently under his breath.

"I mean..." I stutter. I can feel my cheeks flush. I know, somewhere in my whirling mind, that I should be flattered, but mostly I just feel embarrassed. My disappointment must be etched on my face.

"You were probably hoping for a call from someone else." He paints the wall in angry, broad strokes.

"No, wait. I mean, I—"

"It's not a big deal." He dips his roller into the paint and applies more puke green to the wall as if he were attacking an enemy. "Don't worry about it. I was just calling about signing up for this workday thing. And clearly, you did that all by yourself."

"I'm..." I try to regain my composure. "It's okay." I swallow.

"Whatever. I just hope you're not grounded or something. Your dad was pretty angry." Dave tosses his roller into the paint tray with a loud thud.

"It's cool," I say, all of a sudden talking like Christine. "I'm glad you called." But before I can even get it out, Dave has gone back outside and picked up the hoe again.

23

"My house, my house," Tyler sings into the mic. I groove to the music a little and look over my shoulder again. This is the riskiest thing I've ever done in my life, but so far it's totally worth it. Now I get why people like rock concerts so much. They're amazing. I've seen Tyler lead worship at youth group, but this is something different. Three Car Garage's sound, away from the youth room, is loud and brash and high-energy. I keep fighting the impulse to just start dancing right here as if I'm alone in my bedroom. And Tyler looks so cute when he shuts his eyes, grabs the mic, and sings.

Operation Rock and Roll took a full week to plan. I saw Tyler putting up flyers for the show at church last Sunday. Sure, I knew they had a concert coming up, but the flyers told me exactly when the band would be going on and how long the show would be. Then all that was left for me to do was find a way to get myself there.

Just one problem, of course. Okay, well, two problems: Mom and Papá. Christine and Zoe both wanted to come to the concert, too, and Zoe kept saying, "Why don't you just tell your parents the truth?" Her point was that Three Car Garage is a Christian band, so my parents wouldn't object. But what I couldn't seem to get through to her was that all rock and roll is the devil's music. It's all bad, according to my parents. Plus, this outing would also be forbidden under the "strictly no contact with boys" rule, which trumped all other rules except one: church activities are always okay.

That's where Christine came in and really proved herself again. She and I reasoned that, in some ways, this really was a church event. I mean, where two or more are gathered, God is there. And Three Car Garage has three members. So all I needed to do was present this to my parents as a church activity—not technically a lie, since the band members all go to church—and I'd be allowed to go. Christine had the genius idea of having my parents drop me off at church, which is just a short walk from the café, and then we'd all stroll down there together. This way, I never actually told my parents the concert was at church, but they naturally assumed that it was. Really, the whole thing was brilliant.

But now that I'm here, I'm feeling a little less sure. The stage is set up in the outdoor courtyard in front of the café, and I wasn't really prepared for that. Anyone who drives or walks by could see me standing here, instead of, you know, at church where my parents think I am at the moment.

The song ends with a loud chord, and the crowd goes wild. There is a huge turnout tonight, and girls our age crowd the area near the stage. Some of them I recognize from school, and I suspect we're all here to see Tyler.

"Thank you," Tyler says into the mic as Tommy Chu taps lightly on the cymbals and a girl screams loudly behind me. He winks at her, and I turn to see who it is. No one I recognize. Okay, whew.

"That was our song, 'My House in Heaven,'" he says.

"And it's about, like, how God said that your house in heaven will...that you'll have a house in heaven. You know that verse?" Girls scream and I try to make my voice the loudest one.

Dave grabs his mic. "The song is about John 14:2," he says, looking out over the crowd. "Where Jesus tells us, 'In my father's house are many mansions. I am going to prepare a place for you.'" Dave fidgets with a leather bolo around his neck. "He's talking about heaven here. Isn't it great to know that Christ himself is preparing our future home for us all?" A few people clap when Dave is through.

"Exactly," Tyler says. He brushes a lock of hair out of his eyes. "That's where our band name comes from. Because when I get to heaven, I want my mansion to have a THREE...CAR... GARAGE!" He screams this last bit into the microphone, and the cheers from the crowd are ear-splitting.

"Well, that and Tommy's parents let us practice in their three-car garage," Dave says.

I know Dave sees me out here, but every time he catches my eye he quickly looks away again. He hasn't spoken a word to me since the painting incident. Pretty soon no one will be talking to me at all.

Tommy claps his drumsticks together and they start playing again. Slowly, Christine, Zoe, and I work our way up to the front. Zoe keeps swaying back and forth to the music in a sort of trippy way. Christine and I are really dancing, along with the rest of the crowd, and I forget all about my earlier paranoia. I can be so dramatic sometimes.

And then, much too soon, the show is over. I clap and clap and clap until my hands are red. My throat is sore from screaming.

Christine nods her head toward the café, and we all trudge inside to use the bathroom. We check our makeup in the mirrors.

"What'd you guys think?" I dig in my purse for my Chapstick.

"Tyler's actually a good singer." Christine frowns at her reflection. "I was a little worried that he'd starve to death after having seen his painting, but at least he'll always have his singing."

"That bad, huh?"

"Worse than finger painting." She blots her sweaty face with a paper towel.

"I thought that guy Dave was awesome, too," Zoe says and raises a brow at me.

"He's okay," I try to act nonchalant. Zoe shakes her head. "Let's get walking back to the church. My mom's going to pick me up soon. I don't want her to think I've been raptured and she hasn't." Zoe laughs a little, and Christine looks at me like I'm crazy.

As we walk back toward the band area, though, I can't help but slow down. The guys are packing up their instruments. There's no one else around them.

"Hey, Ana." Tyler is smiling at me. At me! I force myself to stay calm. Dave watches us, placing his guitar in its furry case.

"Hi, Tyler." I give a small wave, hoping I don't look too eager.

"Where's that girl Riley tonight?" he asks, closing the lid of his guitar case. He snaps the buckles to lock it.

For a moment, I can actually feel my jaw hanging open. Do I look like that girl's keeper? "Like I know," I snap.

Tyler nods for a moment, studying me. "Well, maybe we should hang out sometime."

"Um..." What is he saying? Does he mean hang out? Or *hang out*?!

"If you want to," he shrugs. I turn around a little to make sure that I'm not being punk'd. I see Dave staring at us, but I don't spy any hidden cameras.

"Cool," I say, trying hard to channel Christine's calm, detached demeanor. "Yeah, let's hang out."

24

"So you told them you were going to church, but you went to a concert instead." Ms. Moore's hands move quickly, tying red ribbons around the bottom of the plastic baggies. We're sitting across from each other at the table in the front of her classroom, and the Elvis Christmas CD she put on makes the plain old room seem kind of festive.

"Sort of." I tear off a bunch of mistletoe and stuff it into a plastic bag. Keeping my hands moving seems very important all of a sudden. "I mean, I didn't actually *tell* them I was going to church." As it comes out of my mouth, I know how pathetic it sounds.

"I see. So you feel okay about what you told them?" She levels her eyes at me evenly, her left eyebrow rising a tiny bit. I avoid her glare.

It was Ms. Moore's idea (of course—what kid would think of this?) to gather mistletoe, a plant that grows way up in the branches of the trees around here, and sell it as a Christmas fundraiser for Earth First. Ed made it totally easy for us and gathered a ton of it from the trees in Zoe's backyard, but we still have to cut the bunches into smaller pieces, place them in plastic baggies, and tie them up. We hope to make enough money on this fundraiser to save twenty acres of rainforest, but we're supposed to start selling tomorrow and our product isn't ready, and since no one else could make it after school today—Zoe has band practice, Christine has to babysit The Bimbot, and the junior girls have track practice—it's just me and Ms. Moore.

"Ana?" Ms. Moore's brown eyes are still focused on me. Doesn't this lady ever let up? She stops tying ribbons and lets her hands rest on the table. "What's the worst that could happen if you were honest with them next time?"

"They'd probably kill me." I hold a small bunch of mistletoe in my hand and run my fingers over the smooth leaves. "Or ground me forever. Lock me in the closet until I'm twenty-five." She doesn't say anything, so I continue. "They'd never let me go, that's for sure. You don't understand how strict they are."

"Maybe not," Ms. Moore says after a while. She reaches into her pocket and pulls out a tin of Burt's Beeswax lip balm, then dips her finger into the shiny gel. "But I can tell that you're uncomfortable with lying to them, and I wonder if there's a better way." She swipes her finger across her lips quickly, then rubs her lips together.

"Like what? They treat me like I'm a baby."

"You could talk to them about how you feel." She says this so calmly I almost don't notice she's started tying the ribbons again.

"I can just imagine that conversation." My brains spin for a moment, picturing it. "Mom, Papá, I want to go to a rock concert to see a boy I like. See you at midnight!"

Ms. Moore snorts. "They actually might kill you if you phrased it like that. But they just want to protect you, Ana,

and if you want to show them you're old enough to have
some adult privileges, you need to come to them like an
adult. Have a conversation about it and tell them how you
feel."

"Whatever." I notice that my hands are idle. I wonder how
long I've been talking instead of working. It's weird to talk to
Ms. Moore like this. Weird but cool.

"So tell me about this boy."

I freeze. Can I tell a teacher something like this? Do I
want to?

"You don't have to tell me if you don't want to." But
for some reason I almost do want to. "Does he go to this
school?"

"Yes." And with that little word, somehow a dam opens,
and soon I've told Ms. Moore all about Tyler. She thinks she
knows who he is, but she isn't quite sure, thank goodness. I
tell her everything, even the part where he asked me to hang
out a week and a half ago, and how I've been waiting for him
to call (not that that would work anyway) or e-mail or IM or
anything. And how I haven't heard a thing.

"Even when I saw him on Sunday, he didn't mention
hanging out. Do you think I should e-mail him or something? I think he was really serious. Maybe he lost my e-mail
address?" Sure. Fritz e-mailed all of us a youth-group direc-
tory a few weeks ago with everyone's phone numbers and
e-mails, but maybe Tyler accidentally deleted the e-mail?

"Maybe. But aren't you getting ahead of yourself?" She
ties another perfect bow, making it look so easy. "Let's start
with this. What would you do if he did ask you out? What
would you tell your parents?"

I bite my lip. What would I do? I would...I would tell them the truth. I think. Wouldn't I?

Ms. Moore smiles. "Ah, the course of true love never did run smooth." She brushes her hair back behind her ear.

"Huh?"

"That's Shakespeare. *A Midsummer Night's Dream*. We'll get to it next semester." Her eyes crinkle up a bit at the corners.

Okay, I can deal with Shakespeare, but that doesn't exactly clear up what she meant. I am about to ask when the classroom door bursts open and Zoe streams inside, her cheeks red and her long hair flowing behind her.

"Am I too late to help?" She drops her backpack and piccolo case onto the floor. "Mr. Parker made us do, like, a thousand drills today." She pulls a bag of chips out of her bag and bites into a Dorito.

"You're just in time," Ms. Moore says, smiling at Zoe. "Here, why don't you take over? I'm going to go over my lesson plans." Ms. Moore walks toward her desk, and Zoe reaches for the spool of ribbon and the pair of scissors.

I try to smile at Zoe, and I really am glad to see her, but I also can't help feeling a little frustrated that she interrupted what felt like such a private moment with Ms. Moore. It was so nice, just the two of us.

Zoe ties a few ribbons, placing a chip in her mouth between each one, while Ms. Moore writes in a big thin black book on her desk. I focus on the task at hand and try to keep my mind from wandering toward anything that starts with a T. Not tigers, not tremors, not taboos, not...

"Do you really think people will want to buy this stuff?"

Zoe wrinkles up her nose as she holds up a finished bag of mistletoe. I have to admit, it looks pretty cheery with the red ribbon and white berries against the green leaves.

"Sure," I shrug. "Why not?"

"It's just some silly shrub." Zoe pops another chip into her mouth and cuts another piece of ribbon.

"Oh, sure," Ms. Moore says. "People love this stuff. Especially around the holidays, when we could all use a help getting a kiss from someone we care about." I feel her eyes boring into the back of my head, so I don't turn around.

"Ew." Zoe shudders. Zoe and I are the same age, but sometimes it doesn't seem that way. "I don't see what all the fuss is about," she says, shaking her head. I pretend I don't know either, even though I'll probably take a bunch home for myself, just for luck. At least I don't have to worry about her stealing my crush.

There's a low beeping, and Ms. Moore reaches into her purse and pulls out her cell phone. "I have to get this." She stands up and walks toward the hallway. The heavy door thuds closed behind her, and the only noise for a while is Elvis crooning about a blue Christmas.

"So I had a new idea for how to get Riley," Zoe says "It just came to me during drills. I'm not a very good swimmer, and I don't really love the ocean, but I bet surfing isn't that hard. I bet I could—"

"Zoe, what are you talking about?" I say before she gets too carried away. "You're going to learn to surf? Don't you think that's a little weird? That's certifiably stalker material." Zoe looks a little taken aback at my outburst, but I can't stop myself, for some reason. "Why are you so insistent about getting her to hang out with us, anyway? She doesn't even like us. She's made that abundantly clear. And I don't actually like her much, either. I'd be happy if I never had to speak to her again. So why don't you just give it a rest?"

"Oh," Zoe says. She slumps a little and lets her hair fall in front of her face. "I didn't realize you felt so strongly about it."

Guilt overwhelms me. How can anyone be so genuinely nice?

"I..." I mean, I do feel so strongly about it. And yet, I know Zoe is only trying to do what she thinks she needs to do. For whatever reason, she's convinced that there are four Miracle Girls. "I just...I just don't think she wants to be one of us. And I don't want to see you get hurt trying to force her."

Zoe nods, but I can see in her eyes we both know this isn't entirely true.

"We won't have to force her," she says quietly. "She needs us as much as we need her."

"I don't think so." I shake my head. Zoe seems like she wants to say something more, but as Ms. Moore comes back into the room, we both fall silent.

25

've been dreading this all week. I wrinkle up my nose at the Ben-Gay smell that permeates the air at Stonehill Manor and walk slowly down the hall, saying a quick prayer for strength to do this. Mom decided it had been too long since I had visited the nursing home. I've come three or four times, which is more than most of the other church volunteers, but she read in a magazine that regularity is as important as sincerity in the admissions game, so here I am. I know there must be a couple of other church people here, but I haven't seen them yet.

It's not that I hate being here. It's just that I'm not really sure what to say or do while I'm here. I run my hand along the textured wallpaper as I walk down the beige hallway, looking for Sarah Slater's door. Even if she doesn't remember me, I'll know her, and that's something. A hunched-over woman with thin white hair trails behind me, pushing her walker along while she mumbles about dogs, but I try not to act weirded out.

I recognize the plastic wreath on the outside of Mrs. Slater's open door, and I take a deep breath and walk to her room. I can see that she still has her Christmas tree set up, but because this time it's actually December, it feels a little less special somehow. I rap lightly on the wooden doorframe, and she turns.

"Is that Molly?" Her voice is low and quiet. She squints at me and takes a step toward the door.

"No, Mrs. Slater. It's Ana." I read online that you shouldn't ask Alzheimer's patients if they remember you, because it puts them on the spot and they feel bad if they don't, so I watch her face for any signs of recognition. She nods, but her eyes don't show that she has any idea who I am.

"Do you want to see my Christmas tree?" Her face breaks into a huge, toothy smile. I nod and walk into the room. She sits down daintily in her recliner and I plop down on her gray chair. She begins to talk about the whipping she got the time she locked Molly in the bedroom and her parents didn't find her for hours. I sit on the edge of the chair and smile, though I heard this story the last time I came. When she gets to the part about choosing her own switch from the bushes in the backyard, she trails off and stares straight ahead.

"I brought you something, Mrs. Slater." I reach into my backpack and pull out a handful of candy canes. Her eyes light up as I hand one to her, then stand up and hang a few on the branches of her plastic tree. She carefully peels the plastic back from the straight end of the candy cane and slips it into her mouth. She sucks on it, and her mouth makes a few slurping noises, which kind of grosses me out. I stare at her. Now that I've given away my treat, I don't quite know what to say, but she seems happy enough, so I let my gaze travel to the window. She does have quite a nice view, looking out toward an enclosed backyard area with green grass and a pond. A heavy gray fog blankets the grass and obscures the trunks of the trees. There's something almost magical about the way the fog erases the hard edges of the world around here.

"Hey, hey, here's where the party is," says a voice from the hallway, and before I turn to look, I know it's Dave. Today he's wearing a bright red Santa hat in addition to jeans, a Grinch tie, and a green T-shirt that says "Genghis Khan is my homeboy." He has an acoustic guitar strapped to his back. He walks into the room and stands in front of Mrs. Slater, then pulls his guitar off his neck and sets it on her bed.

"Hi, I'm Dave." He holds out his hand to her. She takes it, and though she doesn't introduce herself, she smiles and continues to suck on the candy cane. "What's goin' on, Dominguez?"

"Hey." I bite my lip. I haven't really talked to Dave since the concert—since the youth group workday, really—and it feels a little weird to see him standing here. But he appears to have moved past the awkwardness of that day, and I try to act like it never happened, either.

"So what are you two cool chicks up to?" He walks toward the bookshelf to examine the miniature Nativity scene.

"Did you see my tree?" Mrs. Slater asks, pointing to the tree again.

"Rockin'." He picks up the figurine of Jesus in the manger and turns it over in his hands. He looks from Mrs. Slater, slurping contently on her candy, to me. I cross my legs and stare back at him. "You ready, Dominguez?"

"Ready for what?" I narrow my eyes at him. A lock of brown hair hangs over his right eye, but he doesn't bother to push it away.

"The Christmas carols." He shakes his head at me as if I'm an idiot for not knowing. "You're leading them."

"What?" Did I just screech? I think I might have just screeched.

"Sure. I play and you sing. Isn't that right, Mrs. Slater?" Dave says loudly, turning toward her.

"Oh, yes, certainly." She nods.

"Hey!" I almost say, "That's not fair! She's senile and doesn't know what you asked" but stop myself before making that horrible mistake. Dave's eyes twinkle at me mischievously. It's like he knows what I want to say. "I don't know any Christmas carols," I say finally. Okay, that's not a real lie. It's one of those "white" ones.

"Now, Ana." Dave waves the baby Jesus figurine in front of me. "Lying makes baby Jesus cry."

"So does manipulating." But Dave is already putting the figure back and pulling his guitar strap over his head again. He takes a seat on the edge of the bed and begins to tune it.

"What, no bass today?" I cross my arms over my chest.

"Nope." And without further explanation he strums a few chords, then hums a bit. "And a one, and a two, and..." He turns toward Mrs. Slater and starts playing. It's only a few bars into the song that I realize he's playing "Grandma Got Run Over By a Reindeer."

"You're singing that song?" I hiss. With all these old grandmas here? What is he thinking? Dave just closes his eyes and pretends to be really into the song, in an Elton John kind of way, though the way his lips turn up at the corner makes me think he's actually about to start laughing.

I stand there sputtering for a moment, thinking of stopping him, but then I notice that Sarah is smiling and bobbing her head along to the music.

"Come on, Dominguez." Dave opens his eyes just as he gets to the chorus. "Sing." I start to back up. Oh, no. No way am I getting sucked into this madness. Dave presses on as if it doesn't matter to him one way or the other, and Mrs. Slater starts to hum along, although she doesn't quite hit the same tune. I see a movement in the hallway and stop. A couple of residents have clustered around the open door to listen to the music.

And though all I really want to do is bury my head and pretend I don't know either of them, I have to admit, Mrs. Slater looks happy. And Dave looks so ridiculous, with his hat and his tie, singing as if this song is the most serious and important thing in the world, that I can't help but laugh.

Dave ends the first song and transitions straight into "Rudolph, the Red-Nosed Reindeer," and one person in the hallway starts calling out "like a light bulb" in the wrong places.

Dave smiles at the crowd gathered in the hallway, then turns to me and nods. I turn away, but not before I see him smile. And though I'm looking out the window again, watching the whispers of fog curl around the branches of the barren trees, I start to sing.

26

The Christmas Eve service at church starts at seven, but we're all lined up in our pew by six forty-five, because Mom was insistent that get good seats. Churches fill up at Christmas, and while everyone's welcome and we're glad to see new faces in church and all, Mom isn't going to be caught dead standing up in the back when the pews get full. Papá looks quite handsome in his navy blue suit with his dark hair slicked back, and Mom is wearing a new sparkly red top, which I personally think looks a little too Vegas for Christmas Eve, but then, she didn't ask me. I'm practically brimming over with great ideas, but no one cares.

Of course, I am grateful that she took me shopping last week, and though picking out clothes that we both agree on is tough (she can dress like a showgirl, but she basically wants me to dress like a nun), I feel good in my new cranberry dress. The fabric is clingy but not tight, the strings of the wrap dress tie at the side, and the skirt falls just below my knees. Mom hasn't said anything about the fact that I didn't put on the nylons that she always insists I wear. I hate them—I mean, nylons? I'm not eight or eighty—but up until recently, for some reason, it never occurred to me to just not wear them. Either she hasn't noticed, or she is trying really hard to protect the image of our perfect family by not blowing up at me in church. Either way, I'm not wearing the nylons, so score one for Team Ana.

Maria is here tonight, too. She usually goes to Catholic mass on Sundays, and I can't remember her ever coming to church with us, even on Christmas, but she wanted to come tonight. I don't know if she's still not feeling well or what, but Mom said, "Of course, she's welcome to join us. She's part of the family." Maria's sitting quietly next to me, looking around the sanctuary as it begins to fill up, and I can't help but wonder what she thinks of all of it. The church she goes to is ornate and full of dark wood and beautiful paintings and sweet smells. In contrast, our sleek modern auditorium feels a little naked. The only decoration is a wooden cross, but not the rugged, authentic-looking kind. This wooden cross was made by some fancy modern designer, with dark polished wood and a glossy finish. If Starbucks sold crosses, this would be a venti.

Music begins to filter in through the loudspeakers, and it takes me a minute to realize that someone is actually playing the piano at the front of the church. I try to focus my thoughts on the meaning of Christmas and prepare my heart for worship, but it's kind of hard with so much going on around me.

Dear God, I begin, *thank you for coming down to earth. Thank you for . . .*

Riley's family files into the pew ahead of us. Her mom, with her perfect blond hair sprayed into place, turns around and begins to chat with my mom. Riley slumps down in the pew and doesn't turn or acknowledge me, and her brother,

Michael, mumbles under his breath and taps on the padded part of the pew next to him. I hear some numbers and realize he's counting. Riley's dad looks like a Ken doll, and he puts his arm around Riley's shoulders. Riley slides into her dad and lets her head lean on his shoulder a little. Papá is staring straight ahead, and I can tell by his eyes that he's physically here, but mentally he's somewhere else. I try to focus again.

Please, God, let everything be okay with Papá's business, I pray. *Let him relax tonight and focus his thoughts on what Christmas really means, and...*

Out of the corner of my eye, I see a group of people walk into the sanctuary all wearing green. It's Dave and his family. They file into a pew on the right side of the sanctuary, and I almost choke when I notice that all five of them—Dave, his parents, and his two younger brothers—are wearing matching sweaters. Matching light-up reindeer sweaters, to be exact, all of which are definitely lighting up. Dave even has a light-up reindeer tie to match. Mom notices, too, and clucks her tongue, but I can't help but laugh. Everyone else here is wearing their very best clothes, but the Brecht family is acting as if there's nothing weird at all about their attire.

Dear God, I would love to be so free of concern about what people think of me. Please help me to find my value in you, not what others say, and...

The lights of the sanctuary dim, white projection screens lower from the ceiling, and soon we're all watching a video about the first Christmas. It feels a little weird to me to be watching a movie at the Christmas Eve service, but everyone else seems pretty into it, so I try to imagine what it must have been like for Mary and Joseph to be strangers, alone and out of place, far from home among people who didn't know them and didn't care. I can relate, but—I don't mean to be sacrilegious or anything here—I think this might have been a little more compelling for me a few months ago.

These days, I can't help but wonder if Jesus ever had to tell little white lies to Mary and Joseph to keep them from breathing down his neck all the time. Probably not, since he was perfect. I wish I knew his secret.

The lights come up, startling me out of my thoughts. *Thank you, God, for my family, who—as ridiculous and annoying as they may be—are here.* I glance down the row, and Papá gives me a little smile. I smile back and feel very peaceful all of a sudden. It's been so long since I've seen him smile that this simple gesture fills me with hope. Maybe everything will be okay after all.

"They showed Mary twenty-three times, but they only showed Joseph twelve times," Michael says loudly in the pew in front of us, and I hear a few people chuckle.

The choir gets up to sing, and I lose myself in the music. In this crazy world, we really can have hope for the future because of what happened in Bethlehem so long ago. I thank the Lord that we can hope for better things to come.

It isn't until the service is almost over that I realize Tyler isn't here.

27

"There's nothing to do around here," Zoe moans, draped over her bed on her back. She places her arm over her eyes dramatically, like she's starring in some lame TV drama. Two weeks without school always seems like a really great idea at the beginning, but the truth is, Christmas break gets kind of boring. Once all the excitement of the holiday is over, there's just not that much to do.

"This town is so boring." Christine is splayed out on Zoe's beanbag chair. We're all munching on stale candy corn that Zoe pulled out from under her bed, and the tasteless waxy candy only adds to our malaise.

"So there's no big town celebration or anything?" I ask, but Christine shakes her head. Her cherry-red hair fans out. It didn't used to bother me to spend New Year's Eve at home, watching the ball drop on TV with Maria, but I'm not a baby anymore. There has to be something better to do in this town.

"Nothing. This place is so dull." She tosses a handful of candy corn into her mouth and makes a face. "Your church isn't doing anything, Ana?"

"No." I sigh. Though that would have been perfect. "The youth pastor is away visiting his in-laws, and we don't even have youth group over the Christmas break."

I stare up at the ceiling, which has those ugly sparkly bits in the cottage-cheesey plaster. The uneven brown carpet is pressing into my back, but I can't bring myself to move.

"Zoe? What about your church?" I ask out of desperation.

"No way. They do some weird service out under the redwoods, but trust me, we do not want to go to that." She tosses a candy corn into the air and tries to catch it in her mouth, but it bounces off her cheek and lands on the lavender bedspread. She leaves it there and tries again. "There's chanting involved."

"We could hang out at my house with The Bimbo and The Bimbot," Christine laughs. "You know, make macaroni necklaces and stay up until nine." Zoe and I both know she's not serious, so we don't even bother to answer. It seems like too much work.

"If only one of us could drive." Of course I don't know where we'd even go, but still, driving around would be better than this. How can a whole town have nothing going on? "What's everyone else doing? It's not like we're the only three highs-schoolers in Half Moon Bay." I reach my hand into the candy bag.

"Everyone else is skiing," Zoe says. I realize she may be right. With some of the best skiing in the country only a few hours away in Tahoe, many families take off for their mountain cabins this time of year. It was the same in San Jose, but my parents aren't exactly the outdoorsy type, so I've never been. Zoe's never said anything about it, but I kind of suspect money is tight for her family, which explains why they're sticking around, and Christine...well, she's always the wild card. "We could hitchhike to Mexico." Zoe grabs some more candy corn.

"We could order takeout and watch Molly Ringwald movies all night," Christine says.

"Who?" Zoe looks around, but neither Christine nor I have the energy to explain who Molly Ringwald is.

"We could fly to the moon," Zoe says.

"We could eat Taco Bell until we puke." Christine smiles.

"We could sleep on the beach," I say.

Apparently that was the wrong thing to say, since they both turn and look at me. Okay, I'll admit it was strange, but I didn't think it was any weirder than suggesting we fly to the moon.

"That's it!" Zoe pushes herself up to a sitting position. "We should go camping on the beach."

"Oh, no," I say, shaking my head. "That was a joke. You know, like hitchhiking to Mexico?"

"But we could." Zoe stands up and starts pacing. "My parents have all this camping equipment we never use. We totally could."

"Beats Taco Bell," Christine says, shrugging.

"Seriously?" They both nod. "You guys, my parents would never let me. Never in a million years. I'm sorry."

"Hm," Christine says. I kind of like her new hair color. It makes her look dangerous. "Well, would they let you camp out anywhere else?"

"We could do it in the backyard," Zoe says. This idea might sound lame if it were my backyard, which is a perfectly manicured patch of grass bordered with pansies and impatiens in tasteful pots, but Zoe's backyard is the forest.

It would be like really camping. "My parents would totally let us camp there, and we could make a fire and roast marshmallows and stuff out there. They wouldn't care." She turns to me. "Would your parents let you do that, Ana?"

If Dreamy and Ed were in the house, we'd technically be supervised even if we were in the yard. I'm not sure Mom and Papá would go for the sleeping outside bit, but I could just tell them I'm sleeping at Zoe's, which is technically the truth.

"Oh, come on," Christine says, her eyes pleading. "It would be so fun."

Zoe nods. "It would be really cool. We have the sleeping bags and everything, too, so you wouldn't need to bring anything, if that helps."

"I'll ask." It's the best plan we've come up with so far. They have to say yes. They just have to.

You can tell a lot about a person by how they roast their marshmallows. Christine is the kind of person who sticks the whole thing straight into the fire and lets it ignite, then eats the blackened gooey mess in one bite. Zoe is impatient. She lets each marshmallow get warm and a little golden, then plops it in her mouth and quickly moves on to another. I like to take my time and let each marshmallow get perfectly and evenly brown.

Zoe's parents don't know we're even roasting marshmallows. They don't approve of marshmallows, since they're made with gelatin, which comes from animal hooves, apparently, but Christine, always a forward thinker, brought a bag along just in case. Zoe's parents did provide tofudogs and rice pilaf for us to cook on their camp stove, and for the dessert they gave us chunks of spiced pineapple to roast. I don't think I have ever tasted anything so good in my entire life—it's sweet and hot all at the same time. But there's something about marshmallows. You need them when you're camping. And illicit ones taste even better.

"You guys, I think I'm going to ralph." Zoe clutches her stomach as she finishes a marshmallow. She reaches for another one anyway.

"Ha," Christine cries. Delight registering on her face as another marshmallow goes up in flames. "Take that, sucker." She waves it around until it is extinguished, then blows on it until it's cool.

I nibble on my own marshmallow and sigh. This is so perfect. The only thing that would make this more perfect would be if someone male were here, holding my hand, but since that's likely never to happen, I'll settle for this. I don't think I've laughed this hard in ages. The air is cool and moist, and we're all wrapped in layers of clothing and big, thick blankets. We're surrounded by towering trees, and you can just make out a few stars up there through the branches. *God, you sure make some cool stuff.* I take a deep breath of the pure sweet air. The night is so still and peaceful, it almost seems like we really are somewhere out in the middle of the woods, and though Zoe's house is only a few hundred feet away through the woods, we're so decked out that we could survive out here for weeks, if we needed to.

It shouldn't have surprised me that Zoe's family takes camping seriously, but I'm still kind of in awe. I've never seen a tent so big. This thing has three rooms. *Rooms.* In a tent. I can stand all the way up in here without hitting my head. It's crazy. And of course they have high-tech sleeping bags and air mattresses, and they're even letting us use their camp stove and lanterns.

Even if we owned these things, my parents would never let me use an open flame, but Zoe knows about all of this stuff, so her parents let us be. She knew how to pick a good spot for the tent—she found a place where the ground was flat and not too rocky. She instructed us on how to set the tent up, and we had it up in no time. She knows how to work all of the equipment. It's nice to see Zoe in control, not just because Christine and I are so useless we'd probably die out here on our own, but also...it's just nice to see Zoe in the role of a capable leader. I don't know that I've ever really seen that before, and it's cool.

"So you're really not going to come?" I ask Christine. Sure, she just told me she wasn't going to come, but I guess I'm in denial. "I thought it would be the three of us, like always."

It was almost eleven by the time we were done with dessert. Thankfully Zoe offered to extinguish the fire while Christine and I climb inside the tent-mansion to change into our pajamas.

"You think I don't want to? Trust me—I'd rather do anything else in the world." Christine is completely unselfconscious as she changes into a pair of men's boxers and a white men's undershirt.

"Maybe ask your dad again," I say.

"It's freezing!" She dives into one of the sleeping bags we set up in the main room earlier. I laugh as she shivers dramatically in her sleeping bag, then turn away a little as I change into the blue silk pajamas I got for Christmas. Since Mom thought we were sleeping indoors, I couldn't really get away with packing hardier sleepwear, but luckily, silk is actually very warm.

"Dad says that The Bimbo put a lot of thought into this girls' weekend, or whatever she's calling it."

"Girls' weekend?" I jump into my own sleeping bag, shivering.

"Yeah, I think The Bimbo is going to try to tackle me and paint my toenails pink."

"Well, we'll miss you. Won't we, Zoe?" I stare up at the trees through the vent in the top of the tent.

Zoe comes in and zips the tent up carefully behind herself. "Miss what?"

"The church ski trip. I begged my dad, but he said I have to go on this stupid girls' weekend with The Bimbo. It's some big surprise she's been planning to torture me with. Did I tell you we have to go to a spa? They're going to, like, touch me and stuff. Though I suppose it couldn't be worse than the time she made me sit through one of her peppy yogi-woo-woo-lates classes."

"I cannot imagine you at a spa." Zoe laughs for a moment while she collects her pjs and then disappears into one of the other "rooms"—separated from the main chamber by a piece of nylon—to change. "Riley's still coming, right?" She yells through the wall.

It's probably good that she can't see my eyes roll. "Unfortunately."

"Speaking of Cheerleader Girl, did you guys hear that

she's now dating that football goon, Zach?" Christine spends a lot of time just watching and listening to people, and somehow she seems to glean a ton of information this way.

"Really?" So Riley is *not* dating Tyler. "Do you really think so?" Zoe yells through the wall, even though it's not like it's difficult to hear through the piece of nylon. "I kind of get the feeling she's not actually interested in dating anyone—she just likes to flirt."

Christine and I exchange a suspicious look. What kind of person isn't interested in dating anyone? And it's not like Zoe is really an expert in this field.

"I don't know. I can't keep track of that girl," I say quickly. Maybe I can change the subject. I don't want to talk about Riley all night.

"Have you figured out how to get out of your *quince* yet?" Christine asks. Mom and I had a meeting with the party planner last week, and a little thrill of excitement ran through me when she showed me pictures of some previous *quinces* she's put on.

"No," I say, grimacing. "But it might not be so bad, after all."

Zoe emerges from the other room, wearing a pair of baggy gray sweats, a sweatshirt that says New College, a giant rust-colored robe, and hideous red plaid slippers, and for some reason, this sets us off into hysterics. We're a bit slap-happy by this point in the night, it's true, but seeing Zoe all bundled up like an old person is more than Christine and I can take. Zoe isn't sure whether to be amused or offended by our laughter. But she decides to go with amused, and soon we're all rolling on the ground.

"Okay, guys." Zoe sits up on her sleeping bag. "It's time to be serious." She takes a deep breath and tries to compose her face, but she bursts out laughing again.

"Yeah, serious," Christine says, smiling. "We'll need provisions." She reaches into her backpack and pulls out a box of Cheez-Its and a package of Red Vines. "Okay, who's going first?"

"Going first for what?" I reach out to take the box of Cheez-Its. I slide my finger under the lid and pry the cardboard open, then begin to work on the inner plastic bag.

Christine bites the package of Red Vines open. She pulls a long red strand out and points it at Zoe. "Truth or dare?"

Truth or Dare? Why do girls always end up at Truth or Dare? Am I the only girl in the world who doesn't like this game? Why would I want to choose between doing something stupid, dangerous, and/or embarrassing and spilling my innermost secrets? But Zoe is already answering "truth," so I guess we are playing, like it or not. Zoe pulls her legs up so her knees are under her chin and wraps her arms around them.

"Who do you like?" Christine asks, shining a flashlight in Zoe's face.

And why does this game always go there? It's inevitable. Zoe smiles, and her cheeks don't even flush red.

"That's easy," Zoe says, shaking her head. "No one. Next?" She points her finger at me, then Christine.

"Wait, wait, wait," Christie says. "Stop right there. I don't buy it."

"What?" Zoe grabs a handful of snacks and pops them in her mouths. "I really don't."

"You really, seriously, don't like *anyone*?" Christine leans in to study Zoe's face. On the one hand, I kind of agree with Christine here. There's got to be something Zoe isn't telling us. But on the other hand...this is Zoe. Maybe there's not. "No one in marching band?" Christine presses, but Zoe shakes her head. "Not in any of your classes? There's no one you think is cute?"

Zoe shrugs, her cheeks turning a little pink. "Sorry." Christine continues to eye her skeptically, but then turns to me.

"Who do you like, Ana?" She shines the flashlight in my face now.

Zoe groans and rolls back onto her sleeping bag. "You're supposed to ask something you don't already know."

"Hey, isn't it Zoe's turn to ask a question?" I laugh. I look from Christine to Zoe, but neither one seems to care too much about the eternal rules of Truth or Dare.

"I'm just curious." Christine refuses to back down.

"Oh, come on," I say, pulling the sleeves of my pajamas down over my hands. Our body heat has warmed up the air in here significantly, but it's still pretty cold. "Why do you want to ask that? You guys already know."

"If we already know, this should be easy to answer," Christine says. Zoe nods and sits up.

"Do I really have to answer?" I cough into my hands for a moment, buying time. "I mean, I didn't even really pick truth here. Maybe I was going to say dare."

"You weren't going to say dare," Zoe laughs, and I feel my face redden a little, because we all know it's true. I'm not really a "dare" kind of person.

"Fine." I sigh and begin to pull at a loose thread on my

sleeping bag. I'm stalling, and I suspect Christine is the only one who really realizes why. "Tyler," I say quickly, and then read their reactions. Zoe is nodding, but Christine is watching me, not moving.

"Your turn." I take a handful of Cheez-Its and turn to Christine. "Truth or dare?"

"Dare." She doesn't take her eyes off me. I'm beginning to get a little uncomfortable. I said Tyler. Why can't she let it go?

"Um." What kind of dare can you do out here? And why doesn't it surprise me that she picks dare? She's obviously the least concerned with appearances, but it's more than that. Christine has this way of not revealing much. "Call Tyler," I say, giggling at the prospect. I know she has his number. She told me. This is the perfect idea. Christine just shakes her head.

"No cell service."

"Yeah, you can't get a signal this far out," Zoe says.

"Okay." I could do something with the horses, but Zoe would freak out. I could have Christine play a trick on Zoe's parents, but they're being so nice to us that that just seems mean. I could...well, I don't know what else to do. "Streak from here to those trees and back." I gesture to where the clearing ends and the redwoods begin again.

"Streak?" Zoe falls down onto her sleeping bag, laughing at the very idea, but Christine just shrugs, steps out of the tent, quickly drops her clothes on the ground, and begins to run. Ten seconds later, she's back inside the tent bundled into her sleeping bag trying to get warm again, but she doesn't even seem to be at all winded or embarrassed.

"There's no one out there." Christine shrugs. "No big deal. Now...who's next?"

"Hey." I hold up my watch. "It's almost midnight."

"Yay," Zoe says, clapping. Whew. Saved by the bell. We drag ourselves into the left side pocket of the tent, which we have deemed the party room, and don party hats and pick up the noisemakers my parents sent along. We jump around a little to keep warm, testing out the noisemakers a few times, and open the bottle of sparkling cider Zoe's parents brought us earlier. We pour ourselves big glasses, then count down the last minute on Zoe's digital watch. At the stroke of midnight, we lift our glasses in a toast to the Miracle Girls, then toss back the cider. It's light and bubbly and a little sweet. It tastes great and feels so grown-up, and before long we're falling over ourselves laughing again.

It's close to one in the morning when we climb back into our sleeping bags, and my eyes are heavy, but I feel good. We line up our sleeping bags close to each other for warmth and settle in, feeling worn-out and comfortable and happy. Maybe this wasn't the coolest way to spend New Year's Eve, but I can't think of a better one. *Thank you, Lord,* I pray as I begin to drift off to sleep. *Thank you for good friends.*

I'm almost asleep when I hear it. Christine isn't loud on any day, but she's especially quiet now. "I like Tyler," she whispers, then turns over in her sleeping bag and doesn't say anything more. I don't know if Zoe heard it, and the more I think about it, I'm not even sure I heard it. Did I imagine it? But I can't stop thinking about it from every angle, over and over again. I wonder what it means to me, to Christine, to Tyler, and to the Miracle Girls. Slowly, my thoughts dull, and I drift off into a fitful sleep.

28

We're sitting around Christine's kitchen table, eating string cheese, when we hear the front door open. Our heads turn toward the unexpected sound, and out of the corner of my eye, I see Christine stiffen. No one is supposed to be coming home for hours.

"Emma?" Christine glances at the living room, but The Bimbot is staring, glassy-eyed, at the television. The girl can't get enough of *Hannah Montana*. It's always on in this house. Christine stands up, tentatively, and grabs a rolling pin from a drawer, then begins to sidle toward the door.

Zoe and I came over a little while ago to help her babysit The Bimbot. Okay, maybe "help" wasn't exactly what we were planning, but she was stuck staying home with the kid on a perfectly beautiful Saturday afternoon while The Bimbo went to teach Yogalates (which sounds like a torture device, but is actually a form of exercise—so, basically the same thing). It was only going to be a few hours, so she begged us to come over and keep her company. Things have been a little weird ever since she confessed she likes Tyler, and neither of us has mentioned it, which has kind of made it worse, and inviting me over seemed like a really good sign that she didn't hate me, so I took her up on it.

My parents made me swear up and down that I would

get my homework done tonight, since I would be wasting my Saturday afternoon (prime studying time), and I had to spend all of Friday night practicing the piano just to be allowed to come over. But now that someone is sneaking into the house to kill us, I kind of wish I had just stayed home.

The door slams shut, and Zoe and I jump. Christine holds up the rolling pin, takes a deep breath, then walks out of the kitchen and disappears into the hallway. We hear heavy footsteps. Zoe's eyes are wide. She motions to the door. We both stand up and begin to follow Christine. All I really want to do is hide under the kitchen table. I take a step, then freeze when I hear Christine screeching. Zoe drops to the floor and puts her arms over her head as if an anvil is going to drop on her like in a cartoon. But my body is flooded with a surge of adrenaline. I run toward the sound, ready to pummel Christine's attacker.

When I round the corner, I see Christine hugging some strange man, not dead on the floor, so I immediately put on the brakes. I can't stop in time and run into the two of them. What's going on?

The man pulls his arms away from Christine, then blushes. I step back and try to regain my composure, though I'm still struck dumb. He's wearing a gray suit and a tie, and his short black hair is slicked back. Christine laughs at me a little.

"I didn't mean to scare you girls," he says, laughing. Christine looks sheepishly at the rolling pin in her hand, then turns to me.

"Ana," she says, using the rolling pin to gesture toward

me, "This is my dad." She sweeps it toward the man. "Dad, Ana."

"It's nice to meet you." He holds out his hand toward me. His face is soft and pleasant.

"Hi," I say, uncertain what else to say. As a local politician, Christine's dad is never around. He's always off at some supermarket opening in Half Moon Bay or attending to state business up in Sacramento, the state's capital, so I've never seen him before, but he's hardly what I expected. Considering how much Christine hates to be at home, I guess I thought he would have horns growing out of his head or something, but he seems perfectly nice. Kind of soft-spoken. Handsome, even.

"Hi," Zoe says, peeking her head around the wall. Her cheeks are bright red.

Mr. Lee chuckles when he sees her. "Christine, you've got friends stashed all over the house."

"Zoe's the last one. Dad, this is Zoe."

Zoe shakes Mr. Lee's hand and keeps her eyes down.

"The legislative session finished early," Mr. Lee says, placing his hand against the wall. He uses his right heel to push off his left shoe, then begins to slip off the other one. His socks are black and have a gold seam at the toe. "So I hopped in the car and headed straight home. And Candace called to say her last class was canceled, and we had a brilliant idea," he says, smiling at Christine. Her face falls. I can practically see the thoughts running through her head. Her dad wants them all to spend time together. One big, happy family. Mr. Lee is too busy hanging his black trench coat on the coat rack by the door to notice her sour expression.

"I thought we could go to San Francisco. Didn't you say you wanted to go ice skating?" He looks at Christine, his face hopeful.

"I thought Candace didn't like ice skating," Christine says, her voice sullen and thick with sarcasm. In the space of thirty seconds, Christine has gone from delighted to the angry girl we first met in detention.

"She's not coming." Mr. Lee smiles. "She'll stay here with Emma. You and I are going. Just the two of us." Christine squints at her dad, almost smiling. "And your friends, too," he says quickly. "Just the four of us. How does that sound?"

Christine looks at us. Zoe shrugs, and I try not to look too eager. San Francisco! Of course I want to go!

"Candace is really not coming?" Christine spins the rolling pin around the handle and watches him.

He shakes his head. "It was her idea."

Zoe is surprisingly nimble on ice skates. I guess that shouldn't have shocked me, since Zoe is probably the most athletic one of all of us (which really isn't saying much), but for some reason, seeing her there on the outdoor skating rink, her long gray skirt flying out behind her, is strange. She skates smoothly but listlessly, her wavy hair tumbling around her shoulders. It's kind of like seeing one of those prim prisses from a Jane Austen novel on a Harley motorcycle. Christine, on the other hand, is quick and sure, and she zips around the ice as if she owns it. Apparently she once had aspirations of being the next Michelle Kwan. Mr. Lee bops his head as he circles the ice, smiling and laughing, though he looks like he might fall over at any second. Me, I try to focus on the patch of ice directly ahead of me. I just put one foot in front of the other, and every so often I look up quickly to take in the sunshine and the smell of the sea air and the palm trees.

The Bay Area doesn't get cold enough to have a natural ice skating rink, but every winter the city of San Francisco builds one here, just outside the Embarcadero Center. There are some indoor rinks you can go to any time, but because this is outdoors and only up for a few months out of the year, it seems more special somehow. We walked by here last year after Mom and I went Christmas shopping at Nordstrom, but she doesn't know how to ice skate, and we were running late for some appointment or another, so she refused to let me give it a try.

As I make my way around the ice, rail-hanging every step of the way, there is just one thing ruining this perfect moment. In the pit of my stomach, I have a nagging feeling that Mom and Papá might be kind of annoyed with me. When I called to ask if I could go to San Francisco, no one answered the phone at my house. I tried their cell phones, but they didn't pick them up.

I take a deep breath and try to relax. They're the ones who wanted me to make some friends, and this is a totally supervised, male-free (except for Christine's dad, but I somehow don't think he counts) day. What could be bad about that? Plus, I'll get my homework done, like I promised I would, and I left a message about where I was going, exactly who was coming, and when I'd be back. I try to suppress the doubt that tugs at the edges of my mind and remind myself that this is the day that the Lord has made and to rejoice and be glad in it.

After we pile off the ice rink, sore and tired, Mr. Lee declares that he is taking us all on a date. We hop a cab to a café in North Beach, which is the Italian neighborhood of San Francisco, and get a table for four at a charming restaurant. Mr. Lee selects a table by the window so we can watch the people going by, and orders us a big plate of steaming hot garlic bread. We devour it and compare bruises. Zoe wins hands down because she's one of those people who bruises if you look at her wrong.

As Zoe tells a story about her brother and a rattlesnake on the ranch, I sit back and study the restaurant. It's the kind of place I would like to come to on a real date someday, with the white tablecloths, great Italian food, and the sophisticated atmosphere. I try to picture what it would be like in here at night with the lights aglow. I'd be wearing my new cranberry Christmas dress, and he'd be wearing a white collared shirt, his brown hair combed back....

Our main courses arrive—I chose fettuccine alfredo, since I can't think of anything better than noodles with cheese and butter in one dish—and we all dive in. Mr. Lee has a few bites and then regales Zoe and me with a story about the time Christine had to go to the hospital to get an M&M out of her nose when she was a baby. Zoe guffaws and slaps the table, I nearly choke on a noodle while I blink back tears, but Christine stays quiet, like she's been all day. I stare at her for a moment. It's clear how much Christine loves her dad, and yet she's so introverted when he's around. She blushes but doesn't laugh at the story.

Mr. Lee asks us about our hobbies and what subjects we like in school, and then listens to our answers as if he really cares about what we have to say. He's so charming, even Zoe is talking her head off. But Christine just nibbles on her lasagna now and then and doodles on her ticket from the ice skating rink. She's sketching out teensy-tiny figures. I have to squint to see them. So far she's got a man and a girl with dark hair and matching straight-lined mouths that make them seem perplexed or lost, or maybe even slightly angry, and she's working on a third person. Mr. Lee doesn't seem to notice. I guess Christine doodles so much that it's easy to tune it out.

Mr. Lee asks about our families, and Zoe stops devouring her eggplant parmesan for a moment and talks about how her grandmother is coming to visit from Arizona. Maybe it's just me, but she seems a little too excited about seeing her grandmother. I mean, I like my grandma and all, but Zoe's been practicing a special song to play her on her piccolo, and she goes into excruciating detail as she describes the recipe for oatmeal cookies they always make together. It's a little strange, if you ask me. I half-listen as I watch Christine put the finishing touch on her drawing: the third figure is a woman with a million perfect details—dark hair, little tiny fingernails, a cute outfit—but she has no face. I get the willies but then lean in for closer look, and Christine freezes. She slowly crumples up the ticket in her hand and excuses herself to the bathroom, crushing it in her clenched fist.

It's so obvious, seeing them together today, that Mr. Lee loves Christine. But I find myself wishing her dad, charming as he is, spent a little less time in his own world and more time in hers.

29

We're all in good spirits as we ride back to Half Moon Bay. What a great day. In the past, when I've gone to San Francisco with my parents, it's always been to shop or to see a show, never just to play. Zoe, Christine, and I laugh in the back seat of Mr. Lee's SUV and talk about school the whole way home. I don't even notice how quickly we're getting back until Mr. Lee asks me how to get to my house. My heart sinks when I realize that we're on Highway 1 again. I sort of meant to borrow Zoe's phone and give my parents a heads-up that I was on my way home, but now it's no use. I'll be home in two minutes. I give him directions to Ocean Colony and relax a little as we turn onto my street. The house is all lit up, and it looks warm and cozy. It's all going to be fine. I'll go inside, curl up on the couch with a warm blanket and some hot cocoa, and tell Maria all about this perfect day.

"Chez Dominguez." Mr. Lee pulls up into the driveway. I open the door and climb out.

"Thanks so much." I wave at Zoe and Christine in the back seat, then smile at Christine's dad in the front. He grins and gives a little wave, and I shut the door and jog toward the house. It's gotten chillier since the sun went down.

I push the front door open and though the lights are all

on, something feels dark about the house. It's too quiet. Where is everybody?

"Hello?" I call as I take my shoes off and walk across the plush beige carpet.

"We're in here," a low voice says from the kitchen, and though I recognize it as Papá's, it doesn't sound right. I swallow hard and drag myself into the kitchen, knowing the writing is on the wall.

"Papá?" I turn the corner, walk into the kitchen, and freeze. Mom and Papá are sitting at the kitchen table. "What's wrong?"

"Where have you been?" Papá asks quietly. His shoulders are slumped, and he's resting his forearms on the table as if he can't hold himself up on his own.

"Are you okay?" I walk toward him, but he lifts up an arm, as if to hold me at bay. I stop.

"You told us you were going to be at Christine's," Mom says in a shrill voice, clasping her hands together on the kitchen table.

"I was," I say, quickly. "But then I called you. Didn't you get my messages?"

"You told us you would be there, and you left. We did not give you permission to go anywhere else." Mom draws her lips into a tight gather.

"But I called you, and no one answered, and her dad was taking us, and I thought—"

"You did *not* think." Papá slams his hand onto the table. "That's the problem. You don't think. You don't know what's best, and you don't think about the dangers."

"But I..." I want to argue, but I let my voice trail off. I

don't even know what to say. I can tell by the pale tint of Papá's face that they're not just a little upset here. This is serious. "I'm sorry," I say, but I know it's not enough. I wonder if anything will ever be enough. I'm going to be grounded for life.

"Sorry is a start," Mom says.

"You lied to us." I can hear the quiver of worry behind his angry words.

"No, I didn't!" I look at Mom, hoping for a little support, but she shakes her head. I really didn't lie, at least not intentionally, and the indignity of being accused of lying is maddening. I didn't. Not this time.

"We had no idea where you were," Papá says. "We went to Christine's." He scratches his finger across the smooth surface of the table. He dropped me off there this morning, so he knows where she lives. "Some strange woman answered the door. We didn't know who she was. You told us Christine's mother was dead, but there she was. We don't know what to believe from you anymore."

Tears are trying to fight their way out of my eyes, but I push them back. "Her mother *is* dead." My voice falters as tears try to come. I take a deep breath. I have to get this point across. I have to show them that I wasn't lying. "That was..." Any way that I spin this, they're not going to like it. I decide to go for the truth. "It was her dad's girlfriend." I take a deep breath and try to prepare what I will say next.

Papá shakes his head, and Mom sucks in her breath sharply. I can see the wheels in my mother's head spinning—calculating how long it's been since the accident, making assumptions about Christine's family.

"The girlfriend doesn't live there," I say, as if that's going to change Mom's opinion about anything. Why do I feel the need to defend these people all of a sudden? I don't even like Candace. I'm sworn to hate her as a friend of Christine's.

"What kind of man does that?" Papá continues to scratch at the table. I start to get indignant, and I try to remember the verse about casting the first stone, or that one about the plank in the eye so I can quote it at Papá, but as he continues, I realize it's not Mr. Lee's love life that has him so riled up. "What kind of man just takes someone else's child away in his car without even talking to them first? What kind of father has so little respect for another man's daughter?"

"George." Mom puts her hand on Papá's arm, and he stops, but he doesn't look up.

"I'm sorry," I squeak. My throat hurts from biting back tears. Papá suddenly seems so old. I look at Mom, and I know, deep in my bones, that I messed up. I hurt them today. It's going to take a long time to win their trust back. And somehow I don't even care about the fact that I will never, ever be allowed out of the house again. What bothers me is the ache of knowing that I've failed the people who love me most.

"I'm so sorry." The tears begin to spill out, and I move forward and put my arms around Papá. He slides his arms around me and squeezes, and for an instant I think this all might have been worth it, but then he pulls back and takes a deep breath. I stand up awkwardly, my arms hanging uselessly at my sides, as he composes his face and begins to speak.

"The reason we were trying to find you," he says, letting a

breath of air out slowly, "the reason we came to Christine's looking for you..." He runs his hand through his thinning hair. His hesitation tells me that I don't want to hear whatever he's about to say. "Is that Maria is in the hospital. They don't know if she's going to make it."

The biggest lie adults tell is *everything's going to be fine*. They only say this when everything is obviously not going to be fine. They reserve it for wars, bankruptcy, deaths, and stuff like that. As we drive to San Mateo Hospital, Mom just keeps saying, "Everything's going to be fine, Ana," again and again and again. And each time she says it, I get more nervous.

Maria started feeling a cold coming on a week and a half ago. But people get colds, right? It's not the end of the world. I wasn't even worried. And then, a week later, when her cough was very deep and sounded like it was rattling around inside her bones, I still didn't think much beyond "that's a bad cough." How was I to know that she was getting pneumonia?

Wikipedia says that pneumonia is serious and that people with "compromised" immune systems can die from pneumonia. You know who has compromised immune systems? Babies, old people...and people with diseases like lupus. I had just enough time to figure all of that out while I was waiting for Mom to get off the phone with Maria's family in Mexico. Her youngest niece is trying to book a flight up here right now.

Of course, Half Moon Bay doesn't have a hospital, so we

have to drive to San Mateo to see her. The dark hills whiz by as Dad speeds along the twisting road, tapping his fingers on the steering wheel. He tunes the radio to a Christian station, but I don't pay much attention. I spend my time in the car praying. Well, if you could call it that. It might be more accurately described as giving you-know-who a little taste of what's-what:

Hey! You! Up there! In case you forgot, I'm Ana. You created me, and now everything's coming undone. Maria's in the hospital with pneumonia. Look, I know people die. I get that. But you can't take Maria. Please?

When I see Maria lying weak and pale on the hospital bed, I burst into tears. I'm only allowed in her room for a couple minutes because the doctors say that the thing she needs the most right now is rest, but it still helps me immensely to see that she's alive, even if she is very weak.

"Anita," she whispers, and smiles.

I slip my hand into hers and let the tears roll down my face. "You have to get better, Maria."

She nods slowly.

I put my head on her hand. "I need you to come home soon, okay?"

"Okay," she says, her voice low and quiet, and smiles again. "Your tiara came in the mail today."

I look at Maria. *This* is what she's thinking about on her deathbed? My stupid tiara? Isn't she supposed to give me words of wisdom I'll always remember? Or moving parting words about how important I was to her? She moves her head up and down, just a little, and I sigh.

"Thanks." I don't know what else to say.

"It's going to be so magical," she sighs, and closes her eyes.

"Yeah. Magical." She doesn't hear me, because she's already asleep.

30

As the singing on the front row nears ear-piercing decibels, I try to stay calm. We've still got two more hours before we reach Sky Mountain retreat center, but I'm not sure I can make it that long. I don't know whose idea it was to put the boys in one van and the girls in the other, but I'm guessing they didn't know that Kelly Clarkson's new album had just come out. Even Judy, up in the driver's seat, seems like she's a bit tired of it all, and I don't think I've ever seen her without a smile on her face. It doesn't help that the Central Valley, which we have to pass through to get to the Sierra Nevada mountains, is flat and boring with nothing to look at but decrepit farms and ugly housing developments. Staring out the window, pretending to be somewhere better, would be a lot easier if there were anywhere better to look at.

Despite the fact that I'm basically grounded for life, I am still allowed to go on the Martin Luther King weekend youth group ski trip, because my parents would never keep me from church. How will I see the error of my ways without church?

I know I'm supposed to be grateful, and I am, a little bit. At least I get to leave the four walls of my room, which have been pressing in on me since the San Francisco trip last weekend. But Zoe, who had been planning to come with me on this ski trip, backed out at the last minute because her grandmother was having so much fun, she decided to extend her stay. I'd never do that for my grandma, so clearly there is something really wrong with me, which I suppose I knew already.

At first, I was going to cancel on the ski trip, too, because Maria is still in the hospital. How can I go off skiing while she's dying? That's different than your grandma just having way too much fun. But the doctor told me she'll be fine. I guess they're just keeping her for monitoring at this point. But on the other hand, everyone knows you can't trust what doctors tell you.

And then there's the issue of my grades. Our report cards arrived in the mail yesterday. I knew it was a close call in math. I broke into a cold sweat when I saw the open envelope sitting on the kitchen table after school. Mom had already seen it. I closed my eyes and prayed they were good, then reached for the envelope. A huge weight fell off my shoulders as I let out a long breath and said a heartfelt prayer of thanks. I was ecstatic. I mean, I technically got an A– in math, but the A+ in English balanced that one out.

It wasn't until I looked up at the top of the paper that I realized why Mom hadn't greeted me when I walked in the door that day. She was in her bedroom, giving me the silent treatment. It was just one little number, but I knew—and Mom knew—that it meant so much more than any of the others. Overall Rank in Class: 2.

The air whooshed out of my lungs as I realized that even with straight A's, I wasn't the top student in my class. I was second best. I felt myself starting to hyperventilate as I realized that Princeton doesn't let in second best. I took a series of long, slow breaths and tried to get myself under control. I tried to remember that it didn't mean anything, that it's only the first semester of freshman year, that there's plenty of time to catch up and overtake number one, but none of it helped, because even though the report card didn't tell me, I had a sneaking suspicion that I knew who was ranked ahead of me. The humiliation of being beaten by a cheerleader was almost more than I could bear.

So I'm not exactly psyched to be squashed into a fifteen-passenger van with Miss Perfection right at this moment. My only consolation is that she looks miserable, too. I don't know what bug got up her butt, but she's not sitting with the older girls, and her friend Tanya doesn't seem to be here. Riley's squished into the back seat, staring out the window with her headphones on. Her eyes are closed, as if she's sleeping, but the way she twitches every time the girls in the front seat hit a high note makes me think she's just faking it.

I start to panic when I realize that I'm going to have to spend the weekend alone. No one is going to talk to me. Okay, wait.... Stay calm, Ana. Who can you be friends with just for this weekend? That quiet sophomore Jamie in the second row seems nice enough. Maybe I can hang out with her. She joins in on the chorus of the current song, though, and I reconsider. My eardrums are about to burst.

Only two more hours.

"You've got to be kidding me," we say in unison. I never thought I'd see the day when I agreed with Riley, but now we've got a jinx on our hands and are staring at each other in repulsion. I thought God was supposed to be merciful. Now it just appears that he has a warped sense of humor, like my uncle Ernesto, who always tells jokes that make everyone else uncomfortable.

"Since you both had roommates signed up who didn't make it, you're both singles now," Judy says, smiling as if she's said something amazingly clever. "So we put you together in one room."

I'm going to kill Zoe. She was supposed to be my roommate. We started dreaming about this months ago. We were going to stay up all night laughing. But apparently, since Riley's roommate of choice, Tanya, isn't here, we're stuck together. Perfect.

Riley glares at me, as if I had something to do with this. I rack my brain for a solution. Doesn't anyone else on this stupid mountain need a roommate? Maybe I can sleep on the couch in the main lodge?

I have a brilliant idea. What about that sophomore? "Does Jamie—"

"Already has a roommate, kiddo." Judy knows my thoughts before I even think them. I try not to panic. At least there are two beds in here. If I had to share a queen with Riley, she'd probably kick me all night long and pretend she was asleep.

"Why don't you two settle in and unpack." Judy smiles at us and I know that she thinks that this whole thing is like God's Big Plan for Healing Among the Catty High School Girls. I'm dying to pull Judy aside and tell her exactly how this war began. Riley. It was all Riley.

"Group worship time starts in an hour in the main room. See you then!" Judy turns and bustles out the door. She closes it behind her, and I want to yell after her, "You'll pay for this!" but she's already gone and I don't have the guts anyway. That's more of a Christine move.

I turn around and look at Riley. She rolls her eyes, then tosses her backpack onto one of the beds. The flowered bedspread bounces up and down for a second.

"I take showers at night," I say to fill the silence. "Are you a morning person?"

"Whatever." She flops onto her bed, closes her eyes, and slips her headphones on.

"Look, I didn't exactly request this either, but we're stuck here, so let's at least make this as painless as possible." I drop my bag onto the empty bed. "I'll shower at night, and you go in the morning. We'll eat at different tables. We'll stay apart during the day. We'll hardly have to see each other at all."

She lies still on the bed, pretending she can't hear me.

"Riley, your iPod isn't even turned on." I take a deep breath and blow air out through my nose. She doesn't move.

Okay, God. I sit down slowly on the edge of my bed and look around. *Ha ha. You've got us here. Nice job. Now please keep us from killing each other.*

I wait for a moment, hearing nothing, and especially not Riley's iPod. God apparently doesn't feel like talking today, because I feel nothing except an overwhelming urge to go home. I lie back on the bed, pushing my bag out of the way, and stare up at the ceiling.

Maybe if I stay really still, they'll forget I'm even here. They'll go on with worship and meals and skiing all weekend, and I can just lie here. I think about how nice that would be, and then my mind wanders and I realize that somewhere in this lodge, Dave and Tyler are sharing a room. My stomach warms a little, and I try to focus my mind on that, but without warning it goes to Maria. She looked so pale when I saw her in the hospital yesterday. What if she never gets better? What if she dies while I'm gone? I feel a cold sensation in my stomach, and it takes me a minute to recognize it as fear. *Please God*, I pray, *be with Maria.*

"Hey, Riley?" She doesn't move, and I wait. Okay, maybe it's better if she doesn't react. There are worse things than being ignored.

But I can't sit here anymore. I won't be able to go out there and deal with people without knowing Maria is okay. I try again. "Riley? Can I borrow your cell phone?"

Riley doesn't sit up or open her eyes, but she slowly reaches her hand into her bag. She pokes around inside, then withdraws her pink Razr and tosses it carelessly onto my bed.

"Thanks," I say quietly, but she doesn't respond.

31

"You don't need lessons," Tyler says, sliding up to me, dragging his snowboard on one foot.

I feel puffy, and I feel cold, and I feel like I'm about to fall over at any moment, but when I see the brilliant white snow all around me, I can't help but get excited. The mountain is gleaming, and the sight of the bright green trees against the gloriously blue sky is breathtaking. I'm just waiting for Jamie to come out of the rental center. We're going to ski school together.

Dave comes up behind Tyler, looking a lot more confident on his snowboard. "Come with us. We'll teach you."

"Uh, I don't think... I mean, that's probably not a good idea." The last thing I need to do today is die on a mountain.

"Come on, Dominguez. I've been skiing since I was five, boarding since I was eight. I'll teach you everything you need to know." I know it's crazy, but Dave looks so sincere that I start to waver. Maybe I don't need to waste my time in lessons, being humiliated next to kindergarteners. If Tyler and Dave teach me, I can skip all of that. Will they teach Jamie, too?

"Hey, guys." It's Riley, and the chipper tone of her voice tells me she doesn't realize it's me. Under all these layers of puffy clothes and with my hair hidden under my ski cap, I could be anybody. "What're you doing?" She skis up next to Tyler and stops short by sticking her hips out a little bit. I try moving my hips, too, but I realize that since I'm not going anywhere I probably look pretty foolish. She's wearing a tight ski suit, sky blue with white trim. I hate myself for it, but I feel a little jealous. Mom ordered my ski pants and coat from a catalog just a few weeks ago, but I didn't even know they made outfits that don't make you look like a blimp.

"We're about to teach Ana how to ski. Come on." Tyler nods his head toward the line for the ski lift. Her smile falls when she sees me. "You get to explain the snowplow," Tyler says, pointing at her skis. Since Riley is the only other person on skis, she probably will be the most useful person to me today. Fabulous.

She looks me for a second. I can see her weighing her options; then she rolls her eyes and starts to follow Tyler, who is dragging his snowboard, still strapped to one foot, over to the lift.

"You coming?" Dave nods toward the lift.

"I've never done this before, you know." I bite my lip.

He smiles and holds out his arm. I reach for it and grab it with both hands to keep my balance, my ski poles going every which way. I move my right foot forward, then slowly, I slide the left one up too. I look around, but Jamie is nowhere to be seen.

"I need to tell Jamie I'm not doing lessons." I scan the crowd for her. Maybe I can just yell across the way to her? Is she out of the ski rental place yet?

"No problem," Dave says. Dave gently pries my hands off his arm so I have to stand up on my own, then walks quickly to the rental area, and a moment later comes back shaking his head. "I said she could come with us, but she's going to take lessons," he says, shrugging. "Wimp. Now off we go." He moves along slowly beside me as I fumble my way toward the line. After a few yards, I get better at sliding along on these things. Hey, I'm starting to get the hang of this. We get into the line behind Tyler and Riley, and I watch the ski lift to try to figure out how it works.

"It's no sweat. Just sit down when it comes around." Dave points at a five-year-old successfully getting on the lift. Great, no pressure.

"I can do it." I nod and try to look confident.

I can do anything. I feel like I'm on top of the world. Well, I actually kind of am. I'm standing on top of a mountain, and it feels great. Tyler and Riley are already making their way over to the left, away from the ski lift. We follow them, and I don't lose my balance or feel like I'm going to fall once. I am starting to feel pretty good on these things. They're like really, really enormous feet. I don't know why I thought it was so hard.

We approach a small ridge, and before I can even ask what to do next, Tyler and Dave are clipping their feet into their boards and Riley is getting into what can only be described as some kind of "go" position.

What about my lesson? I clear my throat. "So, um, the idea here is..."

"To get down the mountain in one piece." Riley smiles a sugary-sweet grin at me.

I watch Dave. I can tell he hasn't heard me because he's still concentrating on his snowboard, uh, strap thingies.

"Okay, Ana. Just point your skis down the mountain and turn when you want to slow down. It's easy," Tyler says.

I stare at people on the ski slope we're about to try out—which, by the way, is named Brady's Folly, not exactly a good sign—and see how other people are doing it. It's just as Tyler described. You go a little while and turn. Go and turn. Okay, I can do that.

"Here I go." Tyler gives Riley a high five and the two of them take off down the mountain. Predictably, Cheerleader Girl is an amazing skier. She leans out over her skis just a bit and glides gracefully over the snow. Some soft powder sprays from around her skis. Tyler is a bit of a wobbly snowboarder, but he's getting down the slope without falling.

This is it. Baptism by fire, or whatever. I line my skis up at the ridge, point them at the bottom, take a deep breath, and chant to myself, "Go and turn; go and turn." I close my eyes, say a quick prayer, and push forward.

"Dominguez, wait," Dave says, but it's too late. I'm flying down the mountain. I laugh a little as I pick up speed. This is fun! The world is flying by me, the trees zipping by faster than my eyes can register them. Whoa. You go a lot faster than I thought. Okay, no sweat. All I need to do is turn. I try to turn, but realize in a flash of panic that I don't know how. Up ahead, I can see the trail turning and a row of trees coming toward me at a very fast clip. I try to turn again, but my skis start to cross, and I straighten them somehow. Whew. I look up again and realize that I'm going to hit the trees if I don't do something. I'm going to have to stop myself. There aren't any hand brakes on these things, are there? At the last moment, I do that only thing I can think of.

I lean over to the left so far that I make myself fall down. I hit the ground with a heavy thud, then roll over a few times, tumbling down through the snow. I begin to wonder if I'm going to tumble all the way down the mountain, when I finally stop rolling. I sit up tentatively.

Nothing appears to be broken. My right ski is about ten feet away, down the hill, while my left ski is still somehow attached to my foot. I sit there for a moment, stunned and cold.

Tyler snowboards over to me. "Whoa, that looked like it hurt!"

Riley roars up next to him, her eyes wide.

Dave slides up next to me with precision. "You okay, Dominguez?"

"I . . . I think I'm okay." I pat my head, as if to see if it's still there.

Tyler goes down to fetch my ski, then unclips from his board, and starts to walk back up the mountain to bring it to me. I cringe as I watch how much effort it takes to do this. "Thank you!" I yell down to him.

"All right, up you go. Let's get back on the mountain again." Dave gives me a hand and helps hoist me back up on my one good ski. I flail my arms for a moment, like a toddler. This is so humiliating.

"When you need to turn, lean up on the edges of your skis. They'll dig into the mountain." Dave motions to Riley who demonstrates her cool hip shift move again, digging the edges of her skis into the snow.

Tyler comes up with my ski and his board, huffing and puffing. "I really owe you." I feel so bad for him.

"No big deal." He's acting like it's no big deal, but he's clearly a little winded.

I take the ski from Tyler's outstretched hand and struggle to push it back into place on my boot. Dave ends up unclipping one of his feet and bending down to help me. As he's grabbing my boot and pushing it into the binding, I feel so cared for that I can't help but smile a little. I grasp my poles and dig them into the ground.

"I'm fine." I reposition my feet so they're pointing downhill again and nod.

"I didn't have a chance to tell you about the snowplow," Dave says. "That's your backup if the turning thing we showed you doesn't work. You need to position your feet like a piece of pie."

Riley shows me this move. She looks like the most pigeontoed person in the world.

"It doesn't look pretty, but it works. It will slow you way down," Dave says. I move my feet to mimic Riley's and nod. Weird. I never knew there was anything more to skiing than pointing my skis down the hill. This seems like one of those things someone should have told me before I got to the top of a mountain.

"Ready?" Dave watches me from underneath his black knit hat, his lips red from the cold. He needs some Chapstick and I have to fight the urge to hand him mine. Focus, Ana. Tyler and Riley shove off and weave their way down the hill again.

"You go first." Dave does a sweeping chivalrous bow.

I nod, then push off with my feet firmly planted in a snow plow. I'll just go really slow this time so that I stay on my feet. At first it works, but then in a flash, my skis become crossed. I get tangled up and fall over to the side. This fall is less spectacular, and I quickly grab my skis and snap them back on with a little help from Dave. Tyler and Riley are waiting for me far below, squinting back up at us. I push myself up again and try again, and this time I get a little farther before I panic as I see a curve up ahead. I still have no idea how to turn.

I fly through the air this time, and, perversely, I have time to think that the flying part is kind of fun before I hit the ground. I sit up slowly to see Tyler and Riley watching me with concern. I'm almost disappointed. If Riley was annoyed about having to stop repeatedly for me, I think I could handle that, but her pity is almost too much to bear.

Dave slides up next to me and plops down. "You okay?" I see the worry etched on his face.

I nod. Tears sting my eyes, but I push them back. I can do this. I can learn to ski, and I won't let my frustration show.

"The flying part is kind of fun," I laugh, but it sounds hollow, and I can tell no one believes me. "I'm going to get it this time." I try to sound optimistic, but it's really more of a command. I have to get it this time.

The next time I fall, a little ways down the mountain, I start to feel really bad for everyone else. Every time I fall, they have to stop. This can't be much fun for them. Groups of skiers pass us on the trail, staring at me. Rubberneckers. I try to ignore them.

When I fall again, I don't move for a while. I need to get my emotions under control before I sit up and show everyone that Ana Dominguez is not only a bad skier, she's a crybaby, too. The snow feels good against my face. Maybe I'll just stay here.

"I'm sorry," Dave says, plopping down next to me again.

"It's my fault. This is no way to teach someone. I should have known better. When we get down, I'll take you to the bunny slope and show you how to do this right."

I nod, keeping my face firmly against the cool snow. Behind us, I hear a low growl, but I can't bring myself to move even though I'm obviously about to be run over by a snowmobile. The noise stops just beside me, and I'm not totally sure I'm grateful to have been spared.

"Everything okay?" a deep voice says, and I turn my head just enough to see a man in a red jacket with a white cross on it bending over me. I nod. "You need a ride?" he asks. I push myself up.

"I'm fine." I look down at Tyler, who seems a tiny bit annoyed. Riley waits patiently, staring down at the snow. No one says anything, but it suddenly occurs to me that it would be much, much better for everyone else if I swallowed my pride, rode down on the snowmobile, and let them ski in peace. Dave bites his bottom lip. I know that getting on the snowmobile will mean giving up, and that's something I really don't want to do, but I kind of think that for the sake of everyone else, it might be the right thing to do. I close my eyes, take a deep breath, and nod. "I'll take that ride," I say quietly.

The snowmobile driver reaches out his hand and helps me stand up, then sits me down on the machine. His auburn hair is slightly long and floppy, and he's kind of cute, but I don't have the energy to get excited about that. Dave hands me my skis, and I tuck them, along with my poles, under my right arm, then grab onto the back of the driver as he sits down.

I look down at the ground as we drive away so I don't have to see their pity.

32

The main door to the lodge shuts hard, and I turn to listen. Someone stomps her way down the girls' hall and slams a door, but I can't see who it is from where I'm standing. I highly suspect it's another person done in by the miserable sport of skiing. I find a spatula, carefully pry one of the cookies I baked this afternoon off the sheet, and then put it on a paper towel. I'll just take this to the poor soul and make sure she's feeling all right. We'll laugh, compare bruises, and then tomorrow I'll have a friend at the lodge because I'm never skiing again. I round the corner of the kitchen and nearly run smack into Judy.

"Ah!" I scream and the cookie goes flying.

"Ana!" Judy jumps too. "Oh, gosh." She walks across the room to pick up the warm cookie. "Sorry about that. I forgot you came back." She takes it into the kitchen and throws it in the sink. "I didn't mean to scare you."

I take a deep breath. "That's okay. It's just so quiet in here and...I was bringing you a cookie. I made them." I motion proudly at my big accomplishment.

Judy glances at them. "Ana, can we have a word outside for a moment?"

My heart falls. She didn't even look at my cookies.

Judy walks quickly outside. She seems distracted as I grab my coat from the rack by the door and follow her to the front porch, where I perch on a chair. I suspect this porch is a lot more fun in the summer, when youth groups come up here to fish and hike and whatever else you do in the mountains in the winter. The Dominguez family only vacations at manicured beach resorts.

"Ana, I need your help."

I brighten up. "Happy to help. Hey, that's why I'm here, right?" After the words leave my mouth, I remember that technically I'm here to ski and be a kid or whatever, but since I can't ski, helping is a great way to spend my time. Plus, I might go crazy if I have to spend another day locked in that lodge alone.

"Something's happened in Riley's family. I just told her." Judy's face goes dark, and for a moment I realize how hard it must be to be in charge.

I grab my arms as my teeth begin to chatter. "I'll do whatever you need."

"Good, thanks. So you'll stay with Riley for a while?"

"What?!" I yell, and Judy gives me a withering look. "I mean, why?" I say, trying to recover.

"She needs company right now. And I have to go back to the mountain in case of emergencies. Fritz, too." Judy glances back through the glass door, craning her neck to see if she can see anyone inside. "I'm going to tell you what happened because I think you need to know so you can help her, but you can't talk about it with anyone else unless Riley brings it up herself."

I lean in. *Oh, please, God. Don't let anyone in Riley's family be dead.* I may not like the girl, but I know all too well how scary it is when someone goes to the hospital.

Judy takes a deep breath. "Her thirteen-year-old brother is missing."

I gasp as my heart falls.

"He has Asperger's syndrome, which means he's mildly autistic. He wasn't in his bed this morning, and they think he wandered off. Her parents are out of their minds with worry. Her aunt will be here to get her soon."

My eyes well up a little. Michael is so nice. And he's so young and, well, different. How is he going to be okay out in the world on his own?

Judy takes my hand and looks into my eyes. "Look, I'm not dumb. I know you and Riley sort of..." She waves her hand in the air, at a loss for words. "I know you two don't see eye to eye. I just want you to try to be there for her until her aunt gets here. Whether or not she knows it, she needs a friend right now, and it's better if it's someone her own age."

Riley hates me. If I even try to give that girl a hug, she'll probably slug me in the jaw. "It's just that—"

"Ana, remember Fritz's sermon last week?"

I bite my lip, trying to remember. Was it the one about always being a Christian, even at school? Or the one about keeping your thoughts pure? Oh! I remember. "Yeah."

Judy leans back in her chair. "Good. Then this is just what he was talking about. Now is your chance to step up into a leadership role and make this youth group your own."

I look through the window at the eighties-era kitchen with tan appliances and spot my now-cold cookies. "I'll try to help her. I didn't mean I wouldn't." My goodness, the girl's brother is missing. If Judy thinks I should try to talk to her, I will. "I just don't know if she'll accept help from me. I don't know if she'll listen to anything I have to say."

Judy stands up and juts out her chin. "Make her listen. I'm depending on you."

33

Riley hasn't come out of her room since Judy left, and I figure she's sleeping, but after an hour or so I decide to venture into the bedroom to check on her. There she is, wide awake and curled up around her pink Razr phone, which is plugged into the wall. I hesitate for a moment. Should I have brought her a cookie? Should I say I'm sorry? Should I give her a hug?

"I'm fine, Ana," she says and turns over gruffly.

Her voice is low and raspy and tired. I close the door quickly, then walk back out into the living room and start praying for Michael, then Riley, then Mrs. McGee, and finally even Mr. McGee, whom I don't even know, so I have to keep it general with him. I also pray for myself. I pray for strength, wisdom, and boldness. Judy asked something very important—and very difficult—of me, and I am not going to disappoint her. I will be there for Riley. If she hurls insults at me, I will turn the other cheek. If she pushes me away, I will steel myself and try again.

But a little while later, Riley and I are sitting silently in the living room of the lodge, staring at the fire, waiting for her Auntie Kathy to appear and take her back to Half Moon Bay. The boisterous group of skiers and boarders is due back soon, but Riley is glued to her phone. She even took it to the bathroom with her a little while ago. It hasn't rung. I see it in her hand and will it to ring with good news about Michael. But it, like us, stays silent.

We sit like this for at least half an hour, until I finally notice that the fire is about to die out. Mom thinks fires are dangerous, give people asthma, and are messy, so I have exactly zero experience with them, but I still feel compelled to do something about the problem. I go over to it, pick up a small metal shovel from the little carousel of tools, and hit it with the shovel.

"What are you trying to do?" Riley asks.

I turn around and smile. These are the first words I've heard her speak since she emerged from the bedroom. That must be a good sign, right? They weren't "Go away, Ana."

"Well, the fire's getting low and I was sort of liking it, so I thought I'd try to fix it. But I don't really know what I'm doing."

"I'll say." Riley stands up, takes the shovel out of my hand, puts it back on the rack, grabs the pointy stick thingy, and pokes the wood a little. "We need more wood. Hand me some of those pieces."

I scurry across the room and grab two logs. I hand them to her, and she tosses them into fire like it's nothing.

"Usually, when my family goes camping, Michael insists on stoking the fire." She looks up at me. "Two more logs."

I get them from the stack. "That's what they call it. Stoking." I hand her two more logs.

"He really likes to do it. And he's amazing at it. He really gets how the air is supposed to flow for maximum burn."

I nod, pretending I get what she's saying. "How did, uh,

Michael learn that?" I want to keep her going. Talking about him is probably really important right now.

Riley shrugs and dusts herself off. "My dad taught us. He was an Eagle Scout. Michael's going to be one too." She walks back over to the couch and I follow her. She sits down and puts her face in her hands. "Well, I think he..."

Her voice falters, and she looks at me with tears in her eyes. And then, as if it's the most normal, natural thing in the world, I scoop her into a big hug, the kind of hug I've only ever been given by Maria, the one that says, Go ahead, cry now, it will all be fine tomorrow. The moment my arms enfold her, it's like the crack in the dam gives, and suddenly she is sobbing incoherently into my shoulder. I don't say anything. I just keep holding her tight, crying quietly myself. After a few minutes, she pulls back and looks at me sheepishly.

I jog into the kitchen and grab the huge box of tissues, then hold it out to her. "Here," I say, and take one for myself. I blot my eyes and blow my nose. She cleans herself up. And slowly, imperceptibly, I can feel the old awkwardness between us trying to creep back into the room.

"He's fine, Riley. I know it." I feel my shoulders stiffen as I wait for her to yell at me about how I don't "know" anything.

Instead, she looks up slowly with hope in her eyes. "You really think so?"

I relax a little. "He's the smartest person I've ever met." She nods a little and blows her nose again. "And, I don't know, I just have a feeling about this one." I put a hand on her shoulder. I mean what I say. For as long as I can remember, I have been able to just know certain things.

"I feel that way, too," she says, looking at me. "I mean, sometimes I just get a sixth sense about stuff. I don't know what happened to him, but I can feel in my heart that he's all right."

I've never talked about this feeling with Christine or Zoe. I guess I always thought it sounded too, I don't know, God Girl or something. "I know what you mean. Maybe it's woman's intuition or something." I know it isn't, but I don't want Riley to think I'm a total freak.

She shakes her head and fidgets with the tissue in her hand. "No, it's more than that for me. I get this very real feeling..." She glances nervously at me. "Well, never mind."

Maybe Zoe was right. Maybe Riley McGee is a Miracle Girl, as unlikely as it seems, given her slightly evil nature and naturally blond hair. I mean, God wouldn't have saved her from death if she weren't called to do something with her life, right?

Riley's eyes light up. "I think that—"

We're interrupted by a blond woman rapping on the door and bursting into the lodge. She has tears in her eyes, and she rushes to Riley and grabs her into a tight hug.

In the space of five minutes, Auntie Kathy puts all of Riley's bags in the trunk of her car, writes a note to Fritz, and hustles Riley out the door with a quick good-bye to me. I stand outside in the freezing cold in just my jeans and fuzzy slippers and wave as they drive away. And for the first time in my life, I'm actually kind of sad to see Riley McGee go.

34

By the time the weary troops walk back through the door that night, I feel like I might kiss the first person I see, who happens to be Troy, the tenth grader with the really bad zits, so luckily it's just a feeling and not something I actually act on. I'd hate for my first kiss to happen because I'm lonely and stir-crazy in an empty lodge. That's hardly the kind of romantic story you want to tell your grandkids someday.

I try to act calm, peering over people's heads, looking for Dave and Tyler, as I greet the people who come in the door. Maybe I need to give skiing another shot. I had nothing to do after Riley left. I can hang out in this lodge tomorrow and pretend that I don't want to ski, but truthfully, I'm way too hyper to sit still all day. Finally, I see Tyler and Dave walking up and I have to resist the urge to run up and give them both a big hug. I see another person with them and realize that it's Jamie. The sight of my three closest friends on this trip makes my heart light and free.

"Hey, guys." I swing open the door for them. "Welcome back!"

Dave musses my hair. "Dominguez." His voice oozes exhaustion.

"Pinnacle day on the mountain?" I wiggle my eyebrows at him. "Just a little peak pun for you."

Dave chuckles weakly as he hangs up his coat. "So, Jamie, we're on for tonight?"

"Definitely." Jamie smiles at Dave, and I recognize it right away. It's the love smile. In an instant, I know that Jamie has a crush on Dave. Poor girl. Just wait until she finds out that he has a crush on me.

"Hey, Jamie." I might as well show her right now how nice I am, so that when she figures this all out, she won't totally hate me.

"Oh, hey, Ana." Jamie hangs up her coat. "Listen, you should really think about taking some lessons. I only took a half day and now I'm able to ski." She throws a glance at Dave. "Well, kind of."

Dave leans over her shoulder to me. "She's amazing. I picked her up at lunch and she kept up with me on the greens all day long." He tugs on one of her long braids. "Just a half-day in the Dave Brecht Finishing School and she's skiing like Picabo Street." I try to smile.

"Hey, Ana," Tyler says over his shoulder as he heads off to the men's wing. "Missed you this afternoon."

"Uh, thanks," I say to him as he disappears. I'm still trying to process what just happened with Dave. He skied with Jamie all afternoon? I turn back to the coat rack, where Dave and Jamie are comparing their biceps, both swearing they could beat the other in arm wrestling. I stomp away from them and plop onto the couch, expecting Dave to notice that something is wrong. But this plan fails miserably. Instead Dave and Jamie hang out in the lodge's living room, laughing and joking around until I have to leave before I vomit all over them.

When I get back to my room, I throw myself down on my bed in the lonely, empty space and try to think. My mind is racing. He's just Dave. He's nothing like those McSteamy-type guys you see on television. He's not blond and surfer-cool like Tyler, and he doesn't dress as well as Tyler does, either. He's average height, and he's not fat or slim. His brown hair is straight and cute, but sometimes he goes too long between haircuts and it looks a little wild. His brown eyes are warm, but they're not the kind of thing you notice right away. For goodness' sake, he wears a tie every day. The one he's been wearing this whole trip has a polar bear on it. And yet, there's just something about him. He's really caring, and true, and funny.

I hear Jamie's high giggle and put a pillow over my ears. This is not the way it's supposed to go. Jamie's older than him! Why can't she prey on guys her own age? And I'm, well, I'm *Dominguez*. She's just some girl he started hanging out with on the ski trip. They've never even talked before, to my knowledge. He's always hanging around me.

Slowly, it begins to dawn on me. This is exactly what I deserve for being such a quitter. I sit up on the edge of my bed. Well, I'm not going to be quitter anymore.

After dinner, I put my plan into action. Phase one involves getting a seat right next to Dave during worship. In order to accomplish this, I have to hang around the living room, in the very spot where we had worship last night, so that the moment Fritz announces it's time, I'll be poised and ready to pounce.

Unfortunately, tonight everyone is playing Spoons. This means that I must somehow look like I'm engrossed in doing something by myself, which really stinks because I actually love Spoons.

"Ana, are you sure you don't want us to deal you in?" Tyler calls.

"No, thanks," I yell back. I hold up a magazine that one of the girls loaned me, which is splashed with tween stars. "I'm reading."

Tyler gives me a funny look, shrugs, and gets back to the game. It doesn't escape my attention that Dave and Jamie are both playing, but whatever. Worship time will start in about fifteen minutes, so I can wait. Plus, if you really want to compare apples to apples, worship time is very long. It can go on for an hour straight, and then Fritz speaks, so getting to sit next to Dave for such an extended time will totally be worth it.

I catch up on who Zac Efron is dating, what kind of cereal Miley Cyrus likes, and who exactly Raven-Symoné admires the most in the world. Ugh. How can girls read this stuff? Hello? There are these things called books? And they're waayyyy more interesting than the fact that this person or that likes Super Sugar Cinnamon Os for breakfast.

"Okay, let's bring it in for worship," Fritz calls from the kitchen, where he's inspecting the work of tonight's kitchen clean-up crew.

I don't move an inch and pretend to keep reading. I am already sitting in the very spot next to the fireplace that should put me on Dave's right-hand side. Dave and Tyler sit on the wide stone lip around the fireplace to play their guitars, and we form a circle around them. This means that Tyler will be on his left and I will be on his right. Perfect.

Slowly, the other people begin to file into the room and sit down wherever they plop. Tyler comes in first and nearly gives me a heart attack when he sits near me, but after talking to me for a minute about this "amazing run" he took today, he slides over to his usual spot. Fritz comes in and joins the circle, and Jamie sits down next to me. Ha ha! Vengeance is mine, older woman! And finally, as if he knows he's torturing me here, Dave comes over looking beautiful. He smells wonderful, like soap. His hair is just a bit wet at the edges and when he smiles I can see a faint dimple on his left cheek. How did I not notice that he bears a striking resemblance to Adam Brody? How did I miss that I'm falling head over heels for him? For a smart person, I'm pretty stupid sometimes.

Dave sits down, takes out his guitar, and jokes quietly with Tyler for a moment. I notice a few girls settling in nearby, watching Dave. Well. Isn't he Mr. Popularity these days? Lucky for me, I got here first. I settle in to enjoy my evening. I deserve it. I worked hard for this spot.

"Oh," Dave says, turning to me. "I almost forgot."

"Yeah?" I give him my hundred-kilowatt smile.

"Can you do me a huge favor, Dominguez?" He gives me a wink. Is it just me, or is he a lot more confident than he was a few weeks ago?

"Sure." I twirl my hair around my finger. Two can play at this game, sir.

"Can you switch seats with Jamie? I need her to sit next to me tonight."

My jaw falls open in shock. "What?!" I know I sound a little indignant, but it's rude to ask me to move.

"It's a surprise." Dave strums a chord on his guitar and then turns one of the keys. "I could tell you, but I'd have to kill you."

I look at Jamie, and she looks at the floor and blushes. The little Bathsheba! I'm not moving. But as I glance around the circle I realize that the whole group, including Fritz, is staring at me, waiting for me to move. I force a smile. "Oh, sure. Whatever." I try to act very breezy and casual about the whole thing, but I know I don't quite accomplish my goal.

When Dave strums out the first chord and kicks off worship time, I'm glad, because then people will stop thinking about me and start thinking about God. I try to sing and focus on heavenly things, but I simply can't. My heart is pounding in my chest, and my hands are covered in a cold sweat.

On the third song of the evening, Dave nods at Jamie, and she begins to harmonize with him. I pray that the world opens up a big chasm and swallows me up so that I never have to see any of these people again. Jamie looks so petite and pretty as she harmonizes with Dave that I know I have no chance with him. He's already over me. I failed, and he moved on. He found someone better, someone who doesn't suck at skiing and can sing like an angel and appreciates his attention.

As their big duet comes to an end, everyone claps and cheers except me. I just sit there, hoping to die.

35

check in the back of my book for the answer to the problem. 284. Wait, what? How on earth can it be 284? I have been solving this little bugger—which doesn't even look like math, it's all parentheses and the word "log" and the letter X again and again—for a half an hour, carefully following every single step laid out in my Algebra 2 textbook on how to do this kind of problem, and I got 248. I wish someone had warned me that math gets really, really hard when it starts looking like your English homework. I think I actually miss numbers. At least they were straightforward. Maybe this is one of those typos you occasionally find in books. 284, 248. That's close, right?

Riley's smiling face flashes in front of my eyes, and I crumple up the piece of paper I've been working on. I pull out a fresh sheet and start to solve the problem again. I'm halfway through it when I realize it's time for another Diet Coke. I get a new glass of ice and another can from the pantry.

It's already midnight, but I don't care. Tomorrow is a huge test in Algebra 2 and I'm really struggling on this exponential and logarithmic functions chapter. Only old Mackey is mean enough to schedule a test for the Tuesday after a long weekend. I'm going to stay up until I get it down cold. That's the only way to beat Riley, even though, let's be honest, she's got a huge head start on me, since her dad is Smarty McMath Pants for some dot-com company, so she's been endowed with a super-genius math brain.

I sit down and rearrange my book and paper and glass of soda just so. Okay, here I go.

When we got back from the ski trip on Sunday, Riley IMed me with the awesome news that her brother was found shortly after she left Sky Mountain. Apparently Michael loves roads, train schedules, flight patterns, and bus routes. It's something about the repetitive numbers. He had been thinking about his grandmother Friday night, so when he got up in the morning, he took a Greyhound bus to see her, and it didn't occur to him to tell anyone. He got off the bus in Reno and called his grandmother from a pay phone. She immediately called everyone to let them know that he was all right and drove him back to Half Moon Bay, though he couldn't understand why everyone was so upset. I was relieved to hear that he was fine, and I was kind of surprised to get an IM from Riley. I want to believe that things will be different between us now, but I've thought that before and nothing has ever come of it in the past, so I'm trying not to get my hopes up.

Even though I don't hate her anymore, I still have to be number-one in the class, so I need to study all night long to beat her. It's not personal. I just need to get into Princeton.

I jump as the lights in the kitchen turn on.

"Anita, your eyes." Maria wags a finger at me. She walks over and kisses my head. "You study with it so dark in here. You're going to go blind." Maria came home from the hospital yesterday and she's still pale, and thinner than she was a week ago. She swears she feels fine, but she moves slowly, and I'm not sure I believe her.

"Oh yeah." The truth is, I like to study with just one light on and the rest of the house dark. That way, I'm not as easily distracted, and people are much less likely to interrupt me.

"And it's so late. I wish you wouldn't do this." Maria shakes her head at me. "You're so hardworking. Just like your father." I smile at the idea that I might take after Papá. "Want some *carnitas*?" She pulls a Tupperware container out of the fridge and begins to pry the lid off.

Actually, I want to keep working so I get this, but I am kind of hungry, I guess. My mouth begins to water just thinking about the super-slow-roasted pork. "That sounds good."

Maria heats up the *carnitas* in the microwave and digs in the pantry until she finds some tortillas. She stops the microwave before it dings so she won't disturb my parents and dishes some pork and a little *pico de gallo* onto a tortilla on a paper plate for me. She slides it over to me, and I shut my book. I sink my teeth into the tender meat and feel better instantly.

"So why are you up?"

She waves a hand in the air. "My new steroids make it hard to sleep at night."

I pat her hand. I researched all of her medication on the Internet. For some reason, I'm very fascinated by medical stuff...unlike logarithms. "It's a very common side effect. But do you feel better on the steroids?" I take another bite and watch her as I chew. Steroids are supposed to help her stay healthy and reduce her inflammation problems. Treating lupus is a long process, and finding the right drug combination can take years and years, while the patient suffers and continues to get sick.

Maria nods. "Yeah, I feel a little better. These pills are better than the last ones." She begins to make herself a plate of *carnitas*, too. "I thought I should have a snack to make me sleepy again."

I nod and look back down at my paper. "I wish you were a math whiz. I'm really struggling over here."

I hear a voice behind me. "You need a math whiz?"

"Papá," I say, trying to keep my voice down.

He rubs his stubbly face. "I smelled *carnitas*." He shrugs and smiles. Papá has a serious weakness for *carnitas*.

Maria smiles proudly. "I'll fix you some right now."

I down my last bite and take a big gulp of soda. Mom is always saying that one of these days my metabolism will slow down and I'll have to watch what I eat. I seriously hope she's wrong.

Papá peers over my shoulder at my math problem. "Where are you stuck?"

I sheepishly uncrumple my paper and show him how I did it last time. "I'm not stuck, exactly. I thought I did it right, but I have the wrong answer."

He sits down next to me. "Can I have your pencil and paper?" I slide everything over to him, and he begins to scratch some stuff down.

"Here you go." Maria slides a paper plate of steaming hot *carnitas* toward him. He inhales deeply. "You're a genius, Maria."

She smiles and then goes back to the fridge to put the

Tupperware away. I drag my chair over to Papá's side and watch for a while as he works on the problem.

"Aha!" he says finally. I look up and notice that Maria has silently slipped away and left us alone. "Here's where you went wrong. If you had simplified the left side of the equation, I think you would have gotten it."

I peer over his shoulder and suddenly see my mistake as clear as day. "Thanks, Papá. I had no idea that you still knew how to do this stuff. I plan on forgetting it as soon as I don't need it anymore."

He laughs. "Ana, if you want to be a doctor, you're going to have to take a lot more math than just Algebra 2."

I groan. "I suppose I'd better start learning to love it."

Papá nods. "You will. I always struggled with math, too, but you can get it if you work hard enough. Hard work can fix almost any problem."

I nod. There he goes again. And, really, he's mostly right. The only thing that hard work can't fix is Maria's health. There are some things that are in God's hands, no matter what.

"And you can always become a lawyer like your old dad, if you get really sick of math." He winks at me. "After my sophomore year in college, I changed my major from premed to pre-law."

"Really?" I sit there stunned, trying to picture Papá with a stethoscope and a beeper. "I had no idea."

He shrugs. "I'm glad. Being a lawyer has given me a lot of flexibility that being a doctor wouldn't have afforded me."

I think about all his sleepless nights lately, the wining and dining of local big wigs to build up his practice, the financial stress, and suddenly being a doctor seems like a much better choice.

Papá must see the worry on my face. "Ana, things have been hard, but they're going to get better. I'm not sorry we moved here. Are you?"

I look down at my books and think of Christine and Zoe. I think about youth group, where I actually feel kind of comfortable these days. I mean, at least I don't feel like an outcast anymore. And, for just a split second, I think about Riley. "No, I'm not."

"I left my old firm in San Jose because they wanted me to work longer and longer hours." He puts a hand on my head and studies my face for a moment. "You're growing up so fast." His voice falters a little and his eyes get glassy. I gulp. Is Papá going to cry on me? "I didn't want to miss any more of your life than I already had. That's why I wanted to move to a smaller town, where you would be safe, where I could start my own practice and be around more."

I smile and stare at my lap, a little embarrassed. It's kind of odd for Papá to share his feelings like this, but my heart is soaring. He has always seemed so formal and distant. "Thanks," I say quietly. I like my new life in Half Moon Bay, but most days it feels like this house was built on a sandy foundation and it will all wash away if a big storm comes.

"Papá," I clear my throat. "Is...everything going to be okay with your practice?" My mind whirs with worst-case scenarios of Papá declaring bankruptcy or going to jail, and of Mom having to sell her beloved new home, and of me dressed in tatters, and of Maria being let go.

Papá takes a deep breath and rubs his stubble with his

palm. "Things have been difficult financially. But I am work-ing hard. And we both are praying to God to watch over and protect our family."

I stare at him. Why did I ask? I wanted him to reassure me, but this isn't really very reassuring.

"You pray for us, don't you, Ana?" He stares at me.

"Of course!" I nod vigorously. I do pray for us, but now I'll pray even more, all the time.

"Then we must have faith that the Lord will protect us."

I start praying right that moment just for good measure. *God, please remember my family in our time of trial. Please help Papá to find more clients. Please protect and keep us.*

Papá stands, stretches, and folds his empty paper plate in half. "It will be okay. God will never forget us. I learned that when you were born and he saved you because we prayed that he would." We're silent for a moment; then he clears his throat and looks back down at my paper. "Now what's next?" He moves on to the next math problem.

36

f someone came up behind me right now and said Boo, I'd jump a mile high. Actually, if they said anything I'd probably jump a mile high. I grip my mechanical pencil with all my might, watching Mackey pass out the logarithm test. Is he the slowest walker in the world, or what? He waddles down the first row, passing out the papers, huffing and puffing. It's really not fair. They're going to have at least an extra minute with the test.

I rub my huge spare eraser for security. *God, please help me rock this test. If I'm ever going to use all the talents you gave me to become a doctor and save people's lives, then I need to go to Princeton. And if I want to get into Princeton, then I pretty much have to get an A on this test.* All of a sudden there is a sound at the door, and I look up. It's Riley.

"Sorry," she mouths at Mackey.

Mackey glowers at her under his bushy eyebrows. She shrugs it off and walks casually over to her desk.

I beam at her as she passes me, but she doesn't notice me. She sits down and digs in her purse. I watch her over my shoulder, hoping she'll look up so I can give her a wave or something. Maybe she was late because of something with Michael.

"Do you have a spare pencil?" I hear Riley ask.

I quickly pull my backpack around and start unzipping the front pouch where I keep all of my pencils. I grab the best one out and hold it in her direction. But at just that moment, Jordan Fletcher, who sits behind me, holds out a pencil, too.

"Thanks," she whispers to him, grabbing the pencil and completely ignoring my outstretched hand.

I stare at her for a moment longer. She refuses to turn my way. She's staring at the floor instead.

Oh. I see. So nothing has changed. I force myself to face forward just as Mackey finally enters my row and places a copy of the test on my desk. My cheeks burn. How could I be taken in by Riley again? I shut my eyes for a moment to refocus. As angry as she makes me, I shouldn't be surprised. Why did I think we would suddenly be friends?

I open my eyes and focus on the test, scanning the problems. Papá and I stayed up until the wee hours of the night studying. He even pointed out a type of problem that there were only two examples of in my homework, and we practiced those a little more. I told him how sneaky Mackey was with his test questions.

Quickly, I realize the first five are a snap. I almost laugh when I see them. They're the easiest kind! The next five are a little harder, but I definitely understand what they're asking. The final two might be a problem. They seem to make sense, but one of them, sure enough, is the type of problem that Papá pointed out. I stifle a laugh. This test should be no problem for me. I'm so happy, I almost forget Riley's silent-treatment routine.

I relax a little and begin solving. If I budget my time right,

I might have enough time to solve all of the problems and then double-check them. I've certainly got the pencil lead, scratch paper, and erasers to do it.

Thirty minutes in, I've finished the test and my heart is soaring. I did it. I knew every single one of them. I should get an A! Just wait until Mom and Papá hear. But something Papá said rings in my ears: watch out for careless errors. It's so easy to get a problem wrong because of one silly mistake. I begin to re-solve each equation to look for errors.

Fifteen minutes later, I'm really done. I double-checked each problem and even found one careless error that would have surely cost me a few points. My head feels dizzy, and my heart is light. I can do math. I really get this stuff! Papá had a way of explaining it that really made sense, and staying up late to study with him was a lot better than doing it by myself. I glance over my shoulder at Riley, who has her head down on her desk. I look closer. She is fast asleep. Her test is turned over on her desk.

I'm checking through the problems again when the bell rings. "My little mathletes, time is up!" Mackey smiles a huge grin as people groan. He loves to see us suffer. I imagine his house has framed pictures of tests with big red Fs on them in every room.

"Please stand up right now and turn in your tests on the way out. If your pencil is still moving, I'll begin to dock points."

I hear a few pencils drop, and people begin to pack up. I don't want to get my hopes up, but I really might have gotten a perfect score on this test. As I put my book in my book bag, I watch Riley out of the corner of my eye. Should I give her one more chance? Maybe she was sleepy when she came in and didn't notice me. It was kind of ambiguous earlier, because Jordan's pencil was a little easier for her to reach. I decide to give it one more shot and time my exit to coincide with hers.

"Hey," I say as she walks in front of me, nearly right over me.

"Huh?" She turns and looks at me. "Oh, yeah." She nods for a second.

I don't know how to read her reaction. It's neither warm nor cold nor—

Riley scampers away, as if she doesn't want to be seen with me, practically throwing her test at Mackey as she runs out the door.

I slap my head. What was I thinking? Am I a glutton for punishment? Why on earth am I torturing this girl? I follow her around and beg for attention like a puppy dog. It's sickening. Never again, I vow. I walk over to Mackey and hand him my test.

"How was it, Ms. Dominguez? Challenging?"

I look him square in the eyes and then smile a slow grin. "Hardly."

He raises a huge eyebrow at me, and I breeze past him out the door. Who cares about Riley? I know who I am and where I'm going.

"Big news." I plop down at our broken picnic table. Christine and Zoe are already there. I could hug them. It seems like forever since we've hung out. It's only been four days, technically, since we last had lunch together, but so much happened on the ski trip, and since I'm grounded, I'm only allowed to use the phone for pre-approved purposes. And there are exactly two pre-approved purposes: finding out homework assignments and calling my grandmother in Mexico.

"How was the trip?!" Zoe takes a big gulp of her Dr. Pepper.

"Are you some kind of ski bunny now? Because if so, we might need to renegotiate the terms of our friendship." Christine smiles at me.

I pull out my bagel smeared with peanut butter. "I think I'm in love—"

"What?!" Zoe screams.

"You got your first kiss?" Christine breaks her cool demeanor for a moment and her eyes are wide.

"No, no." I take a bite of my bagel. All that problem-solving made me hungry. "Let me finish. What I was trying to say is—" I take a sip of my water. "I think I'm in love with the wrong person."

"What? Who?" Christine asks.

Zoe swallows her last Nutter Butter. "Is it Dave? So you're finally admitting it?"

I cock my head at her. What is she, all-knowing?

"Is that what you mean?" Zoe is acting like her brain is about to explode.

I glance around the courtyard nervously. I know Dave doesn't go to this school, but still I don't want it out. "Yeah, I guess I'm finally admitting it." I take another bite and think back to the ski trip. He's really very cute. I don't know how

I didn't notice it before. "But it doesn't matter. I think he's dating this girl from his school named Jamie."

Zoe shakes her head. "No way. Dave loves you."

Christine dips a spoon into her yogurt. "Yeah, Zoe's always saying he's Brad Pitt to your Angelina Jolie."

Zoe blushes for a moment. So they talk about me when I'm not here?

I look down at the picnic table. "Used to. Dave *used* to love me. Now he loves Jamie. You should have seen them at the ski lodge. They were giggling so much, it made me want to puke."

Christine slaps her head. "Why do girls do that? It drives me crazy. The minute a boy likes them, their IQ halves."

I take another bite of bagel and feel a shadow fall on me from behind. Uh, oh. Zoe's face registers an expression of pure joy. Christine, on the other hand, is scowling like someone has just compared one of her masterpieces to a velvet Elvis.

"Hey, guys." I freeze. I know that voice. It's—

"Riley!" Zoe claps her hands. "Here, sit down next to Ana. There's plenty of room."

I squint into the sun to see Riley. She gives me a half-smile and hesitates.

"Go on. Have you already eaten? I was thinking of going back to the cafeteria." Zoe digs in her bag. "I could get you something."

"Oh, thanks." Riley plops down next to me. I don't move. What is she doing? "I already ate, though. I was just coming over to say hi."

"Are you sure? It might ruin your rep to be seen with us." Christine squares her shoulders and stares boldly at Riley.

Riley laughs her deep, scratchy laugh and pretends Christine is kidding, then turns to me. "How do you think you did on that math test?" A week ago if Riley McGee had said that to me I would have sworn she was trying to rub in how well she did on the test. Today, I'm not sure. If didn't know better, I would swear that she's just making conversation.

"Yeah. I thought it was, whatever." My mouth won't work. What is she doing? I don't know how to feel.

"I was so out of it when I got there," she says, laughing uncomfortably. "I didn't sleep well at all last night." She smiles a little, and I think I understand what she's really saying. "I like your hair red, by the way." Riley smiles at Christine. "I've been meaning to tell you."

"You do?!" Christine seems a bit horrified and touches her hair self-consciously. "I was thinking of changing it again. In fact, I was thinking of shaving it all off." She gives Riley a defiant look. I almost laugh. Christine is really vain about her hair. Even though she dyes it all the time, it's still long and silky. She would never, ever shave it all off. But this is her routine. She dares people not to love her.

Riley nods. "That might be really cool too. You're so pretty that you could get away with it."

"Awww," Zoe says like a mom. "Wasn't that a nice thing for Riley to say?"

Ms. Moore approaches our table, but then she stops cold in her tracks. She quickly recovers, shakes her head a little, and breaks into a big smile.

"Well, if it isn't my little detention club." She raises her right eyebrow at me.

"Miracle Girls," Zoe says. Ms. Moore doesn't seem to hear.

"Might I ask what the momentous occasion is that brings the most powerful minds in the school together at one humble and, might I add, broken picnic table?" Ms. Moore crosses her arms over her chest. Today she's wearing a pin-striped suit that really shows off her curves. A bit of a pink T-shirt shows underneath the jacket.

"We call it lunch," Christine says. "All the kids are doing it these days. It's the latest craze."

Ms. Moore laughs. "Indeed." Her eyes sweep our table again, and I can feel my cheeks burning. I know I've said some pretty terrible things about Riley to Ms. Moore. "It's actually quite lucky that I've found you all together. I'm trying to recruit for the upcoming beach cleanup for Earth First."

Ms. Moore gives us the details. In a few weeks, the club is going to go down to State Beach and pick up as much litter as we can with gloves and plastic buckets. The more volunteers we can find, the easier the job will be.

Christine spoons some yogurt into her mouth. "So you thought of trash and manual labor, and then you thought of us."

"Always," Ms. Moore says, meeting her tit for tat. "Now, Riley, I know you're not a member of Earth First, but I thought this might appeal to you. Plus, we could really use some more members. You like to surf those beaches, right?"

Riley nods.

"Then protecting them is important."

Riley bites her lip. "I was surfing the other day and an empty milk carton floated past me." She shakes her head. "It was so gross."

"So come out and join us for the cleanup. I'm sure these guys will be there." Ms. Moore nods at all of us. "Right?" she says loudly.

"Oh, right," I say. Hey, my mouth works again.

"Okay, see some of you in class. You'd better hope and pray that you made Raskalnikov your new best friend over the long weekend." Ms. Moore walks away, laughing.

I look at Christine. "Pop quiz on *Crime and Punishment* in Ms. Moore's. You can depend on it."

"It's about a wacko who kills his landlord. What more do you need to know?" Christine polishes off the last spoonful of her yogurt.

"Hey, are you guys going to the Valentine's Day dance?" Riley asks. We all turn and stare at her like she just asked, "Are you guys all wearing your bras on the outside of your clothes tomorrow?"

Christine laughs. "I would go, but I can't decide which of my suitors should have the honor of escorting me."

Zoe shakes her head back and forth as if she's just tasted something sour and rotten. "Oh, no. No, no, no. I don't dance."

Riley gapes at us. "Guys, it's the biggest dance of the year, aside from prom. You can't skip it. Ana, tell them." She nudges me with her arm.

"I—" Suddenly it occurs to me why there would be some advantages to having Riley as a Miracle Girl. The truth is, I kind of do want to go to the Valentine's Day dance. I know I didn't used to like dances, but that was before, when I didn't really know anyone and I didn't really understand Dave yet. Zoe doesn't really like guys yet and Christine is so...Christine. But I see now how dances could be romantic. Anything can happen. Pretending I don't want to go can only last for so long before someone finds out it's another lie. "I don't know," I finally say.

"Look, the cheerleaders are sponsoring it, and they all say that everyone goes in big groups. You don't need a date. I'm not taking one." She looks around the table at us. "Just think about it. You don't want to look back and regret not going."

"Riley?!" someone screams from across the courtyard. I freeze. Ashley Anderson marches her way over to our table. Ashley always tries to overcompensate for being one of the less cute cheerleaders by being twice as mean. Her father is a doctor, and she dresses like she lives in L.A.

As she approaches, her flouncy skirt swings wildly. "What are you doing?" she whispers through her teeth to Riley, but she makes sure that we can all hear her.

I swallow. This could get ugly.

Christine leans back to watch the scene with a very satisfied look on her face. "Good question. We were wondering the same thing."

Riley shrugs as if she couldn't care less. "Talking to some friends."

Zoe breaks into a huge grin. "We're just talking to *our* friend, Riley, okay?"

The bling around Ashley's neck nearly blinds me. She crosses her arms over her chest, and then glances at me, as if noticing me for the very first time. "I didn't know you were friends with God Girl. Isn't that cute?"

It takes everything I have not to throw my applesauce at Ashley. I take deep breaths and remind myself that I am not afraid of being called a Christian. I am one. And I'm proud of that.

"Her name is Ana." Christine stands up and levels her eyes at Ashley. I smile for a moment, until I realize that Christine, like some kind of shark, can smell cheerleader blood about to be spilled. The look on Christine's face scares me.

At this point, a normal person would make nice and retreat. But Ashley is one of the queens of the school, and she is not normal. She continues to ignore me.

Ashley pulls at her necklace. "I guess I didn't know that you were some kind of religious freak, too."

Riley's confidence seems to waver for a moment. Her shoulders droop.

"Maybe you could write a new cheer for us." Ashley steps back from our table a little bit and starts to clap "Who's got sandals and hair down to here? Goooo, Jesus!" She nearly doubles over laughing at her own joke.

Riley walks around the table and stands directly in front of Ashley. I suddenly realize how different Riley is from the other cheerleaders. I had always lumped her in with the others, but now that Riley stands next to this unathletic beauty queen–type, I see that she is nothing like them. Riley is tanned, muscle-bound, and has a casual, natural beauty that she seems unaware of.

Ashley and Riley stare at each other for a moment. What will I do if they start to tear each other's hair out?

Luckily, a group of football players walks by, carrying trays piled high with fried food. "Zach! Andy!" Ashley calls, waving at the hulking quarterback. Zach turns his thick neck, squints at Ashley, and nods. Andy smiles at Riley. "Hang on!" But Zach keeps walking.

"Well," Ashley says, shrugging. "I guess I should be going. See you at practice, darling." She runs after the football players, her red ponytail bobbing up and down.

Riley flares her nostrils and watches Ashley go with her fists clenched. Zoe is practically in tears, but Christine is studying Riley.

Riley turns to us. "I have to go, too." She picks up her bag and purse. "But maybe I'll see you guys at the dance."

We all mumble good-byes and watch her walk away from us. The usual swagger is gone from her step.

37

say a quick and, I'll admit it, very selfish prayer right before I pop my head into Mrs. Slater's room.

"Knock, knock." As I walk in, my heart sinks. It's still Christmas in here, and Dave is nowhere to be found.

"Becky!" Sarah pushes herself up in bed. She seems to have no doubt about who I am today. "You made it. I thought your flight was delayed. Well, no matter. You're just in time."

"In time for..." I walk over to her bed and help her get up. She's in such a state. Her face is bright with joy. I get her safely onto her feet, and she pulls her housecoat around her body and pats her hair.

"Your father likes to keep it so cold in this house. I told him, I said, It's Christmas Eve. And, you know, Peter is from the South. He'll freeze to death."

Oh. It's Christmas Eve.

Sarah walks over to her little Christmas tree and plugs it in. It sparkles with bright, multi-colored lights.

"Now what is keeping Peter? Does he need help with the luggage? I could send your father out there, though he threw his back out again."

I study her for a moment. I think Becky was one of the little girls in that photo. Becky must be Sarah's daughter.

Sarah goes to sit in her favorite chair. "I'm so thankful you married into a family without back problems. It will give your kids a better chance of not suffering like your father. But where is Peter?"

I sit down across from Sarah and pretend I'm plotting a novel. Okay, I'm Becky and I'm married to Peter. Sarah is my mother. It's Christmas Eve, and Peter is supposed to be here with me. Why isn't he here? "His flight was delayed. He'll be here later."

Sarah shakes her head. "Poor Peter. Flying is so miserable."

I nod, and we sit in companionable silence for a moment. I hope that she's not getting confused again. It's easier for me when she's stuck in one moment in time instead of skipping around. I can't make sense of the characters when she changes scenes.

I've been trying to figure out a way to hang out with Dave all week. Calling him on the phone is out of the question because (1) I'm grounded and thus not allowed to use the phone, (2) even if I weren't grounded, I'm not allowed to call boys because that is a sin, though don't go looking for it in the Bible, and (3) calling him would be humiliating since he's probably already engaged to Jamie by now.

But if I were to run into him, well, then, that would be something else. Then I could figure out what's going on with him and Jamie...and me...without angering my parents or exposing myself to too much risk of embarrassment.

And truthfully, I almost waited until youth group tomorrow. I'll definitely see him then. But the more I thought about it, the more I realized that that wouldn't work. There are way too many people there to talk about anything serious. So I hoped I might run into him here with Mrs. Slater. Only, now that I'm here and I see how happy she is to see me, I feel like a jerk. I'm worried about a boy, and this poor woman doesn't even know what year it is.

"Peter! You made it!"

I turn to the doorway and see Dave holding a bouquet of flowers and wearing a Rudolph the Red-Nosed Reindeer tie. He bows deeply at the hips and kisses Sarah on the cheek.

"Flowers for the ultimate hostess." He gives them to her.

Sarah takes a big whiff of them. "They smell wonderful. I'll just put them in a vase." She walks across her room and then stops. "Becky, take your husband's coat, for goodness' sake!"

I stand up and glance at Dave. Am I really supposed to pretend he's my husband?

"Becky?" Dave says, arching an eyebrow at me. "Have you completely forgotten your manners?"

I glare at him. How can he think this is funny? "Well, of course not," I say through my teeth. I walk over to Dave and help him take off his navy blue pea coat. As I stand behind him, I realize how tall he is and how broad his shoulders are.

"Mrs. Slater was wondering what kept you." I hang his coat on the rack by the door. "I worried you had flight trouble. But maybe you had other plans?" Plans with Jamie? Hmm, Dave?

"Wait!" Mrs. Slater screams, staring at us. We both freeze. "Just stay right where you are! I have to get my camera!"

She digs in drawers and eventually pulls out an old disposable camera. I doubt it has any film left.

"I caught my two little lovebirds under the mistletoe," Sarah sings.

I look above my head in horror. Sure enough someone has hung some fake greenery with white berries over Sarah's door.

"That's right," Dave elbows me. "You caught us!"

I stare at him in horror and, truthfully, in hope. Is he going to kiss me? My heart starts racing. Will he do it on the lips? I need time to prepare for this, study up. I didn't think my first kiss would come so unexpectedly. What about Jamie? Is this cheating?

"Becky, go on. Kiss your new hubby! I know you guys are crazy for each other. That's why I've already got a grandbaby on the way."

My face turns beet red and I hear Dave stifle a laugh. I know she doesn't mean to imply that I'm fat, but just the thought that I'm . . . omigosh, this is so embarrassing.

Sarah comes over and peeks at us through the viewfinder of her camera. "You two are the cutest couple in the world."

Dave grins broadly and puts his arm around me. "Thanks, Mrs. Slater. I couldn't agree more."

I look up at him to see if he meant it. He's still smiling, and I suddenly feel very warm, and a little pleased. I also feel like I'm about to throw up.

"Peter, I don't have all day. Please kiss Becky for me. She's too shy." Mrs. Slater points her camera at us.

"I—" I don't even know what I'm going to say. I'm trying to stall. But then I feel Dave squeeze me tighter and put his soft, warm lips to my cheek.

"That's it, now hold it." Mrs. Slater walks forward to get a closeup. "Oh, you two are a hoot."

I shut my eyes without realizing it. My heart is pounding in my chest. Nothing has ever felt so good. And then, in an instant, it's all over. Sarah snaps the photo, Dave drops his arm, and awkwardness hangs in the air.

"I'll get you a copy. Don't worry." Mrs. Slater walks back to the drawer to put the camera away.

"Mrs. Slater, I hope you'll forgive me for kissing and running, but I have to go now." Dave walks over to give her a hug.

"Now, don't you worry. I know doctors have very irregular hours." She gives Dave a hug. "Thank you for coming. You made Christmas Eve the best it's ever been."

Mrs. Slater walks Dave to the door. My shoes feel like they're sewn to the carpet. He's just leaving? What? For the life of me, I'll never understand guys. I have to do something. "I'm going to walk Da...Peter to the car. I'll be right back."

"Okay, hurry back." She shakes her head at me. "The roast is going to dry out if we wait too much longer."

Dave and I step outside, and he stops for a moment. "I love her." Dave shakes his head.

For a moment, my ears hear "I love you," but then I figure it out. "Yeah, she's great." I stand there, staring at him. What do I say?

"Listen, sorry I have to run. I'm meeting Jamie at our practice pad. She's auditioning to join Three Car Garage, so I've really got to be there."

My whole face crumbles. I feel like the wind has been knocked out of me.

"Dominguez, what's wrong?"

"I, uh . . ."

"You like her, right? I thought you guys were friends." Dave watches my face. I try to control it so that he won't see how crushed I am.

"Yeah, she's great."

Dave looks relieved. "And what a set of lungs, right?" He gives me a pat on my shoulder. "Okay, see you around."

"Right," I say to no one, as he walks out the glass front door.

38

Maria parks our SUV in the garage. I tear open the passenger side door, open the door to our kitchen, and start screaming.

"Mom?" I call. My voice almost echoes back.

Maria shuffles in behind me. "She was here when I left."

"*Mom?*" I call again. I wait a few more seconds and begin to draw another huge breath when I finally hear soft footsteps on the staircase.

"My goodness, Ana," Mom says as she steps into the kitchen. "Why are you screaming bloody murder?"

"Because of this!" I raise my right arm and show my mom a piece of paper with the three best numbers in the world on it: 1-0-0. "It's my logarithms test that Papá helped me with."

Mom slides her reading glasses down to the tip of her nose and takes the paper out of my hand. Mackey wrote a note at the top that says, "Keep up the good work!" I nearly fainted when I saw it.

"Ana," Mom whispers with reverence. "You did it! You did it!"

Spontaneously we both jump around for a moment to celebrate while Maria laughs at us.

"Well, this is just really something." Mom starts shuffling papers on the front of our fridge and then tacks my test up there with a magnet that says 'Think Thin Be Thin.' It's kind of lame—what am I? Four? But on the other hand, it's kind of awesome. I worked so hard on that test.

Mom turns around and wraps me in a big, if a bit unpracticed, hug. "Just wait until your father hears. He'll be so proud."

"Thanks, Mom." I shut my eyes and thank God again. When Mackey handed me my test back, I thought there had been a mix-up. I felt good while I was solving the problems, sure, but I've practically never made a hundred on a math test. "It feels really good." I walk over to the pantry and search for a suitably naughty celebration snack.

"And you know what else this means?"

I turn back to Mom. She raises an eyebrow at me.

"You're no longer grounded."

"Really?!" I can't help myself. I start to dance right in the pantry. This is so huge! I can have my life back. My parents said that my grounding would come to an end when they felt like it, and I was beginning to fear that that meant after I got married and started a family.

"Really, Ana." She comes over and gives me another hug. "You deserve it. You have really buckled down on your studying, shown us the maturity we were looking for, and been thoughtful and considerate around the house. Now just remember to practice your piano more, and you'll be right on target for the goals we set for you."

I grab a package of Oreos and a paper plate. No one is allowed to eat without a plate in our house, no matter how small the bit of food. If Jesus himself came over and asked for a cracker, my mother would insist he used a plate. "I really never even thought I could do math, but Papá just knew how to explain it better than my math teacher."

Mom smiles. "I'll bet you'll beat out Riley for the number-one spot in your class yet if you keep up this hard work."

I shrug. Beating Riley would be nice in theory, but now that she's kind of my friend, it's a little more complex.

"By the way, Ana, the event coordinator at the Ritz-Carlton called about the ballroom. I really think it would be fabulous for your *quince*. Then we wouldn't have to restrict the guest list at all. We could easily do a full sit-down meal for six hundred there."

I almost drop the bag of Oreos. "What?!"

"Please don't get crumbs on the floor."

I stumble over to the counter in shock, trying to remain calm. Did she just say six hundred people?! I know, like, ten people total. "I thought we agreed to make it a small party."

Mom sighs. "Well, I liked that idea. But as you know, your court is supposed to have fifteen couples for the waltz. So we're going to need a dance floor I think. Plus, your father got me his list of invitees, and it was extensive."

I stare at the round Oreos on my plate, thinking about how to articulate my complaints. Mom and I are having such a good day. I don't want to ruin it. "Maybe I don't need to have *damas*. I could just skip the court thing." *Damas* are your best friends who are a part of the court. But I don't have fifteen best friends who all just so happen to have boyfriends. I mean, hello? I just moved here, and it's definitely not raining men in Half Moon Bay.

Mom comes over and smoothes my hair. "Will you just come and look at the Ritz-Carlton with me? Then we can talk about it." Her eyes are pleading.

Wow. That really worked. I stayed calm. I didn't make any wild accusations, and she actually heard my opinion. "Sure." I nod. "Let's check it out and go from there." There's no way on earth that I'm going to have it at the Ritz, but it will make my life easier if I play along.

"Thank you, Ana," Mom says, and wipes her hands on a dishtowel. "I think you might be impressed with it."

I begin to unscrew the top layer of my Oreo. I don't see how people can bite right into them and eat all three layers at once. I scrape all traces of frosting from the top cookie and think about how Ms. Moore told me to be honest with my parents and cut out all the lying. Maybe she's right. Mom did just say I was showing newfound maturity.

Still, do I dare?

"Listen, so there's this, uh, event coming up at school…" I look up tentatively. Mom narrows her eyes a little. I peel the frosting layer off the bottom cookie carefully and set it on the plate. "You see, the thing is, Riley McGee invited me to go."

Riley's been stopping by our table at lunch now quite regularly, and she's got all of us convinced that the dance might be kind of fun. Once Zoe realized we'd be going together as the Miracle Girls—without dates—she was all for it. And Christine gave in all too easily to our pleading. I'm pretty sure she's counting on Tyler being there. I shove the bottom cookie into my mouth and look up hopefully.

Mom smiles like a politician. "I'm so glad the two of you are finally becoming friends."

I nod. "Right. So Riley invited all of us, you know, Zoe and Christine and me—"

"And *I*. Zoe, Christine, and I—"

Actually, it's me. But I can't risk correcting her right now. I take a deep breath and blurt out the rest. "She invited us to the Valentine's Day dance and I was hoping I could go."

My mother's face begins to darken as if a storm cloud is rolling over it. "What?!" she hisses. She grabs my arm tightly and I twist my body to get out of her grasp. "What did you ask me?"

I see Maria hightail it out of the kitchen and I want to scream, Come back! "Mom, it's just a school dance. It'll be chaperoned."

Mom shakes her head slowly at me, as if she can't believe I'm even standing there in front of her with the gall to ask permission to actually go out for once in my life. My hands clench and I set my face.

"We agreed that you would go to the youth group Valentine's Day party." She says this so calmly I want to punch her. She agreed I would go to the youth group party. I agreed to nothing.

"I don't want to go to the lame church event. Why can't I go to the dance?" I flare my nostrils. "Everyone else will be going."

"What does that matter?" Mom throws her hands up in the air. "Do I care about everybody else? No. Did God entrust their safety and well-being to me? No. Only you. You are the only one I am supposed to take care of, and this dance is absolutely out of the question."

My eyes begin to well up. And God help me, I know I shouldn't say it, but I can't help myself. "You can't keep me locked in this stupid pink palace."

Mom tightens her lips and looks like she's about to throttle me. "Stupid?"

"It's a prison, Mom. I'm almost fifteen. You can't keep me from doing everything."

"You want to bet?" Mom walks across the room and grips the granite countertop. "Ana, I can't even believe you asked to go to this dance. You know the rules of our house. No dating until you're sixteen. These dances are dangerous. Lewd dance moves, people pouring alcohol into the punch, kids getting high!"

I force myself not to laugh. Mom's fears seem to be exclusively based on bad eighties movies. "They're nothing like that! The teachers are really strict." Mom turns away from me. "Be reasonable. I came to you like an adult. I asked for permission. I'm trying to have a discussion about this."

Mom turns around quickly. "That's it, you're grounded again. I don't know when you started thinking you're an adult, but you're not. You're still fourteen. And you will obey the rules of this house, young lady."

"Argh!" I throw my hands up in the air.

Mom starts to speak again, but puts her nose in the air and stomps out of the room instead. I stand there for a moment, clenching and unclenching my fists. It's all so unfair. I did everything just like Ms. Moore said. I was honest and mature. And it didn't work. In fact, it made everything far worse. I could have passed the Valentine's Day dance off as an event for Earth First and gotten to go, no problem. But now, all of my friends will be there, having the kind of fun normal teenagers have, and I'll be at some stupid church party with all the other losers.

I see my math test on the fridge. Suddenly the hundred seems to be laughing at me, taunting me, saying, I can't believe you thought that would work, you idiot. I rip it off the fridge, crumple it up, and throw it in the trashcan.

39

What are the chances Valentine's Day would fall on a Saturday? Actually, I'm pretty sure it's one in seven. Mackey would be so proud. Unfortunately, Mackey is probably at the school dance right now, monitoring all my friends, while I am desperately trying to channel Christine (also at the dance, by the way) and act like I don't care. The closer we get to the church, though, the harder it's getting. After seeing girls at school carrying around bunches of roses and balloons all day Friday, the last thing I want to do is go out and face people.

I guess I'm supposed to be grateful that Fritz organized a Valentine's Day party for those of us with nothing better to do, but somehow it just feels like a pity event, where all the losers without dates come to make each other feel better about the fact that Jesus loves us even if no one else does. I know that both Tyler and Tommy Chu are going to our school's dance, and Jamie mentioned she was going to the dance at her school, which means Dave will be at that, hence there will not even be a praise band tonight. We'll probably sit around and read 1 Corinthians 13 and cry out of loneliness.

But Mom insisted I come tonight. Even when I tried to back out over dinner, she shook her head and said I had to go. And since Mom and I aren't exactly on the best of terms right now, I decided I'd better not argue with her or she might put me up for adoption.

As Mom pulls into the church parking lot, I scan the cars and quickly realize how few there are. I feel even more pathetic. I get out as quickly as I can.

I walk to the door and try to muster the courage to go inside the youth room. It's awfully quiet in there. What if I'm the only one who showed up? What if I'm the only one in the whole youth group who doesn't have a date on Valentine's Day? Judy and Fritz will have to sit around all night, smiling at me, trying to pretend that they don't wish they were having a romantic candlelit dinner.

I tentatively push open the door. Okay, I'm not the only one. There are not as many kids as on a typical Sunday night, but there are about twenty people inside, and after hanging out with most of them at the ski trip, I don't feel like a total freak walking into the room.

I casually walk up to a group of junior girls. Tricia, whose mane of thick golden hair puffs out around her face, is telling a story about how someone had a singing telegram delivered in her history class on Friday. The lights are low—mood lighting I guess—and I look around the room and take in the paper hearts strung from the ceiling and the retro love songs playing on the stereo system. The snack table supports a giant pink cake, and there are confetti hearts all over the floor. I try to make out the faces on the other side of the room. I squint. Is that...?

My heart soars as Dave waves at me, a ridiculous shiny red necktie hanging down the front of his shirt. I smile back, command my stomach to stop turning flips, and scan the room quickly. Where's Jamie? I can't make out every face, but I don't think I see her. Dave starts walking toward me, but before he gets very far, Fritz puts his fingers in his mouth and whistles an ear-splitting call. Everyone freezes. Fritz dances his way to the front of the room, then gestures for the music to be turned down. I have a very bad feeling about this. I thought this was supposed to be a party. No one said anything about activities.

He welcomes us to the festivities, then gestures to Judy, who begins to hand out slips of paper. I take one as she goes by and unfold it uncertainly.

COW, it says.

Oh great. I'm a cow. Exactly what I wanted to hear. Maybe this game is meant to explain why we're all dateless on Valentine's Day? Dear Ana, it's because you're a big fat cow with a dim bovine brain. Moo.

"Each slip of paper lists an animal," Fritz says from the front of the room. "There are four kinds of animals. You want to be with your kind." I freeze. I can see where this is going. Is it too late to run? "You'll find them by making the noise the animal makes. Go."

Immediately, the room is filled with people quacking, oinking, mooing, and meowing. I watch incredulously as two pigs find each other in the chaos, then together set off to find more pigs, oinking in delight.

Why do they always do this? It's like the youth leaders sit up all night thinking of ways to embarrass us. They probably dream about whipped cream and wiffle balls.

I stand still and listen carefully to determine where the

other cows are, then when I see a group forming, I go over and join them silently. Dave is a cat, as it turns out, a role he embraces enthusiastically. It only takes a few minutes for the group to divide itself into barnyard clans, then Fritz gets on the microphone again.

"Now you're in your teams," Fritz says. "Each team will get a clue. And frankly... I think it's about time." He laughs, though no one else does. "This clue will lead you to your next clue, which will lead you to your special Valentine's Day prize."

A scavenger hunt. How romantic. Why couldn't my parents have let me stay home? What was wrong with hiding in my room and being miserable there?

I assess my group. There's a weird freshman guy named Phil who's apparently a champion diver, but whose freakishly blond hair seriously needs to be washed. Troy, the pimply sophomore, Tricia of the pouffy hair, and Stacy Meeker, the long-legged senior who is gorgeous and by all rights should be somewhere better than this tonight. We talked a little on the ski trip, and she's cool.

As I puzzle out the liabilities of my team, Judy hands around slips of paper. Fritz announces that each team has the same clues, just in different orders, and that the final clue will lead us to a great treasure. He blasts an ear-splitting air horn, and we're off.

"Come on, guys!" Phil yells, gesturing for us to follow him. My group takes off after him out the youth room doors, ignoring my weak protests. We don't even know where we're headed. They stop a few feet outside the door, apparently realizing the same thing, and Stacy starts to read from the small slip of paper in her hand.

"We'd all appreciate if you'd quit your crying," Stacy reads. Out of the corner of my eye I see the Cats running off toward the Sunday School classrooms. "Quit your crying. What does that mean?"

"The nursery!" Phil runs down the hallway. The others follow after him, and I go, too, despite my doubts. It says quit crying. The nursery is where all the crying happens. We scramble across the courtyard and enter the main building, then run down the hallway. When we get there, the room is dark and empty. There are no clues to be found anywhere.

"There've got to be clues here somewhere," Troy says, picking up a bag of diapers to check.

"Do you guys think it might mean the soundproof cry room?" I say.

'That's it!" Phil gives me a high five. We run en masse to the little glass box at the back of the dark sanctuary, where moms are supposed to bring their fussy babies so no one else has to listen to them. Inside, there are four little envelopes. I pick up the one that has the word COWS on it.

That was kind of fun. I start to wonder how the other teams are doing. Have they found their first clue yet? I pick it up and begin to read.

"The only room named after a man." I look up at the group.

"The john?" Phil asks, shrugging his shoulders.

"That's it!" Stacy says.

"Wait." I hold up my hand. They freeze. Rushing around from guess to guess will waste huge amounts of time. We could win this if we use our brains a little.

"It can't be the john." I shake my head. "There's like a thousand bathrooms in this place. There's no way they'd make us search them all." I stare at the clue, trying to figure out the hidden meaning. My competitive side is starting to take over. I read the clue to myself again and break into a smile. This one was so easy it was hard.

"It's the gym," I say, and the team begins cheering and runs out of the cry room. I race ahead and get there first, passing the Pigs going the other way, and fling open the door. Taped to the back side of the door is an envelope that says COWS.

"Before you sing, to here you will bring." Stacy says, reading the clue uncertainly. Okay, that doesn't even make sense, but the answer is pretty clear.

"Where do they keep the choir robes?" I haven't been here long enough to know where everything in this church is.

"My mom's in the choir. Follow me," Troy says and then runs off toward the stairs. I think we're doing pretty well. We could really win this thing. What other kinds of places would Fritz think were good hiding spots? I make a list in my head as we run toward a closet behind the sanctuary.

Any one of the Sunday School classrooms is fair game. There's the church office at the back, but they wouldn't let us go in there, would they? There's the playground. The welcome desk. The kitchen.

Stacy flings open a door, and rows and rows of hanging choir robes greet us. She reaches around behind the door as the Ducks run by, then pulls out an envelope.

I think about the music room and the bride's lounge. What was it that Fritz said we are looking for? Great treasure? Then it hits me. I snap my fingers. That's it. Of course. Why didn't I think of this before?

"No whining," Stacy reads, squinting at the clue. "That's all it says." Confusion registers on her face. "What does that mean?"

I keep mentally running down the list of locations, but none of them seems right for this. "How's that spelled?" I ask, an idea forming.

"Whining?" She looks at me quizzically. "W-I-N-I-N-G."

"There's no H?"

Stacy shakes her head.

"The communion supplies. There's no wine. They only use grape juice." The group starts cheering, but as they run off, I stay behind. There's another place I want to check out.

"Come on, Ana," Troy says, but I shake my head.

"I'll be right there," I say. He shrugs, then runs off with the group.

It's so obvious. I can't believe I didn't realize right away where the final clue would lead us. I'll just go make sure I'm right, then I'll meet up with the rest of the group and have them skip the rest of the clues and head there. We'll be sure to win. We'll sit there and laugh and wait for the rest of the groups to finally figure it out.

The hallways are quiet as I make my way to the lobby. No one else seems to be around. Perfect. I test the door to the sanctuary, and of course it's unlocked. It had to be. I slip into the dark, quiet room and take a deep breath.

It's so peaceful in here. The only light comes from the green EXIT signs, and the shadowy corners of the room feel a little mysterious. There's something magical about it, like the mysteries of the ages would be answered if only I could stay here long enough.

I squint at the front of the sanctuary and make out the sleek edges of the cross hanging above the stage and then begin to walk slowly down the center aisle. My footsteps echo in the cavernous room, and the sound feels raw, a little too loud, but somehow I don't mind. It kind of feels right. I guess that's kind of like life, I think, touching the edge of a pew for reassurance as I walk by. Faith is kind of like the quiet, peaceful sanctuary, mysterious and magnificent, but life is loud.

I get to the front row of pews and step tentatively toward the stage. There, under the shiny cross, I see four envelopes. I step up slowly, reverently, then walk toward them. Halfway across the stage, though, I turn around and look out over the rows and rows of empty pews stretching out before me. Is this what the pastor sees every Sunday morning? It's totally different from this angle, but the sanctuary is still blessedly quiet, and I sigh. God must have known that I needed this tonight. He knew that it would refresh me to be in this sacred place, utterly alone.

"Hey, Dominguez."

"AAHH!" I don't normally think of myself as a screamer, but it escapes from my lips before I can stop it. What is that? I squint out over the sanctuary and see a shadow move a bit on the front pew. I watch it for a second. It appears to be . . . waving?

"Dave?" I walk down off the stage quickly, then move toward the shadowy figure. As I get closer I can see him sitting there, arms crossed over his chest, smiling. "What are you doing here?"

"Same thing you are." He shrugs and pats the empty space on the pew next to him. "Have a seat."

"You figured out the scavenger hunt?" I take a step toward him. My cheeks are burning, and suddenly I'm really glad it's dark. He nods.

"When someone in church tells you the prize is great treasure, you can bet they're talking about the cross," he says, rolling his eyes. "Especially on Valentine's Day. True love and all that. So I came here right off the bat to watch the fun." He pats the space next to him again, and I tentatively lower myself down. As my eyes begin to adjust to the dim lighting, the big blob on the stage takes the shape of a grand piano.

"You've been sitting here in the dark this whole time?" I let my body relax a little as I lean back against the padded pew.

"It's nice." He lifts the end up his necktie and plays with the tip. "Me and God had a chat."

"Sorry to interrupt."

"I'm not sorry." He shifts a little and settles himself on the pew. If I'm not crazy, he's a fraction of an inch closer to me than before. I must be crazy. "It's nice to have company."

I sit still, afraid to move. If I move, he might realize he's sitting with me, not Jamie, and he'll leave.

"So." He twists a little to face me. "Valentine's Day. Why aren't you at the dance at your school?"

I shrug. "Why aren't you?"

"Don't like dances."

"But Jamie must like dances." I bite my lip.

"Maybe." He shrugs. "I don't know."

"But weren't you supposed to..." I trail off. This is awkward. How do I say this? "Weren't you taking her to the dance?"

Dave laughs. "Nah. Not my style." He twists again, and this time his arm settles on the back of the pew. He's not touching me, but I can feel the heat of his arm on my shoulder. "Besides," he says, leaning forward a bit, "I'd rather be here with you."

I laugh quietly, but everything in me hopes he doesn't mean this as a joke. I lean back a little, and my shoulder just touches his fingertips. He doesn't pull them away.

"But aren't you and Jamie..." My mouth suddenly feels very dry.

Dave sits up suddenly, pulling his arm away. Uh-oh. Why did I do that?

"I don't know why everyone thinks that." He shakes his head, but his voice doesn't sound upset. It's soft, kind of sexy. "She's just singing with us. That's it." He leans back against the pew again, but this time, his hand lands on the bench part of the pew, just a few inches from my hand.

"Oh." I don't know what to say, but I'm also afraid to say anything for fear he might move again. I feel my muscles tense as I lean to the left a tiny bit.

We sit in silence for a moment, and slowly, so gently I almost don't feel it at first, his pinkie brushes against my hand. I wait, and a few seconds later, his hand touches mine, lightly. I'm staring straight ahead, afraid to move, but out of the corner of my eye I see Dave watching me.

"I keep waiting for the movie to start." He laughs, and I vaguely comprehend that he's making a joke about this room being like a theater. I smile and let out a slow breath as he places his hand on top of mine, then twists my hand over. He rubs my palm lightly with his fingertips. I start to relax, but cringe as I hear voices out in the hallway. There's laughter and yelling, and it's coming closer, and I quickly realize that the winning team is about to burst into the sanctuary and destroy this moment. Dave threads his fingers though mine and gives me a quick squeeze. I think he's about to pull away, but as the Pigs burst through the door and start storming down the aisle, he simply holds my hand.

40

'm practically skipping up the walkway toward my house, but I try to control myself so Papá, trudging up the path behind me, won't suspect anything. If he found out that I held a boy's hand at church tonight, I'd never be allowed out of my room again. Luckily, Papá seems distracted and doesn't notice much of anything as he unlocks the door to the dark house, then locks it behind us. He walks off to his bedroom without a word.

You'd think that if you can afford a house this big, you could also afford some lamps, but for some reason there are never enough lights on in our house. I replay the scene in the sanctuary over in my mind as I walk into the kitchen, flip on the light, and pour a tall glass of Diet Coke. He really held my hand. And he sat next to me for the rest of the evening, even when we went back into the youth room. And he promised to e-mail me tomorrow. I giggle a little and dance around, picturing his face in my mind, then take a long sip and jump around some more.

I'm so full of nervous energy, I can't go to bed, so I take my glass and begin to head toward my bedroom. I wonder if anyone is still on IM. I can't wait to tell Christine about what happened. But as I leave the kitchen, I see a strip of light under Maria's door and decide to stop in and fill her in first. She'll be so excited for me.

I knock quietly on the door, then push it open, and freeze. Maria is in her bathrobe, her hair in curlers, bent over her suitcase. Her clothes are strewn about the room, and there are boxes everywhere.

"Anita," she says, straightening up slowly. "You weren't supposed to see all of this." Her face is pale, and there are dark circles under her eyes. Has she always been this frail?

"What's going on?" I set my glass down on Maria's dresser quickly so I won't drop it. The air is suddenly gone from my lungs, and my heart falls. I don't know what's happening, but I know this is not good.

"I thought you were out tonight," she says.

"I was. I just got back." Goosebumps raise on my arms. "Were you trying to leave while I was gone?"

Maria turns and lowers herself onto her bed slowly. She sighs as she sinks into the flowered comforter. "Your parents thought it would be better if you didn't have to see this," she says. "I'm not leaving for a while, not until after your *quince*, but I'm shipping most of my things ahead." She gestures around the room vaguely. "I wanted to have it all packed up by the time you got home."

"What?" Suddenly, Mom's insistence that I go tonight makes a lot more sense. She wanted me out of the house. "But..." I swallow and bite back the tears. "Where are you going?" Even as I speak the words, I know the answer.

Maria touches my arm. "I'm old. I'm sick. I'm tired." She runs her hand across the bedspread. "It's time for me to go home."

"But you are home."

"My heart will always be where you are, but Mexico is my home."

"But..." My bottom lip trembles. "But you can't leave. You're sick! All the best hospitals are here. Here, you'll get better. If you go back there..." This is madness. My parents won't let her do this. They came to America because they wanted the best treatment for me. They'll put a stop to this.

"Anita, you don't need me anymore. And I'm a huge drain on your parents."

"I need you!" I shriek. I know I'm starting to sound a bit hysterical, but I don't care.

"Now, with the lupus, I'm costing them so much. It doesn't make sense," she says quietly.

I am stunned. Maria is a member of the family. I can't live without her. How could my parents just let her go? Is it really because of the high cost of her medical bills? I can't believe them!

"Oh, that's it," I say. I turn on my heel and storm to the door, flinging it open. The hypocrites! All their talk of love and God, and then when someone finally needs their help, they just let her walk away. As if they can't afford to pay for a few pills. I'm going to drag their sorry butts out of their big soft bed and scream at them until they realize what horrible people they are and change their minds.

"Anita," Maria calls, but I ignore her as I stomp through the door. I hope the noise wakes up their pitiful selves. I hope they never get back to sleep. "ANA!" The pained tone in Maria's voice sends chills down my spine, and I freeze. I turn back to look at her. She holds out her arms to me, and she looks so small and frail there on the bed that I walk back to her. She stands up and wraps her arms around me and holds me like she did when I was a little girl.

"Anita. Your parents have been very generous."

I sniff back the tears and drag my sleeve across my eyes.

"Being here, watching you grow up, has been the best thing that's happened to me. But you have grown into an amazing woman. You are not a child. You don't need me anymore."

"Of course I need you," I say, hot tears running down my cheeks. "We can't survive without you. Please don't leave me with those horrible people."

"You don't need me. You need your parents, and they need you." She wipes a tear away from her eye. "With me gone, you'll all finally realize that."

"I'll come with you," I say suddenly. Yes, that's what I'll do. "You took care of me, now I'll take care of you." It's perfect. I'll finish high school via correspondence course. I'll learn to make real tamales. I don't like this cold weather anyway.

"Your place is here. And mine is there." She sighs. "I miss my home." She says it so quietly I almost think I've misheard her. "I miss my family." I gasp, and she shushes me. "You're my family here," she says, rubbing her hand on my shoulder, "but I miss my kids, too." She pulls back and looks me in the face. "I have grandchildren I've never met. It's time."

I watch her face, lined and pale. When did she get to be so old?

"Seeing you cry breaks my heart," she says, stroking my hair softly. "Please, let me go quietly."

41

It's Monday at lunch when we come up with the idea. Well, I guess technically the idea was born in the high school gym at the dance last Saturday, when they were having such a good time that they decided to schedule a big night out, but it's when we're talking on Monday that I resurrect the idea of camping on the beach.

"I don't know." Zoe crunches into a Nutter Butter. "I don't think my parents would go for it unless we had an adult with us."

"We don't need an adult." Riley rolls her eyes. "Nothing bad's going to happen."

"Besides, that's the whole point," Christine says, sucking on the end of a Dorito. "To get away from our parents." Christine's feelings for her dad don't seem to be cheered much by the fact that she apparently danced with Tyler for a little while on Saturday. They didn't dance to any slow songs, but still, dancing is dancing. I was so happy for her when they told me. And apparently Riley spent a good part of the night dancing with Zach, which didn't make me quite as happy. That guy rubs me the wrong way.

Zoe looks unsure, and I feel a bit uncertain, too, if I'm honest. I know my parents would never let me camp on the beach, even if I weren't grounded for life. I guess maybe that's part of the appeal. I don't feel any need to follow their rules anymore. I'm an adult and it's time that they respect that.

"I can't do it this weekend." Christine's hair is now a light shade of green, which doesn't go as well with her skin tone as the red but still looks pretty cool. "I have to babysit The Bimbot while my dad takes The Bimbo to Napa." She rolls her eyes. "But the weekend after that?"

"Sure," Riley says, polishing off a cheese sandwich. "I'm always free. My parents are so busy running Michael to therapy these days, they don't care where I am."

"You guys, I'm not sure it's a good idea." Zoe is so plaintive and sincere, it's hard not to feel bad for her.

"You can all tell your parents you're staying over at my house," Christine says. I nod, though I'm not sure how well that's going to work. For one thing, that would mean talking to my parents, and for another, I'm grounded, but I'll figure this out before then. I don't owe them anything.

"But what about all the camping equipment? How am I supposed to sneak that by my parents?"

Riley waves the question away as if it's an annoying bug. "Say we're camping in Christine's yard."

"I don't want to lie," Zoe whines.

"Besides, we won't need nearly as much stuff as last time," Christine says. "It was freezing then. But it's warm enough now that we'll only need a few blankets."

"I—" Zoe looks around at us. She tries to smile, but she still looks unsure.

"Come on, Zo. It'll be okay," Riley says, her face breaking into a smile. "Nothing's going to happen. We're the Miracle Girls. We're invincible. God will always be on our side."

Zoe pops the last of her Nutter Butter into her mouth and chews thoughtfully. She swallows, then takes a swig of her soda. Finally, she seems to make up her mind. "I guess so."

42

f Mom calls it "Bloomies" one more time, I might scream.

"What about this one, Ana?" Mom holds up what basically amounts to a wedding dress. It's white, ankle-length, and pouffy. "It's by Vera Wang." She nearly drools as she says "Vera Wang" and the saleswoman—pardon me, personal shopper—looks like she might pop a button on her suit.

The dress is too expensive and too...bridal. I'm not getting married; I'm becoming a woman. Well, theoretically I'm becoming a woman. I'm flattered that in Mexico I could be considered a woman at fifteen, but here in the good old U. S. of A, I'll be a baby until I graduate and go off to Princeton and get far, far away from my parents. That's just the reality of things. I'm surprised Mom and Papá haven't looked into putting bars on my windows so I can never leave.

"It's okay," I say. I might hate my mom right now, but I do still want to look good at my *quince*, so I'm trying to play along a bit here. If you had asked me before Valentine's Day what I was going to wear to this thing, I probably would have said a burlap sack and a bag over my head. But now, Dave is going to be there.

We only see each other at youth group, and sometimes at Stonehill Manor when we hang out with Ms. Slater, but we stay in constant touch over e-mail. Dave can write an e-mail that will make your socks melt. And I'm learning so much about his family, like the fact that his dad restores old cars and his mom makes her own stationery. She actually makes the paper. I was blown away by that. And Dave dreams of doing special effects animation for Pixar movies someday.

Plus, I'm trying to play ball with Mom because she caved in on the whole Ritz- Carlton idea. We've compromised on having it at home, but in huge tents in the backyard. Mom finally decided it would be more "intimate." Personally I think she just decided that showing off her palace would be a good way to impress people.

Bloomingdale's is our first stop in the city today. Up next is Nordstrom, and then we're off to hit up a few boutiques, most of which are bridal shops that do a small side business in *quince* dresses. It's not like I'm the only Latina in the Bay Area, after all. I suppose I should be thankful for that. I've seen some pretty hideous dresses online in my research. Just be thankful you don't live in Nowheresville, Ana.

"But what about this really cute pink one?" I walk across the immaculate Bloomingdale's floor and unhook a hot pink and black lace number that is...maybe a bit low-cut. She'll never go for it, but maybe we can compromise on something that doesn't look like it's from the 1800s.

"Good taste, my dear." The personal shopper crosses her arms across her birdlike chest and grins at me. "That's a Betsey Johnson."

Mom glares at her. "But I don't think it's quite what the occasion requires."

"Right." The personal shopper comes over and twists the hanger under my neck so that the dress drapes against me. "Your mom is absolutely correct. However, some of our *quincean...quinceanaararara* girls prefer to change into something more fun after the dinner portion of the evening."

I smirk. Even if she can't pronounce *quinceañera* to save her life, this woman is good. She's trying to sell us two overpriced frocks now. "Well, I could just go with that one, frankly." Why did Mom insist on shopping for dresses in San Francisco? It's so pricey here. I don't even want to think what the party is costing poor Papá now, between the rented tents, the DJ....

"You *are* having a dinner, I presume?" The personal shopper's tone drips with snottiness.

"No—" I say firmly.

"Ana! Yes, of course we are." Mom glares at me like I've forgotten my manners entirely.

"It really is expected." The personal shopper nods with Mom. Any minute now, these two are going to make it official and become best friends forever.

"Well, it's *my* party, and I don't know if I want a dinner." I hang up the cute pink dress and put a hand on my hip. Maybe if I make it seem like my idea, Mom won't be embarrassed by not having a full sit-down meal. And no meal would save Papá thousands of dollars. "I read online that appetizers are what's cool now," I say, lying through my teeth.

Mom flares her nostrils. "Let's discuss this later. Today, all we need to do is find the dress of your dreams. The party is just three short months away now." Mom walks over with the white Vera Wang dress and holds it up to me. A jaded smile crosses her face.

I pick up the pink dress again. "Great. I found it. Let's go ahead and get it."

Mom takes the pink dress from my hands. "I said no, Ana. You must choose something else. That dress is too skimpy."

"Why can't I just have 'the dress of my dreams'?"

"I'll just give you two a moment." The personal shopper splashes a fake smile on her face and disappears.

"Ana, what has gotten into you?" Mom hisses under her breath.

"I don't want to look like I'm getting married. I hate this dress. Do you even care that I don't like it?" I jut out my lip. Do you even care that you're kicking Maria out in the cold? No, you don't because you only think about yourself.

"If you want a pink dress, then fine. But you can't have this dress. Your Papá would faint the moment he saw you in it."

I frown. I definitely don't want to make Papá uncomfortable. He's actually been showing a lot more interest in me lately. His practice seems to be picking up a little momentum and he's really been getting into this *quince* stuff. At your party, you have a special dance with your dad. Last Saturday he came to me with a CD in his hand, saying how excited he was that he'd finally found the perfect song for us to dance to. I'd never heard of it, but he played it for me and I kind of liked it. I was touched that he'd put so much thought into it.

"Fine," I say and put the dress back. I don't know why I even try. No matter what I do, this is really going to be my mother's party to show all the snooty-tooty people of Half Moon Bay that we're good enough to be in their clubs, even though my grandfather was a farmer and no one in our family came over on the *Mayflower.*

"Honestly," Mom says, shaking her head. "I don't know what's gotten into you lately. The closer you get to becoming a woman, the more childish you are."

43

ifty-five degrees feels a lot colder than it sounds. Fifty-five percent is more than half. Fifty-five is almost old enough to retire. But fifty-five degrees on a wet March night on the beach in Half Moon Bay is cold, even if you are wearing two sweatshirts and gloves. It's not raining exactly, but the air is misty and the beach is nearly deserted. We're huddled around the fire Zoe managed to build, but even though we're far away from the water and the high rock walls behind us shelter us from the wind a little, it's still pretty chilly.

But, hey, we're all here. That's kind of amazing. Zoe managed to convince her parents to let her take the tent and sleeping bags to Christine's, Riley said she was staying at my house, and I had the brilliant idea to tell the jailers that Riley and I were working on something for church and I would crash with her. Since it was for church, they relaxed the grounding for one night, and besides, I think they're feeling pretty bad about the fact that Maria is moving right after my *quince*. I suspected I could use that to my advantage. And what I told them wasn't technically a lie. I am crashing with her...on the beach, and we will talk about church at some point. For now, the warm glow of the fire makes our small circle, huddled against the misty night air, feel happy and safe, and the rhythmic pounding of the waves against the shore is comforting.

I've just gotten my second marshmallow a perfect toasty brown when Zoe asks me about my *quince* plans.

"It's coming along," I sigh. "It's tricky to plan without actually speaking to my parents." I bite into the marshmallow, and the gooey center leaks onto my fingers. I lick it off slowly. "My mom is being, like, an evil dictator on steroids. She's completely obsessing about the chocolate fountain she's decided we must have. But she hates the quality of the chocolate the caterer tried to put past her. Plus, we're having an all-out war about the throne." I stuff the rest of the marshmallow into my mouth and savor the hot sticky sugar.

"Throne?" Zoe asks.

I roll my eyes. "During the party, your *madrina*, who is like a godmother, presents you with a tiara, and Mom actually wants me to sit on a throne for that."

Riley's eyes are wide. "You're kidding."

I point at Riley. "Exactly my reaction. Mom says I'm being so unreasonable about it. She keeps saying, 'Ana, think of the pictures!'" I do a dead-on mimic of my mother's voice and Zoe and Riley squeal with laughter.

"I'm probably going to cave in about it. At least she agreed to hire professional dancers. I spared you guys that. You would have danced a full waltz with some random guy."

Zoe's face flushes bright red at the very thought. "Bless you, Ana."

"Whatever. It's fine, I guess. I just thought this was supposed to be my party, you know?"

"Parties are always for the people who throw them." Riley

shrugs. She holds her hands up to the fire, trying to warm them. Riley doesn't eat marshmallows. "My cousin told me that at her wedding."

"That's becoming abundantly clear," I say, my voice a little higher. "It's just an excuse for my parents to show off, make a good impression. It's not about me at all." I put the end of my stick into the fire to burn off the melted parts that always get left behind. "It makes me so mad. Don't pretend like you're doing this great thing for me." I roll my eyes and see Zoe nodding. "I just wish my mom would leave me alone sometimes."

I push a new marshmallow onto my stick and pull the sleeves of my sweatshirt down farther on my wrists. It feels so good to get that out. I reach the stick out over the fire but then notice that Christine's head is down, the strings of her hoodie pulled tight so that only a small portion of her face is showing.

"Christine?" Riley touches her arm, but Christine doesn't look up. I hear a wet sniff.

Christine mumbles something, but with the wind it's hard to hear what she says. She gestures with her hand for us to go back to our conversation. In other words, stop looking at her.

"Christine," I say quickly.

She looks up slowly, and I see she has tears in her eyes. Riley and I stare at each other with the same wide-eyed terror. Zoe, God love her, is already reaching out her arm to Christine, but Christine pulls away. Her face is red and her eyes watery, but her voice is very calm as she speaks.

"I wish I had been nicer to my mom."

Oh God, help me. How could I complain about my mom in front of the girl who just lost hers?

"I didn't mean—" I am the biggest oaf. How can I be so utterly insensitive? Why do I say such stupid things all the time?

I listen to the lonely whine of the wind as it rushes down the sand.

"Anyway," Christine says, quickly wiping the tears away. She sits up straight and tries to pull herself together. Like a switch, she's back to being tough, cynical Christine. "Dave said he'd come to your quince?" She reaches into the bag for another marshmallow, then thrusts it onto her stick and puts it straight into the fire. She doesn't look up at any of us.

"Yeah." Christine has been the most excited about how things are going with Dave. I think it finally gave her permission to like Tyler. She probably knew I didn't really like him for a long, long time, but now it's out in the open.

The marshmallow catches fire, and Christine waves her stick around until it goes out, then blows on it carefully.

"Hey, you should be sure to invite Tyler," Christine smiles shyly. She wipes her hand across her eyes again, then puts the marshmallow into her mouth.

"He's on the list." I nod. "Don't worry. Mom invited everyone I've ever met or even breathed near."

"Are your friends from San Jose going to be there?" Zoe asks. I think she means to sound curious, but her voice is a bit wary.

"A few of them." I wonder why I don't feel sadder that more of them aren't going to make it out for the party. It's really not that far of a drive. But I haven't really made the trip out to see them either. I haven't even talked to most of them since I left. I wonder if it feels as far away—and I don't just mean miles—for them as it does for me.

A rustling occurs far off in the distance.

"Did you guys hear that?" Riley is staring down the beach, squinting into the darkness.

"I thought I heard something." Zoe stands up. "It sounded like voices."

"Male voices," Christine says. She stands up, sniffs, and looks down the beach.

I stare into the inky darkness, but I can't see anything, and all I can hear is the crashing of the waves. "It's probably nothing," I say, my voice a little braver than I actually feel. The beach is so big and dark beyond our little fire. Anything could be out there.

"It's definitely something," Riley says, walking away from our little group a bit. Then I hear it too—low, deep voices. The sound seems to be obscured by the mist, and the unknown only makes it more frightening. The indistinct voices grow louder, and Zoe tenses, then scurries toward the tent and begins to unzip the door. I look at Christine, who stares back at me, her eyes wide. She pulls her phone out of her pocket and flips it open. Then slowly, almost imperceptibly, figures begin to emerge from the darkness: two big, dark figures walking down the beach toward us.

All of a sudden, I know this was a very bad idea. I thought camping on the beach would be a fun exercise in rebellion, but now I have a sinking suspicion my parents might have been right. Maybe they had a very good reason for wanting to keep a close eye on me. I wish with all my heart that I had listened. There's no one else out here. No one else was crazy enough to camp out on a cold, drizzly night. With a shudder, I realize that there's no one to hear us scream.

"Well, well, well," one of the men says, and the guy with him chuckles a little. "What do we have here?"

Riley tenses up, and lifts her arms up like in one of my mom's kickboxing videos.

"What a nice little surprise," the guy on his left says. As they step closer, I see that these guys are huge. Should we all just make a run for it?

"We're armed," Christine says quickly, and I hear a thud as Zoe hops inside the tent.

"Get in here, guys," Zoe whispers, but no one follows her into the tent.

"Fresh meat," the biggest one says, coming closer, and I freeze.

"Leave us alone!" Zoe shouts from inside the tent.

That guy almost looks like—

"Zach?" The tension on Riley's face drains away, and she drops her hands and starts to laugh. I wonder if it might be too soon to relax, seeing as how we're still on the beach with two huge guys and no one else within calling distance. "Zach? Andy! What are you doing here?"

Zach laughs and gives Andy a high five. They smell like beer.

"You scared us to death," Riley says. She laughs a little too loudly as the guys scan the area quickly, then look back at her. Apparently we're uninteresting and don't merit further investigation.

"Your fire is the only thing lit up on this beach. We could see you miles away," says Andy.

"And when you stand up like that against the light," Zach says, reaching out to lift a section of Riley's bright blond hair, "it's pretty easy to tell who you are." Zach laughs. "We thought we'd come give you guys a little scare."

"You did that on purpose?" Riley screeches, which the football players think is hilarious.

"We're just having a little fun," Andy says, but Riley has shifted into cheerleader mode and is laughing and slapping at Zach playfully. I'm so relieved that we're not about to die that I don't even care that she's playing dumb.

"I can't *believe* you." She reaches out and punches his shoulder lightly. "How could you do something like that to me?" She flips her hair over her shoulder. For once, I don't really mind fading into the shadows. And then, suddenly, I wonder if Riley invited Zach out here. She wouldn't, right? This was supposed to be only for the Miracle Girls.

"You just made it all worth it," Zach laughs, holding his waist as he doubles over laughing. Zoe climbs out of the tent and stands up slowly.

"Whatever. I'm going to get you back." Riley slaps at his face, but Zach doesn't even flinch. He simply picks her up, throws her over his shoulder like a sack of potatoes, and begins to walk away.

"AAAH!" Riley screams, but her high-pitched shriek sounds more like laughter than anything else. "Put me down!" She slaps his back uselessly.

Zach puts Riley down a few yards from our little circle, and she immediately lunges toward him. He jogs away, surprisingly nimble for a guy his size. Like a shot, she's after him, laughing as she chases him down the beach. Andy follows, jogging along behind. Within moments, Riley has disappeared from sight, vanishing into the dark, empty night.

"What on earth was that?" Christine's face registers her disgust. "Did she really just giggle and run away?"

"Do you think she's okay?" Zoe asks, looking toward the sound of shrieking.

"She sounds okay," Christine says, rolling her eyes. "She can always just cheer her way out if she gets in trouble." She curses under her breath. "I can't believe they scared us like that on purpose."

"It's okay," I say quickly. "We're fine." Once again, I try to make my voice sound sure.

"Do you think we should go after her?" Zoe scrunches up her face, but Christine shakes her head. We hear Riley shriek again, but this time sound echoes off the wall of the cliffs behind us.

"She'll be back when she's done with her *other* friends." She sits back down in the sand and pulls her legs up, then wraps her arms around them. I follow suit, and Zoe sits down tentatively. We sit in silence. The night is cloudy, so the moon and stars are obscured, but the steely gray clouds still look majestic. It's just so big.

A few minutes later, we hear Riley scream again, but this time there are no deep voices responding. Zoe turns her head, then looks back at us. "I'm going to go check," she says.

"Go for it," Christine replies, staring into the fire.

Zoe nods, then pushes herself up. She brushes the sand off her hands and begins walking. I stand up quickly and move to follow her, and finally Christine, apparently aware that she's about to be left alone, reluctantly stands up and begins to follow. We've gone a little ways when we hear another shriek, and I gasp when I make out dark figures on top of the cliff. Their shadows seem so small against the dark sky.

"Riley?" Zoe calls, and it isn't until she laughs again that I realize Riley isn't one of the figures at the top of the cliff. The noise comes from the middle of the cliff, and as I get closer I can see a dark figure halfway up the sloped rock face. It's not a completely vertical face, but it's steep enough that no one in their right mind should be trying to climb up what are bound to be slippery rocks on this wet night.

"Is she trying to kill herself?" Christine hisses. Riley finds a foothold and pushes herself farther up.

"You climb like a girl," Zach says, egging her on. Is that how the guys got up there?

As my eyes adjust to being away from the fire, I see a trail a little farther down that leads from the beach up to the top of the cliff. I quickly measure the distances in my head and realize that the guys must have used the path, but Riley, to save time, decided to scramble up the rocks instead.

"Riley?" She doesn't seem to hear me. She moves slowly up the rocks, and the wind howls. I hear some low laughter from the top of the cliff.

"Riley!" Zoe yells, cupping her hands around her mouth. Christine shakes her head.

And then, somehow, the dark shadow on the rocks slips. She almost catches herself, then loses her grip again. There is a moment of shocked silence; then I hear a scream followed by a sickening thud. Riley falls to the ground. My heart stops.

She can't have just fallen. I start running as fast as I can toward the dark shape on the sand. She's not moving.

A deep voice curses, and suddenly I'm grateful the guys are here. They can help us. They're big enough to carry her to their car. But before I can register what's happening, they turn and begin to run, and soon I see headlights illuminate the night. The tires squeal as they drive away.

I run as fast as I can, but even as I pump my arms, I know it's ridiculous. I am too late. Still, I pray. *Please, God, please, God,* I whisper over and over again, until my breath becomes choppy and I have to gasp for air. But I still keep saying the prayer in my head.

Maybe a fall onto a sandy beach isn't so bad.

But I know enough about physics to understand that even if you fall into the ocean from that height, you'll be in serious trouble. And Riley's body is so still and peaceful—too still. A weird mournful sound escapes my body. I know she is dead. I can just see it. I don't want the others to see her like this. I stumble back a few feet and stop them.

Zoe immediately pulls her phone out of her pocket and calls 911, and while she's talking to the operator, her voice high and scared, Christine and I avoid each other's eyes. She's weeping, and I don't know how to react to that right now.

Quietly, Christine pulls out her own phone and hits a button. I try to understand what Zoe is telling the operator, but she's not really making any sense. Christine hangs up and tries her call again. I watch her to avoid having to look at Riley's still form. Her movements are sluggish and her eyes are panic-stricken.

"Dad, it's me," Christine says into her phone. "It's an emergency. Please call me back as soon as you get this." She flips the phone shut and holds it in her right hand.

"She's not *moving!*" Zoe shrieks into her phone, and Christine opens her phone up again and retries her call.

It's funny the things you notice when time stands still. I can feel the tiny drops of water hit my face as the fog swirls around us, and I hear that the deep pounding of the waves hitting the shore actually has a high-pitched undertone.

Christine's call is dumped into voicemail again, and I slowly reach out my hand. She hands me her phone without meeting my eye. I hold it, running my finger along the smooth plastic edge as Zoe explains to the 911 operator where we are again. I cast a quick glance at Riley, then look away. I open the phone and take a deep breath.

As it rings, I wonder if I am doing the right thing. There's no turning back from here. But still, somehow, there's nothing I want more right now.

"Mom," I say as soon as she picks up the phone. I suck in a jagged breath. "Riley fell. I'm scared." She gasps, but I plow ahead before she can ask any questions. "We're on the beach, near the cliffs. Please come."

44

've been sitting on my foot for so long that it feels like there are ants in my sock, but that's not enough to make me move. I feel like I'm trapped underwater, and even when I do try to shift my position, my movements are slow and weak. It's easier to sit here and stare at the linoleum floor. I don't feel sad, and I don't feel angry, and I don't even think I feel scared. Actually, I don't really feel anything, except numb.

My mother has been glaring at me from across the emergency room for an hour straight. No doubt she's making a mental list of people to call to cancel my *quince* and figuring out how to find the best locksmith in town so that she can lock me away for good.

Papá keeps bringing everyone fresh cups of terrible coffee from the hospital cafeteria, but I haven't even looked up to say thanks.

Mr. McGee paces the floor. He hasn't stopped moving since the moment he walked in the door. He appears to be unable to sit still. Every time a doctor enters the waiting area, he stops and looks at them in hope, only to be disappointed as they pass straight through the waiting area, attending to something else. It's heartbreaking to see his face fall again and again. Mrs. McGee is perfectly coiffed and is keeping busy helping Michael with his homework, but neither of them seems very focused on California history. Her voice is strained and tight, and Michael is asking rapid-fire questions about Riley.

Zoe has been sobbing for an hour straight, Christine left a dozen messages for her dad and has now locked herself in the bathroom, and still I sit here. I feel nothing. No, I feel something. I feel empty. I can't even find the words to pray. This must be what shock feels like. Or doubt, maybe.

I hear a noise and look up. Dreamy and Ed rush in, Dreamy's long ponytail streaming behind her. Ed's Birkenstocks slap against the linoleum as they run to Zoe and throw their arms around her. Even from here I can see tears glistening in Ed's eyes, and Dreamy smoothes Zoe's hair and whispers to her for a long time. Zoe doesn't lift her arms to return the embrace. I look back at the floor.

It's been two long hours. Yesterday, the worst day of my life, is now over, but today looks no better in these small hours of the morning. The doctors haven't updated us on Riley in ages, and people's nerves are beginning to fray. I wonder how much longer Mrs. McGee can take it. Her face is pale, there are dark smudges under her eyes, and she can't stop wringing her hands.

A dark-haired doctor walks in, and immediately a hush falls over our section of the waiting room. He clears his throat quietly and then motions for the McGees to follow him. They rush to the nurses' desk, and none of us—not even Mom—can turn our eyes away. Mrs. McGee has her hand over her mouth and Mr. McGee has his arm around her shoulder, as if preparing for her collapse. Michael is unusually quiet and clawing at his mother's only free hand.

The doctor says something quietly, and Mrs. McGee lets out a small, joyous gasp. She hugs her husband and son. Then the doctor says something more, and they nod. The stifling tension in the room lifts a bit, but still we wait. Finally, he leads the McGees away, and we all look at one another in confusion. Dreamy and Ed whisper quietly with my parents. Zoe keeps her head buried in her mother's shoulder, and I stay completely still, focusing on the ants in my foot.

Five minutes later the doctor comes back and sits on the coffee table in the middle of our group. He smiles kindly.

"The McGees asked me to update all of the friends of the family."

Everyone in our group leans in closer. I brace myself. The ants go wild.

"She has woken up."

"Praise the Lord!" Dreamy shouts and throws her arms around the doctor. He pats her on the back in a professional manner, as if he learned all about this in medical school.

Dreamy lets him go and wipes tears from her eyes. "Please go on. I'm sorry."

The doctor smiles again, his white teeth bright against his olive skin. "We're not entirely in the clear yet, but she is able to respond and she asked for her parents."

As I listen to the doctor's calm, factual tone, I feel like I'm waking up from a long sleep. Suddenly, the pain in my foot is nearly unbearable, and I move it out from underneath me. The sensation of fresh blood pumping into it again is comforting.

"She'll need some staples in her skull. She has six broken ribs, some internal bleeding, and a broken arm. But she will most likely make a full recovery."

My mom leans over and hugs Dreamy, and if I were more awake, this would probably strike me as odd, but I can't stop myself from smiling. Riley will be okay. She's not going to die.

"Her family suggests that you all go home and get some rest now, and they thank you for your support." The doctor stands up and smiles again. "Riley McGee is one lucky girl." He glances at Zoe, and then looks at me, his eyes kind.

An incredible, oppressive guilt presses down on me again. This is all my fault. I promise God right then and there to never, ever disobey my parents again, no matter how strict they are. I may never go out again, but least I didn't kill Riley.

The doctor excuses himself and disappears down a long hallway. Mom hoists the strap of her purse and slides it carefully over her shoulder, then looks at me expectantly. She and Papá walk toward me, and Ed wipes his eyes and gestures toward Zoe to stand up.

"Christine is still in the bathroom," Zoe says quietly, shaking her head. Mom glances at Zoe, then up at Dreamy and Ed. Papá looks around slowly, as if realizing for the first time that Christine's dad isn't here.

"I'll take care of it," Dreamy says quickly, brushing a wisp of hair away from her face. "We have... I think I know what to say."

Mom looks like she might protest for a moment, but then puts her arm around me, almost making me jump. "Okay, then. Thank you. I can't imagine where her father must be." Both mothers tsk-tsk under their breaths for a moment. "I'm going to get Ana home now."

Papá stands up and hugs Dreamy and shakes Ed's hand. Mom hugs them both. Zoe and I both stare at the ground. It's not that I don't want to hug Zoe. I do. But I'm just, it was just . . . I can't right now.

"C'mon, Ana. It's time to go home," Mom says with something like tenderness in her voice. I follow her out the door in silence.

45

I jump when I hear a knock at my door. I can see muted sunlight coming in around the edges of the curtains. I still feel exhausted. As soon as I got home this morning I passed out. I wouldn't really call it sleep. I just can't account for those hours. I was out, gone, completely knocked out. Oblivious. I suddenly wish I could go back to that more than anything.

"Ana?" Mom's voice is muffled by my door.

I blink at the clock. It's two in the afternoon. I sit up slowly, shaking my head. I guess we're not going to church today. I need to write Dave. He'll be worried when we don't show up.

"May I come in?"

I nod, though obviously she can't see me. She pushes the door open anyway, and I pull the covers up to my chin. I feel naked, even though I'm in my pajamas. I haven't had time to think about what she's going to do to me. I needed to prepare. Why didn't Papá come too? He's the reasonable one.

Mom sits down on the side of my bed. "Zoe's mom called earlier. Christine's dad finally showed up and took her home. He rushed back from Sacramento."

I nod and wait for her to go on. She clears her throat.

"Ana, I want to talk about what happened last night."

I notice a bump on my arm and start to pick at it.

"I guess you see now why your father and I have so many rules for you."

I bite my lip and continue to scratch at my skin. Mom puts a hand on my arm, and I look up slowly. Her face is pale and there are dark rings under her eyes.

"What you girls did last night was very risky—"

Riley's face flashes into my mind. How could we just let her walk away from us with those guys? Why did we even go to the beach in the first place? What kind of Miracle Girls are we?

Mom rubs my shoulder for a moment, and it almost doesn't feel awkward.

"Ana, I know that you have learned a lesson. I hate that you had to learn it this way, but I do hope that now you'll see just how serious the consequences of lying can be."

I nod. "I'm—" My voice is deep from sleep, and I clear my throat. "I'm so sorry. I didn't think anyone would get hurt. She just started climbing, I was too late, she fell—"

"I know, Ana." She scoots closer to me and holds out her arms. I watch her for a moment, then lean toward her a bit. She holds me in a hug. I want to pull away, but at least she isn't watching me anymore, and the scent of her perfume, just noticeable up close, makes me feel safe. "I don't know what I'd do if I lost you."

Her voice is so earnest and unguarded that I feel a little embarrassed, like I caught her in her nightgown or something.

Mom pulls back slowly. "But that's not what I came in here to say." She takes a deep breath and composes her face.

Suddenly, I know what she came in here to say. "Mom," I start before I have to hear her say the words, "I know I don't deserve a *quince* now. It's okay."

Mom squints at me. "What?"

I wipe my nose on the sleeve of my sweatshirt. "I know my *quince* is canceled. I understand."

"Ana, that's not what I've come here to say at all."

I look up. Uh-oh. I'm in serious trouble now.

"I wanted to tell you that Papá and I have been thinking about it, and we learned something last night, too." She smiles a little bit, though her eyes are far away. "We've started to think that maybe we've been too hard on you."

"What?" I know I'm losing it. She didn't just say…

"What you did last night was wrong. But once Riley fell, you did the right thing. You showed great courage and honor."

I spent all last night in the hospital thinking about what a horrible friend I was because I didn't stop Riley from falling, and now she's telling me that I'm honorable? *God, is this your version of* Wife Swap? *Where's my real mom?*

"Papá and I want you to feel like you live in a fair household. You shouldn't have sneaked around and lied. But maybe we made it difficult not to." I watch her as I consider this. Did they make it difficult not to? Or was I just being selfish? "We want to be tough, and truthfully, even a little strict, but we don't want to be unreasonable. We want you to do the right thing, live the life that we expect of you, and that will lead to trust, respect, and even some freedom."

My heart begins to beat faster. No way. Am I going to get off scot-free?

Mom crosses her arms across her chest. "But that doesn't mean that there won't be a serious punishment for last night."

I smile a little. I guess that's fair.

"We have discussed it and would like to present you with a compromise." She waits for my reaction.

"I have a say in the punishment?"

She smiles. "You do. We're going to give this plan a try. It's what you've been asking for, right?"

"Well, yeah, but..."

"Because of the severity of what you did—lying to us, lying to the other parents—and because one of you was seriously injured, Papá and I think that you should be on probation for a year."

I gulp. Did she just say a year?

"During probation, you can only go to a limited number of pre-approved social events. School events, church functions, chaperoned dances..."

"Okay!" I say, a little too quickly. I can go to dances!

"But if you are caught lying, telling half-truths, or otherwise skewing the truth even once during this year, you will be grounded for the rest of the year, with no hope for parole."

I look down at my covers as my face burns with shame. I do kind of have a lying problem. How did it start? I'm usually a very honest person. It just kind of happened.

"And then when you're sixteen years old, you'll be off probation. That's when you can have full car and dating privileges."

My heart dances. I can't help but throw my arms around Mom in a huge hug. "Oh, thank you, thank you, thank you."

Mom leans back and smiles a little at me. "Now, do you find this deal fair?"

"Yes!" I almost scream. For a moment I realize that most kids would think this is the world's worst deal, but at my house, it's positively lax. "I accept your terms and find them to be quite fair."

Mom nods. "Great, I'm happy to hear that. We put a lot of thought and prayer into it."

"Okay." I pull nervously at ends of my wet sleeves.

"Now get up. It's the middle of the day," she says, laughing a bit, but even though I know she's trying to make a joke, I only feel panic. I just realized something.

"Mom?" I say, but my voice comes out as a bit of a squeak. I know I need to tell her. It's not really a big deal, but if honesty is what she wants, I need to confess. I whisper a quick prayer that Mom meant what she said.

"There is...something." I bite my lip for a moment. She tilts her head a little and her smile fades. "A...boy, I guess. A guy I like at church. I don't think we're dating but, um, we might be. I'm not sure."

Mom's eyes widen, and she suddenly looks as white as a sheet.

I start talking quickly, not really knowing what I'm saying. "His name is Dave, and he really loves God, and he's really kind and funny and nice." I can feel my cheeks burning. "And I think Papá would really like him. And I just see him at youth group stuff. And—"

"Ana." Mom puts her hand on top of mine. "Thank you for telling me."

I let out a huge sigh of relief. I thought there was still a chance that she might send me off to a nunnery.

"This changes things." She watches me, and her face softens a bit. "You're too young to date," she says, and I nod. I knew she felt this way, and though I'm disappointed, I still feel okay. Free, in a way. At least it's not a secret anymore. "But maybe this boy could come over for dinner sometime." She forces herself to smile a little. "We'd like to meet him, of course."

"He could come over?" I ask. I think I need to hear her say it again, just to believe it.

She smiles, her eyes a bit watery. "I guess you're really not a child anymore."

I throw my arms around her again and give her a big, full-throttled hug. I haven't hugged her like this since I was a little girl, and it feels good.

46

"Louie, Louie," I scream, and Riley laughs. She sways carefully to the music while I secretly watch the space behind her, making sure none of my guests accidentally knock into her.

I have to admit, the backyard looks pretty stunning. The night is clear and warm, and you can just see the ocean past the long slope of the lawn. The patio is decorated with lots of candles and white lights, and the tables under the huge tent spread out across our lawn are covered in white damask and topped with tons of flowers. Mom and Papá's friends are laughing, and a few of them are even staggering around and slurring their speech, which Christine finds endlessly amusing. Servers are bustling in and out of the crowd, refreshing everyone's drinks, but as the sun sets on this gorgeous evening, the real action is on the dance floor under the tent.

Zoe pretends to swim over to us through the crowd and then leans in to sing, "Ay-yi-yi-yi."

"This is kind of a weird song," Christine yells over the loud music, but even she is bopping around a little. The Miracle Girls are my *damas*, so they're all wearing matching navy blue dresses. Christine is practically swimming in hers while Zoe's is stretched tight across her hips. They all look beautiful.

I pull them into a big group hug, and we keep singing "Louie Louie" at the top of our lungs. Riley is next to me, and I try to be gentle with her.

We're only a few days into summer, but after weeks in the hospital and months at home, the doctor gave Riley the okay to come to my party. In two and a half short months, she has made great progress. Her broken ribs are technically mended, but still a bit sore. The staples in her head are gone—which is good because the entire concept sort of creeped me out—and she got the cast off her arm a few weeks ago. She's still not allowed to surf, run, or do anything too strenuous, but apparently she told the doctor that she absolutely couldn't miss my *quince* and he cleared her. I think her mom is still a bit nervous because she lingered at the door when she dropped Riley off, but Riley is practically back to her old self again.

"Hey, look who's coming over here," I yell into Christine's ear. The DJ has the music turned up so loud that only she can hear, but I see her tense up when she notices that Tyler is walking our way.

Christine immediately looks at the floor and acts as if she's trying to disappear, which is kind of hard to do when you have hair as green as a booger. I snort. How can such a bold girl be so afraid of a guy?

Tyler is so near Christine could almost touch him, but still she doesn't move. This calls for drastic measures.

"Oof," I gasp and pretend to trip on absolutely nothing. I "fall" onto Christine and shove her backwards, directly into Tyler's arms.

"Oh, gosh," I say to Tyler, who looks a little stunned. "I'm such a klutz." I turn tail and run, leaving Tyler and Christine staring at each other. He's got to talk to her now.

I peek back over my shoulder and see her giggling—giggling!—and tucking her hair behind her ears.

"Dominguez!" I turn quickly and run directly into Dave. Now it's my turn to blush. "You're supposed to walk with your head facing forward."

"Oh, sorry." I try to act natural, but my breathing still gets a little off when I look at Dave, and it doesn't help that he's absolutely gorgeous tonight. He has just a hint of a tan and his dark eyes are sparkling. His brown polyester suit is slim and tailored, and it pulls across his chest and flares a tiny bit at the ankles. Underneath the jacket, he's wearing a light yellow shirt and a brown and yellow striped tie. Basically, he looks like a businessman from 1975, and on anyone else it would look ridiculous, but on Dave it works. Works quite well, actually. Everyone else here is wearing plain old gray and black suits, with plain ties, and he stands out like a . . . well, like a guy in a cool retro suit.

"The monkey suit is my dad's," he laughs, pulling at the wide lapels. He winks, and I feel my cheeks burn a bit, and I'm thankful he can't read my thoughts. "Bought it when he got his first job." His eyes sparkle. "You look great."

My stomach tingles, and I feel my face flush. Mom ended up letting me get a different pink dress, longer and less low-cut, but still fun, and I got to wear (sort of) high heels tonight. She even loaned me a string of pearls that has been in the family since the age of the dinosaur. I feel grown up, which I guess is the point.

"Thanks." Dave has tucked a yellow handkerchief into his

pocket, which draws my eyes to his broad chest. I need to get my mind off this. I glance over his shoulder and quickly point at what I've done. "I'm playing Cupid."

Dave looks in the direction I'm pointing. "Christine likes Tyler?"

"Shhh!" Guys are so clueless. "Are you trying to get me killed here? Keep your voice down."

"Christine likes Tyler," he says again, as if considering it.

"Do you think she has a shot?"

He shrugs. "He doesn't know she likes him. He thinks she's a really great artist, but I don't know if he's ever thought about her as more than just a friend."

My heart sinks, but when we turn back toward them, they're slow dancing. Wow. Somehow I didn't even notice that the DJ changed the song. Next to them, Ms. Moore, wearing a cool blue vintage dress and high heels, is dancing with one of my dad's lawyer friends. She winks at me and I wave, but she and her partner turn a little as they sway to the music, and soon she is facing the other side of the room.

Dave bows deeply. "May I?"

I take his hand, and he leads me to the floor. For a moment, I'm worried that he'll do some kind of old people moves, but instead he puts his hands on my hips and I relax. Thankfully, I get to put my hands on his shoulders. My palms are sweating like hogs. Wait, do hogs sweat? Well, they're sweating a lot.

It's nice to be this close to him. He smells very clean, with a hint of aftershave, and some quality that I can only describe as distinctly boy. I take a deep breath and then sigh. What a perfect *quince*.

And I really owe it all to Mom. Ever since our

breakthrough conversation after Riley got hurt, we've both been trying, which greatly helped with the planning. We looked at all the *quince* plans and started compromising on stuff so that we'd both be happy. I got the traditional Mexican theme, the pink dress, and the party in the backyard. She got a sit-down dinner, a huge guest list, and the throne.. Dave's even come to Sunday night dinners a few times. Papá seems to like him, even if he is a teenage boy.

As we sway, I stare at Dave for a moment. I can't believe how much life has changed for me. A year ago, I hated the very words Half Moon Bay, and I was desperately trying to convince my parents to let me stay in San Jose. But now this place feels like home. These are my friends now.

None of my friends from San Jose even made it tonight. A few of my parents' colleagues and church friends came out, but the people I invited...well, it's tough to get over here when you're too young to drive. And for some reason, I'm not *that* disappointed. I think it might have been weird for my two worlds to collide. And I don't know if I could handle seeing how my friends have moved on without me.

The year I started middle school, I went back to visit my elementary school, but they'd painted the whole school brown, and my favorite teacher had rearranged the way the desks were set up in her room, and I was sad for days, because the place I loved was no longer the place I loved. My memories no longer matched reality. I guess sometimes it's safer to keep memories intact.

"Why are you shaking your head, Dominguez?"

I laugh. "I think I just wanted to say something to you...but I'm not sure how to say it."

Dave looks into my eyes for a moment, and I can tell he already knows everything, but still I feel the urge to say it out loud.

"Thank you," I say finally.

He chuckles. "That's what you were struggling so much to say? Thank you?" I bite my lip. He stares at me for a moment, then shakes his head in disbelief. "Thank *you*, Dominguez," he whispers and then pulls me in close so that I can feel his breath in my ear.

We stay like that, floating on air, for what seems like an eternity, but then the song ends and the lights come up. I rub my eyes for a moment. It's been a long day and an even longer night.

"Miss Ana Dominguez? Could you come up here with me for a moment?" the DJ says. I see the Miracle Girls moving toward the stage in their matching dresses.

"Ana, would you please have a seat right here in your throne?" The DJ makes a grand gesture toward the enormous throne, and I roll my eyes and oblige.

"At a *quince*, the young lady traditionally chooses a *madrina*, a godmother who will give her a tiara. Her godmother is someone who has played a crucial role in her life, helping her to become the woman she is on this very special day," the DJ says, reading from an index card. He hands me the microphone.

"Maria? Would you join me up here?" I look out over the sea of faces, and my stomach flips over. Somehow it didn't occur to me that everyone would be watching me.

Maria walks onto the stage, dressed in a gorgeous traditional layered skirt in many vibrant colors and a peasant top.

Her hair is up in an intricate twist around the crown of her head. I put my arm around her and squeeze.

"Most of you don't know Maria," I say, trying not to be get freaked out by the way my voice echoes across the tent. "But she has taken care of me since I was a baby. She has been my second mother, my sister, and my best friend for many, many years. And soon, she is flying home to Mexico, her homeland, to reunite with her family. I chose her to be my *madrina* because I want her to know that her family in America will never stop missing her." My voice cracks, and my eyes fill with tears. "And I will always love her."

Maria throws her arms around me, and we hug as everyone cheers and claps. We hold each other for a moment and cry, and then finally pull back, blotting our eyes. She motions for me to sit down. She takes the mic from me.

"I made this for my Anita. It is her last doll to symbolize that she is now a woman." Maria places a darling, delicate handmade cloth doll in my lap. She is wearing an outfit similar to Maria's.

Mom, just offstage, holds out a tiara, only it's not the shiny new one mom ordered months ago. It's a little dull, and kind of old-fashioned. I squint, and see that some of the stones are missing. But as Maria grasps it and gently places it on my head, I smile. I don't have to be told where this tiara came from. The look on her face tells me all I need to know. Many years ago, in Mexico, this graced the head of a much-younger Maria. Somehow this seems right.

Maria squeezes my shoulder. The crowd cheers, and I look out at the sea of faces. Mom and Papá are off to the right, holding hands and smiling. Ms. Moore stands off to the side, by herself, but the look on her face is satisfied. Dave nods at me. Zoe is dancing around in a little circle, and Christine is clapping, a smirk on her face. Riley, blond hair brilliant in the moonlight, smiles at me, and I smile back.

Looking out at the faces of the people who have come to mean so much to me, I begin to understand that my life is full of miracles.

47

"If my sweet-sixteen is even half as cool as your *quince*, then I will die a happy woman." Riley joins the rest of us on the edge of the patio.

Christine picks up her plastic cup of Diet Coke and toasts in agreement. "That was seriously an amazing party."

"I'll bet it was." I nudge her knowingly. Tyler ended up asking for Christine's e-mail address, and they made some vague plans to go to an art gallery downtown.

The waiters have now taken off their ties and are breaking down the tent and the tables and chairs, and since the girls are spending the night, we're sitting on my back deck, looking out at the ocean.

Christine narrows her eyes at me. "By the way, if you ever call your house a pink prison—"

"Or an Easy Bake Castle—" Zoe adds, swinging her legs. They dangle a good ten feet off the ground up here.

"Or an Easy Bake Castle again, I'm going to call you a liar to your face. This place is awesome. I love that your back-yard was big enough to host five hundred people under a huge tent. What is this place, the circus?"

I look back at my house behind me. "It's not so bad."

"Plus, you're not in prison unless you literally haven't been allowed to leave your house." Riley shakes her head in disbelief. She missed the last few months of school, and she will have to make up all the work this summer, but she's supposed to come back in the fall all caught up. "Michael has taught me the first hundred digits of pi, I've learned that my dad has this weird subconscious habit where he's always whistling, and my mother secretly watches *Days of Our Lives* when she thinks no one will catch her."

Zoe puts her arm around Riley. "We're just glad that you're feeling better."

"Thanks," Riley says. "And I'm still so sorry I got all of you in trouble." She looks around, and we shrug. The truth is, I'm the only one in trouble. Christine's dad was just glad she was okay, and Zoe's parents let her choose her own punishment, so she decided that she has to weed the garden all summer.

"I guess I thought . . . I don't know." She leans back so she's lying on the smooth wooden boards, staring up at the sky. "After God didn't let me drown, I really felt invincible or something. It seemed like he'd never let me fall, that I had him on my side to always pull me out of scrapes. But then I did fall . . . and hard."

"I thought you had a death wish," Christine says wryly.

"I can still remember when you let Zach put you on his shoulders in the hallway," I say. "I remember thinking, this girl is going to crack her head open!"

Riley shakes her head slowly. "I remember that day." She looks up at the stars. "It seems like so long ago. It's been such a weird year for me."

I look over at Christine and see her nodding. It's been a weird year for all of us. Thank God we found one another.

Christine mutters something, but I can't quite tell what she says.

"What?" I'm learning to keep my ears pricked when Christine talks softly. That seems to be when she says the most important stuff.

She clears her throat and takes a deep breath, and then blurts out, "My dad proposed to The Bimbo."

"What?!" We all pretty much screech the same thing.

"But it's only been—" I stop myself. Christine doesn't need reminding that her mom died less than a year ago.

"Yep," she says. "Yep, yep, yep."

"How could he?" Zoe sighs. I'm sure she's crushed. Zoe thinks the very best of everyone, even that horrible guy Zach. I actually heard her wonder aloud if Zach was just going for help the night that Riley fell.

"I'm sorry," Riley says. Her voice sounds far away. I lean back on the deck with her. The boards are warm under my tired back.

"You haven't even met The Bimbo yet. Just you wait." Christine rolls her eyes. "Then you'll see why this isn't just bad, it's tragic."

I watch Christine, but her face is composed, as if she's determined not to show how much this bothers her. Truthfully, Candace doesn't seem that bad, but I still can't see the whole thing working out into one big happy family.

Slowly, Zoe leans back, and we're all stretched out staring up at the sky. It's one of those clear summer nights where the sky is full of thousands of pinpricks. Some of them even seem to have red or blue casts, and several of them seem to be twinkling just for us.

"Did you guys know there are something like 100 billion stars in our galaxy? You can't see them all because of dust inside the Milky Way," Riley says quietly. "And there are millions of galaxies beyond ours."

Christine starts to laugh. "What are you, some kind of science freak?"

"Michael likes astronomy."

I try to visualize the number one-hundred billion, and my brain stalls out. That's ten to the... eleventh power? My mind isn't big enough to wrap itself around that number, let alone what all those stars would look like. I try to focus on the stars I can see, but as I stare at them, their edges seem to fade away a little.

There are times when I have my doubts, but when I look up at the brilliant tapestry spread out before us, knowing it's only a small piece of what's really out there, I know without a doubt that God is there and that his plans are way bigger than mine.

The low roll of waves and the clinking of chairs being stacked on a rental truck are the only noise for a few minutes.

"I can't believe freshman year is over, you guys." I say to break the silence on the patio. "We're officially sophomores now."

Zoe sits up and grins. "And it's the beginning of our first summer as Miracle Girls. We have to do something to commemorate tonight."

"Zo-eeeee," Christine whines. "I don't want to pinky swear or become blood sisters right now."

Riley laughs.

Zoe swats at Christine. "That's not what I had in mind. Let me think."

"We could always make up a secret handshake," Riley says and elbows Christine. We all snicker.

Zoe ignores us. "Oh! I've got it. Let's all say one goal we have for the next year."

I look at her earnest face. Has anyone ever had as a pure a heart as Zoe's?

"A goal?" Christine asks. "Like I'm going to lose ten pounds and give up chocolate or something?"

"Anything you want. Just tell us what you what to accomplish next year. Whatever is important to you. It doesn't matter what you answer."

Christine snorts. "That's easy." She sits up and looks at us. "My goal is to break up my father and The Bimbo."

"Chris-tiiiine." This time it's Zoe's turn to whine.

"What? I'm serious. That's my goal. You said it could be anything."

Zoe waits for a moment and then sighs. "Ana, you go next."

I try to imagine my sophomore year. In my fantasy, the Miracle Girls will have Marina Vista High School eating out of our palms. Dave and I will be sickeningly in love, and maybe my parents will even let us see each other sometimes. Maria will be healthy, and she'll be happy in Mexico. Everything will be going well at home. But there's one more thing I want for next year. Should I say that? I'm not really sure it's a good idea. But Zoe said to be honest, right?

"Ana?" Zoe says again.

"Oh, um..." I look up at the stars, trying to get up my nerve. Well, if there's anything I've learned this year it's that honesty always pays off in the end. "Well, I guess next year I hope to move to the number-one spot in class so that I can get into Princeton."

For a moment, no one says anything. I can hear some bullfrogs chirping. I mentally slap myself in the head. What an idiot I am.

"Bring it, sister," Riley finally says, and we all burst out laughing. "Those staples in my head only made me that much smarter." She rises up from the deck like Franken-stein, and we all howl. Finally, she settles back down next to me, and I'm so thankful to have Riley in our group. I have to hand it to Zoe. She saw Riley's fate all along. She's one of us, our missing piece.

"Your turn," I say, and nudge Riley.

Riley crosses her legs and brushes the dust off her hands. "I'm going to spend more time with Michael. When I was healing, I realized that I've been kind of a crappy big sister to him. So next year, I want to do a better job."

Is she serious? I look at her composed face and realize that she is entirely sincere.

How could I have been so wrong about this girl? Was she always a better person than I am? And did I ever apologize for accusing her of cheating? I know now that she isn't even capable of such a thing. I kick my legs around.

Zoe clears her throat politely. "And now it's my turn, and I know exactly what I'm going to say."

Christine is sprawled out, staring up at the sky. I'm lying on my side, looking at Zoe. And Riley is sitting next to her, listening intently. Here we are, all together, just like it was written in the stars.

"God is so big and mysterious that we can never understand why we are miracles when others...aren't." She takes a deep breath and presses on before any of us can interrupt. "I am going to try with all of my might, with every fiber of my being, every day of the whole year, to keep the Miracle Girls together and make sure that we all realize our special calling...no matter what that is."

I wait for Christine's snicker, but it doesn't come. Zoe's goal is so pure and noble that I feel strangely moved by it, even if it is a kooky, overly serious Zoe kind of thing to say.

And, hey, even though I'm not a "woo-woo, let's sit in a circle and share our emotions" kind of person, maybe she's right. This year we accidentally stumbled onto something very special. I don't think any of us even fully understand yet who we are or what we are capable of, and she's right that none of us really gets why we're still here. But I think we all know that something bigger than us has brought us together, and if we made it through this crazy year, we can make it through anything.

Maybe God will use us for big things someday. Perhaps we are all called for something special. Then again, maybe that something special is already here. As I look up at the enormous sky, I start to suspect that maybe just being here with the Miracle Girls is enough.

about the authors

Anne Dayton graduated from Princeton and has her MA in Literature from New York University. She lives in New York City. May Vanderbilt graduated from Baylor University and has an MA in Fiction from Johns Hopkins. She lives in San Francisco. Together, they are the authors of *Emily Ever After*, *Consider Lily*, and *The Book of Jane*. To find out more you can visit www.goodgirllit.com.

BACK AD (TK)